DJINN & TONIC

JASINDA WILDER

DJINN:

"**Jinn** or **djinn** (singular: **jinn**, **djinni**, or **genie**; Arabic: *al-jinn,* singular *al-jinn*) are supernatural creatures in Islamic mythology as well as pre-Islamic Arabian mythology. They are mentioned frequently in the Quran (the 72nd sura is titled *Sûrat-al-Jinn*) and other Islamic texts and inhabit an unseen world in dimensions beyond the visible universe of humans. The Quran says that the *jinn* are made of a smokeless and "scorching fire," but are also physical in nature, being able to interfere physically with people and objects and likewise be acted upon. The *jinn,* humans, and angels make up the three sapient creations of God. Like human beings, the *jinn* can be good, evil, or neutrally benevolent and hence have free will like humans and unlike angels. The *jinn* are the analogue of demons in Christian tradition, but the *jinn* are not angels and the Quran draws a clear distinction between the two creations." ~ Wikipedia (http://en.wikipedia.org/wiki/Jinn)

Ifrit (say: "ih-freet"): "The Ifrits are in a class of infernal Jinn noted for their strength and cunning. An ifrit is an enormous winged creature of fire, either male or female, who lives underground and frequents ruins. Ifrits live in a society structured along ancient Arab tribal lines, complete with kings, tribes and clans. They generally marry one another, but they can also marry humans. While ordinary weapons and forces have no power over them, they are susceptible to magic, which humans can use to kill them or to capture and enslave them. As with the jinn, an ifrit may be either a believer or an unbeliever, good or evil, but it is most often depicted as a wicked and ruthless being." ~ Wikipedia (https://en.wikipedia.org/wiki/Ifrit)

Chapter 1: A Breath of Wind

Carson

I'm not sure how I end up at The Old Shillelagh, a tumbler of gin and tonic in my hand, watching replay footage of the Tigers beating the Rockies. I left the station hours ago and finally ended up here because I hadn't felt like going home. I'm watching the game, but I'm not really paying attention. It's just something to stare at while I try to clear my mind, try not to think about the case. This is one I know I won't forget any time soon. Miriam al-Mansour is just . . . stuck in my brain, somehow. It's not like I'm attracted to her in a sexual way or anything. It's definitely not that. I mean, she's beautiful, sure, but it's something else. And, anyway, she's with Jack Byrne.

Yeah, it's definitely something else. Something beyond the woman herself. Beyond the facts even. How am I supposed to just let it all go? Just write off the murder of a man as . . . what? Self-defense? Even Miriam herself has admitted that it wasn't self-defense. She said she'd been defending Jack. She said she'd ended up killing Ben because he'd shot Jack—two bullets to the chest. You didn't survive that kind of injury. You just didn't. A sucking chest wound was, by all accounts, one of the most painful ways to die, next to being shot in the gut. But here's the weirdest thing—the part I can't figure out, and the reason I've been sitting in this bar for so many hours: Miriam had been shot in *both* the abdomen *and* the chest, yet somehow she walked away unscathed; four gunshot wounds and she'd survived . . . without any medical attention whatsoever.

Either she was inhumanly tough, or she healed like Wolverine.

There can be no other explanations.

I finish my first drink, raise the glass and clink the ice at the bartender, Leila. She approaches with a sway, a tumbler half-filled with ice in one hand, a bottle of Bombay Sapphire in the other. She smiles at me, a quick, flirting glance, and then pours a generous two fingers-worth of gin into the glass.

"Start a tab?" she asks.

"Yeah, sure," I answer. "Thanks."

"You seem preoccupied, Detective Hale."

She's leaning on the bar in front of me, toying with a book of matches. Her T-shirt has a low-cut V-neck, and when she leans over it's hard to keep my gaze from straying to her generous cleavage. I've made a study of the various ways women bend over: there's the absent-minded bend in which the woman is simply assuming a natural, comfortable position, neither realizing nor caring about how she looks. Then there's the flirting bend where she is aware of what she is revealing, but isn't necessarily trying to accentuate it. Lastly there is the overt seduction bend, where she squeezes her arms together and props them underneath her breasts as she leans over so her cleavage all but spills out.

At the moment, I'm pretty sure Leila is somewhere between the first two. Between the way she's looking at me and her body language there is a definite hint of flirtation, not to be confused with seduction. I'm kind of glad about that, actually; I've been seduced on a number of occasions, mostly by women trying to get out of a ticket or DUI arrest. Occasionally, I might encounter a witness hoping to sway the outcome of an investigation, or sometimes I'm being pursued by a drunk badge-chaser. I've found that the ones who try to seduce me are not the kind of girls

I'm interested in—at least not long term.

I realize I never responded to Leila's comment. "Sorry, yeah," I say. "I guess I am a bit preoccupied."

Leila laughs. "Delayed reaction, much? I was starting to wonder if you'd even heard me."

"No, I heard you, I was just . . ."

"Lost in la-la land?" Leila teases. "It's okay. I imagine your job takes up a lot of brain space."

"You have *no* idea," I say. "Today especially."

The bar is dead and I'm only one of three patrons in the place, so Leila has time to chat. I don't mind; she's a beautiful girl, tall and willowy with thick black hair tied back in a neat ponytail and wide, dark, expressive eyes. She seems to like me, and that makes it even better.

I could use a distraction.

Leila wipes at an invisible spot on the counter. "So, I've been meaning to ask . . . how long have you been a detective?"

I shrug. "Six years on homicide." I feel my phone vibrate in my hip pocket, but I ignore it.

"Homicide, huh?" She grimaces, somehow making the expression look attractive. "You must see a lot of unpleasant stuff."

I finish my drink, and Leila pours me a third without me asking. "Yeah," I tell her. "Part of the job, I guess. Most of it I can forget, but some I can't. Some things people just . . . aren't meant to see."

"I can't even imagine. So, is that what's preoccupying you tonight? A bad case?" She folds the towel without taking her gaze from mine. "I hope I'm not being too nosy."

"No, you're not being nosy," I sip at my gin, and then crunch an ice cube. "It's not one of those gruesome cases that'll give you nightmares or anything, it's just . . . confusing. I'm not sure what to believe, you know?"

Leila just nods, her attention fully focused on me. She has her chin propped on a palm, listening. I find myself wanting to talk about the case, which I know I shouldn't do, especially with some girl I've known a matter of months. But Leila seems . . . different somehow.

Trustworthy, for reasons I can't quite pinpoint. Maybe the gin is beginning to cloud my judgment. She's pouring them stiff, more gin than tonic or ice, and I'm not protesting.

"You mentioned before that this case is tricky, that there's some element to it that you're having a hard time believing."

I nod. "Yeah, and it's only gotten more unbelievable since then."

"Unbelievable how?" Leila asks, unloading glasses from a dishwasher underneath the bar and stacking them to dry.

I swirl the thin black straw around the tumbler, causing ice to clink on the walls. "God, I don't even know where to start. The whole thing is crazy."

"Can you tell me about the case?"

"You have to promise not to tell anyone about this," I say, meeting her warm, friendly brown eyes. "I really shouldn't be talking about this with you. Technically, it's still an open case."

"I won't tell anyone. Promise," Leila says, smiling.

"Okay, well, you better not. I would normally never break protocol like this, but I just don't know who to turn to, what to think, what to believe. I'm so mixed up I can't tell if I'm coming or going, you know? It's just . . . if something goes against *everything* you know to be true, what are you supposed to do then?" I'm slurring a little.

I should slow down on the drinks, I know I should. I just don't want to. I like the warm muzziness, the gentle floating of my mind. Leila's easy to talk to, and even easier on the eyes. It's past two in the morning at this point, and the last customer is weaving out the door.

"Well, what does the evidence say?" Leila asks.

I shake my head. "That's the issue. The evidence is part of what's so unlikely."

"Unlikely, or impossible?" Leila says. "Didn't we talk about impossibilities before? If it's several elements too big to ignore, or pretend they're not what they look like, then you can't just refuse to acknowledge the truth."

I nod. "Yeah, that's what part of me says too." I duck my head, chastising myself internally.

Leila considers for a long moment before answering, which I appreciate. "There's so much about this world and about life that we can't see, you know? Just because we haven't seen something before doesn't make it impossible, does it?" Leila comes out from behind the bar and starts lifting chairs onto tables.

I stand up to help her, a little more unstable on my feet than I'd expected to be. Leila rolls her eyes, pushing me back onto my stool, forcing me to sit down. Her hands on my back are warm, the feeling of her touch electric, sending thrills through me.

"Yeah, you're right," I say. "But that doesn't make it any easier to accept what you always thought was impossible."

She shrugs, then places the last stool on the counter beside me. "Changing your worldview, changing your impression of what is true or possible, I don't think that's ever easy."

"Yeah, but this is . . . extra weird on top of crazy impossible."

"Explain." She's back behind the bar, turning off the TV and wiping down liquor bottles with a bar cloth. I watch her move, admiring the easy grace of her motions. She's so light on her feet, every step smooth, every twist of her body flowing into the next motion.

There's something air-like about her. It's an odd idea, even for me, but it sticks in my head. She moves as if blown by a secret wind, as if she were a leaf. She has a dancer's body; maybe that explains it.

But no. Merely being a dancer doesn't explain the way her hair floats and flutters as if blown by a breeze. Only . . . there are no open doors, no cracked windows, no fans whirring.

But her hair is definitely fluttering.

There's no other way to put it, and even though I'm pretty loaded by this point, I know I'm not hallucinating.

Am I?

I stare at her, blinking, closing one eye and then the other, watching every motion she makes. And yes, her hair is definitely fluttering. The tips wave and blow from side to side; a strand drifts across her face and she brushes it absently back behind her ear. I can't explain it, yet I can't ignore the truth of what I'm seeing.

Apropos, I suppose.

I watch as she stands at the bar, counting out the register drawer, taking her hair out of its pony-tail and shaking it to fall in glimmering black waves around her shoulders. Her hands peel bills from the stack in her hand in quick, sure motions that speak of years of practice. She's standing still, but her hair is moving—most definitely moving. I'm watching her, mesmerized, and I can't deny what I'm seeing. I peer surreptitiously around the bar. The entrance door is closed and locked, and the back door, visible through the double-hinged kitchen doors, is closed as well. There are no windows at all and no A/C. So where the fuck is the wind coming from?

There's no way to ask her about it without sounding absolutely drunkenly idiotic so I keep quiet, but I can't stop staring at her, can't stop watching the gentle, subtle fluttering of her hair in the stillness and silence of the dimly lit bar.

I finish my drink and hand my credit card to Lei-la, who processes the bill. I sign the slip with a sloppy signature, adding a generous tip. Then I accept one last drink. My fourth? Fifth? I don't even know; I've lost count, and I don't really give a shit.

"Okay, so it's like this," I say. "A DPD patrol of-ficer responds to a call from the MGM, they found a dead body in the parking garage. The responding officer shows up on the scene, takes one look, and calls for a detective. So I roll up, thinking it'll be just another dead body with few or no leads. Easy enough, either you find evidence and make the collar, or you don't, and it goes cold. Get a lot of both. Only, what I find when I get on scene is like nothing I've ever encountered before. It's not a dead body, it's . . . just bones. Charred bones, like very literally burnt to a goddamned crisp. Blackened almost to ashes. No weapon on the scene, and no cameras in that part of the garage. Nothing to go on. No way to even identify the body, I thought at first. But it turns out the vic was ex-military, and the teeth were intact enough to get an ID based on dental records. Poor dead fucker was a guy named Ben. So we have an ID on the vic, but that's it. Because there's no other evidence of any kind, except a pool of blood a few feet away, and four shell casings from a nine-millimeter pistol. Not much to go on. No eyewitnesses, no other calls that could be connected."

"So what did you do?"

The room is wobbling a little as Leila shuts off the lights in the kitchen, locks the register drawer in the office, and sits down next to me with a plastic cup of Coke. She's sitting pretty close to me, her shoulder brushing mine, her thigh nudging mine as she absently bounces her knee. I can smell rum in the Coke and on her breath. I'm aware of every point of contact between us. Her presence grounds me in some undefinable way, keeping my spinning world centered.

"I investigated the victim, Ben. Ex-Marine, nothing big on his military record, no commendations but no demerits either. Just an average guy. But then I find out that he's got a girlfriend, a girl named Miriam. And she's nowhere to be found. Further conversations with those who knew Ben revealed that he had a mean streak, liked to knock Miriam around a good bit, and that Miriam in turn had a history with dating abusive assholes. That gives me motive for Miriam as the killer, but shit, I still got nothing whatsoever on cause of death."

"I thought you said the body was burned?" Leila asks, then sips at her rum and Coke.

"Yeah, but *how* was the body burned? House fire? Car fire? Set on fire intentionally? None of those fit the evidence, not even setting the guy on fire with accelerant. Because there is no evidence. No physical clues of any kind. No weapon, no sign of struggle, no sign of fire anywhere else, no reports of someone on fire anywhere within, shit, hundreds of miles. Nothing. The garage itself is clean, too. No scorch marks on the ceiling or walls or the floor or any of the surrounding cars. Nothing.

"But wait, it gets weirder. The ME tells me that in order to burn a human body to the point this one was, so there's nothing left but bones, and even those were toasted to ash—to burn a human body, flesh, muscles, skeleton, hair, clothes, personal effects, you need the kind of heat used to cremate a body. That's fourteen, fifteen hundred degrees Fahrenheit. *Insane* heat. Flame throwers don't give off that kind of heat. And even if it could have been a flame thrower—which isn't something you can just go out and buy, even on the black market—or an accelerant like charcoal grill starter fluid or gasoline, a dude gets set on fire, he freaks out. It's a slow, horrible way to die. I know, I've seen it. They run around screaming, roll on the ground, bump into cars, jump out of the fucking window, anything. But forensics told me the body died where it fell, the way the bones were arranged. It looked, according to the evidence, that the vic was somehow exposed to unnaturally extreme temperatures and was dead within seconds. But . . . that's not possible. There is no weapon, no technology, nothing in nature short of the fucking sun that can produce that kind of heat. It's just not possible."

Leila doesn't answer right away, and there's a tight, sour expression on her face, like she doesn't like what she's hearing. "So then what?"

"So then I keep digging. Look for Miriam. She's the only suspect I could find. No one else had any reason to want Ben dead. No gambling debts, no gang affiliations, no enemies, not even a bar fight. Just his battered, abused girlfriend. And there's a lot on her, motive-wise. A nurse at Mercy Hospital tells me Miriam was brought in a few days before Ben's body was discovered. Someone drove by an alley, saw her on the ground. Thought she was dead, she was so badly beaten. The nurse was emphatic that Miriam should have died. Ribs broken, lungs punctured, fractured cheekbone, fractured skull, severely concussed, bleeding from everywhere. She was brutalized, Leila. So there's the second impossibility: she got up and walked out that same day, *with* the guy who put her in the hospital in the first place. Shouldn't have been conscious at all, should have had months of surgeries, healing, recovery, physical therapy. But she walks out on her own two feet hours later."

Leila isn't looking at me now, running a thumbnail in the Styrofoam of her cup, making abstract patterns. "That is weird."

She knows more than she's letting on, that's my impression. I shake it off, and keep explaining, because I've already gone this far, so why not?

"Then there's the lady who saw a weird glow out her living room window late one night. She went to the window, peeked out the blinds of her second story apartment. She claims—she *swears*—she saw a girl walking down Eleven Mile Road, glowing. She wasn't senile, wasn't suffering from dementia or Alzheimer's or even boredom. No medications that might cause hallucinations. So she must have seen something, right? I have no reason to disbelieve her. So then I have to believe her, right? But . . . a glowing person? Glowing like she had the sun inside her, the witness insisted. Then a motorcycle shows up, swerves, crashes, and the glowing girl goes to the rider of the motorcycle, a guy I find out later is named Jack, who was also at the hospital, begging Miriam to go home with *him*, not Ben.

"So go back to more weirdness: She has a guy who clearly cares about her, who knows she's got this asshole hanging around who likes to hit her, but she doesn't leave with him, she leaves with asshole? What the fuck? That's what I'm thinking. But the motorcycle crash, the glowing girl, who I'm assuming is Miriam, based on purely my own intuition, she glows even brighter, so bright the old woman who saw all this said she had to look away because the glow was so blinding.

"And then, of course there's more. A fancy sports car shows up, a big guy gets out, looks angry, and this is Ben I think. Miriam faces him, they argue, and Miriam—again, according to the eighty-six-year-old eyewitness—catches on fire. But doesn't burn. Like she *was* fire, the lady claimed. Not like she was *on fire*, like someone tossed her a match—and get this, it was raining buckets at this point anyway—but like she was made of fire."

I lift a hand palm-up, shrug, and shake my head. "Okay, so the fancy sports car. Legally registered to Ben, but . . . no proof of sale. It was a Maserati, a car worth a quarter million dollars. And this was a guy who worked at a bar and lived off his USMC savings. No way he'd ever afford a Maserati. No way. Yet it was registered to him. No title in his apartment or in the car, no transfer of funds to show he'd purchased it, no importer or high-end dealer in the surrounding four states with a record of that car's VIN in their inventory. Also highly bizarre, but not really material to the murder. It was found in the casino's parking garage, several levels up from where the body was found. So it wasn't stolen or stripped for parts, despite its value."

Leila glances at me, then back to her cup. "I'm starting to see why you're having a hard time with this case. Nothing adds up."

"No," I agree. "Nothing adds up. Until Miriam herself shows up at the precinct one day and tells me the whole story. An abusive ex-boyfriend, how Ben saved her, they dated, and then he joined the Corps and went to Afghanistan, came back a different man. Meeting Jack, ending up in the hospital, leaving with Ben, getting kidnapped by Ben after she finally had enough of him—did I mention Ben had another girl-friend who Miriam hadn't known about? Yeah, he did. Nice guy, right?

"And then she gets to the confrontation in the parking garage. Ben kidnapped her, brought her to the casino, was going to rape her. She escaped, ran, he caught up to her in the garage. Jack showed up about the same time, but he wouldn't say *how* he'd found them. . . . So there was a big showdown. Ben had a gun, Jack fought him for it, Jack got shot, Miriam got shot . . . but neither of them died, or needed medical attention. And Miriam killed Ben. She said as much, in so many words. It was self-defense, she claimed."

Leila's voice is low and even. "How did she kill him? And how did they both survive being shot? Did she explain that?"

I nod. "She sure did. She healed Jack, because she has magical powers. And then she killed Ben because she's—what was the word she used? A djinni. She claimed she was sort of a mythical or mystical being called a djinni, and that fire was a integral part of her essence. Now, aside from the fact that her explanation fit all the evidence, it sounded like delusional horse shit. Right? Magical powers? The ability to heal gun-shot wounds, to heal herself of brutal injuries, and oh yeah, she also claimed the Maserati was her doing too, because a djinni is where we get the myths about genies, right?"

I glance at Leila, and see that she's gone stock-still, expression blank. I watch her as I finish my explanation. "So of course I'm openly and obviously skeptical. But then she closed her eyes, and when she opened them . . . I don't know how to explain this part. Her eyes were flame. As if the sun lived inside her soul. As if . . . like the old lady said, and as Miriam herself claimed, as if she was made of fire on an elemental level. I *saw* it, Leila. With my own eyes. And then . . . and then this little flame, the size of a candle flame, it comes out of her fucking fingertips, dances across my desk, onto my palm. It was fire, and it was . . . *alive.* On my hand. I felt it. It burned, it hurt, but it didn't consume me. It was just there. And it *looked* at me. I swear it did. But . . . that's impossible, right? Yet I saw it, and I can't forget it. I'll never forget what I saw, but I can't explain it. Not to anyone. You probably think I'm crazy."

I look at her, and instead of laughing at me or telling me how nuts I am, she snags a packet of matches from a glass on the bar, folds the lid over to reveal the striking surface, lights a match, and watches it burn down toward her fingertips. Before it touches her skin it suddenly extinguishes, as if puffed out by a gust of wind.

She glances at me sideways to see if I notice, and I

wonder if she's hoping I did notice, or hoping I didn't?

"I don't think you're crazy," is all she says. A long moment of silence, during which I should ask her why she doesn't think I'm crazy. I don't ask her this, and she sighs. "So what are you going to do? Is the case still open?"

"Yeah, it is still open," I say, avoiding the question of my sanity. "Technically, *legally*, what Miriam did was manslaughter. She should've reported Ben to the authorities and let them deal with him. But, speaking as *one* of those authorities, by the time she did, and we had investigated, he would have vanished. He would've disappeared before we could have caught him and, honestly, there are just so many other more pressing cases to investigate that a domestic abuse complaint is a lower priority. I'm not saying this is right or okay in any way—abuse in any form is despicable. I don't mean it that way at all. I just mean that with all the drug cases and murders and shit like that, her case would just get . . . lost in the shuffle. And although I'm not supposed to say this, all the evidence points to Ben being an asshole who deserved *exactly* what he got." I drain the last of my drink and chew on an ice cube. "I know what I *should* do, what I'm supposed to do, according to the most correct definition of my job, but I just don't think I can. I became a cop to get justice for people. There were other reasons, but that was the biggest one. In the case of Miriam, she did the only thing she could in those circumstances, and I just can't make myself arrest her for it. It's like . . . ethics versus morals, you know?"

Leila nods, bumping her shoulder against mine, and I pretend like the quick, innocent touch doesn't send a bolt of lightning through me. "Hey, all you can do is what you think is right, you know?

Leila has a ring on her right hand that she twists absently. I remember the first time I met her, the way she'd pause before answering a question, and how she often fiddled with that ring, how I thought she was a woman with a story to tell. I have that feeling about her now more than ever. She didn't balk at my story in the slightest, despite how crazy it sounded even as I told it. In fact, she looked like she was finding it all too believable, and disturbing for that very reason.

She twists the ring again, then glances at me. "So you're gonna close the case?"

"Yeah, I think I am," I say. "I'll tell the captain there's not enough to go on. And, honestly, there isn't. There's no physical evidence tying Miriam to Ben's death, and even if there might be plenty of motive to pin on her, there's no way to make a charge stick. It would waste everyone's time and money, and just cause more trouble for Miriam. And she's had enough of that, if you ask me."

"Good," Leila says. "I'm glad."

I hesitate for a moment, and then go for it. "So . . . what's your story? You said before you needed a fresh start, so you came here. What's that about?"

Leila glances at me, and seems uneasy. "Oh, it's a long story, and not a very interesting one."

"You never know what I'd be interested in." I reach over the counter, grab the soda gun and fill my glass with water. "I'm interested in you, for example."

Jesus, did I just say that? I didn't mean to.

I focus on sipping at my water to cover my flush of embarrassment. Leila turns on her stool, regarding me, several emotions flashing across her face: surprise, embarrassment, curiosity and maybe a little fear.

"You are, huh?" she says eventually, with a slight smile on her lips.

"Yeah, that just kind of slipped out." I let out an awkward chuckle, and then decide on further honesty. "But it's true."

"A Freudian slip, huh? What else are you thinking about me that you're not saying?" She's inched over on her stool, just at the edge of my personal space.

I'm hoping I'm reading her body language right. "Oh . . . I don't know," I say, setting my glass down and looking at her. "You're gorgeous."

Leila's laugh is an infectious, musical sound. "Is

that right? Keep going." She crosses one leg over the other, facing me.

"Um . . ."

There are a lot of things going through my mind: her lips look soft, a slight glimmer of lip balm on them; I wonder what her lips taste like.

"I'm wondering what flavor Chapstick you have on. What your lips taste like," I hear myself say. I cover my face with my both hands and speak through my fingers. "God, I suddenly have no filters."

Leila arches an eyebrow. "Filters are a nuisance anyway," she says. "I've always believed in saying what you mean."

Is it my imagination, or is she leaning in to me, ever so slightly?

I'm tipping toward her, thinking how badly I want to kiss her, and if kissing her is a good idea or not, what I would be getting myself into. "Yeah? So what are you thinking? Now that I've embarrassed myself."

"Oh, so it's my turn?" She's definitely closer than she had been a moment ago. Her wide eyes are inches from mine, sparkling with amusement and secrets, and something I really want to believe is desire. "You haven't embarrassed yourself at all. I'm glad you say what you're thinking."

"You're avoiding my question." Leila is facing me

now, her feet between my legs, perched on the rungs of my stool.

I put my hands on her knees, and she doesn't pull away.

"True," Leila admits, a mischievous smile on her lips. "Okay, so what am I thinking? Hmmm. I'm thinking . . . you've got this rugged, sexy look going on, and that I'm digging it. I'm also thinking that you're a little drunk."

Leila's fingers are plucking at a loose string on the collar of my shirt, and then they're playing with a lock of my hair near my neck. It's an odd intrusion into my personal comfort zone; touching someone's hair is a strangely intimate thing. I don't mind, though. Not at all. Not when it's this beautiful girl doing the touching.

"I'm thinking . . . I like you," she says, "and I'm hoping you'll ask me out. There. How's that for embarrassing yourself? Admitting something like that to the guy you're interested in goes against every rule of the dating game I know."

"I've never been too interested in the dating game anyway," I say.

"Me neither. That's part of the reason I moved up here," she says. "I know I'm avoiding your original question, but . . . I don't want to talk about that right now."

"Fair enough."

"Do you have a girlfriend?" Leila asks. "Or a wife?"

I shake my head. "Nah. Would I be here, talking to you like this if I did?"

"You'd be surprised what some guys will try, even when they're involved with someone else." Her eyes harden.

I shrug. "You'd be surprised how much it takes to surprise me. I'm a homicide cop, remember? I've seen just about everything." I move my hands a little higher, from her knees to her thighs. "But, no. Short answer is, I'm not married, dating, or seeing anyone in any capacity." I had been about to kiss her, but the moment seemed to have passed with the turn in the conversation.

"Well, that's good. I wouldn't like to have any surprises come up later on." She glances down, then adds, "if there is a later on, that is."

"Why wouldn't there be?"

"Well, I left you a pretty big opening to ask me out, but you didn't." Leila bites her lip and scratches at a stain on the leg of her jeans.

Drunk dumbass, I scold myself. "Yeah, I guess I missed the boat on that one. Is it too late?"

"You'll never know until you try," Leila says, still not looking at me. But she's smiling a little, and her eyes flick to mine, then away, and back again.

"So . . . do you want to go out with me? For dinner? Sometime?" I shake my head, irritated at myself. "Sorry, that didn't come out right. Lemme try again. Leila, would you like to have dinner with me?"

Leila rolls her eyes. "You're funny," she says, a teasing grin on her face. "Yes, Carson, I would. I'm off this Tuesday."

She's tilting forward again, touching her lips with her tongue. There's an invitation in her eyes. I watch her tongue wet her lips, watch her teeth catch her lower lip and let go.

I let myself fall forward, touch my lips to hers slowly and hesitantly, giving her every chance to pull away. But she doesn't. Instead, she moves one of her hands from her knee to my thigh, and her other slips to my neck, pulling me closer, deepening the kiss.

Her breath is cold, like a winter wind, and her lips taste like cherry lip balm, with a hint of rum and Coke. I could have sworn a breeze had kicked up somehow, blowing through my hair, ruffling my shirt, and skirling Leila's long raven-black hair around us.

Then I feel a quick, sharp pang of pain blast through the back of my skull, and darkness leaps up to swallow me.

As I fade into unwilling unconsciousness, I hear Leila shrieking and cursing, and I try to fight back, try to stay awake, but it's no use.

The world goes black and silent.

Chapter 2: Spinning a Web

Leila

THEY FOUND ME. I CAN'T BELIEVE THEY FOUND ME. I MEAN, I figured they would eventually find me, but not quite so soon.

All I want is to be left alone. Is that so much to ask?

For my father and Hassan . . . yes, it is too much to ask. They think they own me, they think they can determine my life, they think they can make choices for me.

But if either of them think I'm going to just lie down and let them control my life, they have another thing coming.

Especially Hassan al-Jabiri. The arrogant bastard.

I know it was his thugs who came for me, who showed up at the bar and forced me to defend not just myself this time, but Carson. If I'd been alone, things might've gone differently. I might not have used so much . . . restraint. But Carson was there, and I couldn't let him get hurt any more than he already was.

God . . . Carson.

Why did he have to show up? And why does he have to be so goddamn sexy and irresistible? Why did he have to kiss me? I might have sensed them coming. But Carson was there, watching me with his electric blue eyes, roving over me, devouring me. He was there with his spiked brown hair and big, hard muscles coiled like springs under his shirt. He was just sitting on the stool next to me, downing gin and tonics like he wished he could drown in them, tempting me with his hesitant flirtation. His lips touched mine and I couldn't see or think or feel anything else.

I don't know all that much about him, but I think he hides behind his job. He seems most comfortable talking about his work, and I can tell he wants me, but, for some reason, he doesn't dare let himself think it.

I like the desire in his eyes. It's not possessive, calculating, or domineering. It's just simple male desire. Maybe "simple" is not the right word, but it is free of ulterior motives. He wants *me* just because I'm *me*. Not because of my family, or because of my father's wealth and position within the clans. He doesn't even *know* about any of that. I think he knows there's a deeper story behind why I'm here aside from "needing a change." He didn't buy that at all, obviously. He's a cop, after all, so I'm sure he can smell evasions and prevarications from a mile away. Part of me wants to tell him everything about myself. Which is stupid, idiotic, foolish. And dangerous, for him and for me. He doesn't need to know anything about me. He doesn't need my life story. He doesn't need to know why I ran away from a spoiled life of sheltered privilege and endless wealth.

And he sure doesn't need to know what happened at the bar. He doesn't need to know who I really am . . . or *what* I am.

But part of me wonders: should I tell him? Will I end up having to tell him?

Part of me wants to confide in him and throw myself at him simply because of the purity of his desire for me.

Men have always pursued me, flirted with me, charmed me and hit on me, but I could always see the greed and the motive lurking behind their gazes. I can feel it in their hands when they try to charm their way into my pants and into my father's ear and bank account. Hassan, above and beyond all the rest, has motives for wanting me that have nothing to do with who I am. He doesn't want Leila; he wants Leila *Najafi*. He wants the name and the weight behind it, the power that will be his once the alliance between our clans is sealed.

I refuse to be a pawn in their stupid games of power. I am a woman, not a chess piece. I want a man to love me for who I am, not for what I have, or who my father is. I don't care about their alliance. I don't care how powerful our joined clans will be, how much power we will wield over the other clans, I don't even care how vast our wealth will be once— *if*—the alliance is sealed.

The alliance, after all, hinges on me, and I refuse to be a part of it. I have refused Hassan's clumsy, oafish advances. I have denied my father's orders. I ran away from the only home I've ever known to get away from both of them, and their politics and their positioning and their avarice.

Carson Hale, when he fixes those hard, intense blue eyes on me, wants me without knowing anything of that. Perhaps it is only lust at this point, but I'll take that over Hassan's version of desire, which isn't desire but lust for my body, and need for control, and hunger for power all mixed together.

My fear is that Carson will vanish once he realizes that what trails behind me is a freight train of baggage. Plus, he's a cop, and my family runs on the opposite side of the law. Yet another reason I fled Chicago.

It's all so complicated already, and now Carson is, unwittingly, in the middle of it. He has no clue, and he sure doesn't know how confused I am right now. He has no idea how alluring, how tempting he is to me. My heart tells me it's not just lust, though. There's something else in the way he looks at me, in the way he talks to me. He's come to me three times now when he's upset or confused, and he talks to me about it. I like to think he came to The Old Shillelagh as much for me as for the gin and tonic, although I can't say for sure. I mean, there has to be a dozen other places he could have gone to get drunk, all closer to the precinct or to his apartment.

But he comes to *my* bar. That has to mean something, right?

Whether it does or not, I had no business involving him in my tangled-up mess of a life. The problem is, he's now involved, most likely to his detriment.

I should go see him, shouldn't I? I mean, he's in the hospital with a concussion and possibly even broken bones, and all because of me. I should make sure he's okay. I should find out what he knows, what he suspects, and get his version of events.

I have to allay his suspicions, don't I? For his own protection, I have to lead him away from the truth.

Who am I kidding? I'm going because I want to see his rugged face and feel his hands touching me. I'm going because deep down I want to feel his lips on mine again. Knowing that Carson Hale is the last person on earth I should be getting romantically involved with doesn't change what I feel about him.

I'm flushed with lust for him. The only question is whether my prudence will be stronger than my lust. Because that's all it is: lust. It's physical. He's hot, he's strong, and he's a damned good kisser. It's not emotional at all. I don't *feel* anything for him at all. It's simply hormones and pheromones.

Right?

He's sitting up in the hospital bed, the thin white blanket pulled up to his hips, pillows propped behind his back. He's eating green Jell-O. The lights are dimmed, the TV on mute, and he's staring at the TV without really seeing it. The hospital gown is too small and is untied, showing his muscular arms and the bandages around his ribs. I can see the band of his black underwear peeking out from between the front and back of the gown where the blanket doesn't cover him. Even standing in the doorway, watching him, I want to run my hands across his abs, around to the small of his back and under the band of his underwear. I shove my hands in my pockets.

He notices me, and his eyes light up. He sets aside the Jell-O and clicks off the TV using the controller attached to the bed.

"Leila! I wasn't expecting you . . . come in, sit down." He tugs the blanket higher and tries in vain to make the gown close around his side.

If I'm being honest, I'm glad it doesn't close. I like the glimpses of his skin, of his powerful physique.

"Of course I'd come and see you," I tell him, pulling the plastic guest chair closer to the bed. A little closer than it needs to be, probably, close enough that I can reach out and touch him if I want to. My hands are clutching my purse so hard my knuckles are white—a lame attempt at keeping myself under control.

He smiles, showing absurdly straight, white teeth. "Well, I'm glad you're here." It's a slightly awkward moment.

I'm not sure what to say, and neither is he. I can see a million questions flitting around behind his eyes, coupled with his desire for me. All of this is communicated in the way he glances at the TV screen, as if wishing it was a means of distraction, and in the way he plucks at the loose threads of the blanket.

I find myself wishing that his hands would busy themselves with me.

"How are you feeling?" I ask him. "Are you hurt badly? How long will you be here?"

He shrugs, lifting the gown up to show more of his bruised abdominal muscles. He has cuts on his face and a square of gauze is taped on his forehead. "Eh, I'm fine. Some bruised ribs and a concussion. I've been hurt worse playing football, honestly, but I'm a cop so I can't just leave. I'll be here for another day or so to make sure my ribs are healing and so they can keep an eye on the concussion."

"I saw that wince when you shrugged," I say. "So let me ask you again. How are you really, Carson?" I lean forward, and my hands are on the edge of the bed, inches from his own.

He glances down at my hands, takes a quick look and then glances away. He's aware of our proximity, which means he wants me to touch him, I think. I try to hold my hands still, but one of them finds itself brushing against his knuckles, nudging his fingers aside so my hand is beneath his. He wraps his hand around mine, a reflexive motion.

I like how this feels.

Why am I holding his hand? I shouldn't be doing this, but . . . I can't seem to summon the will power necessary to make myself let go.

Carson is searching my face, and he answers my question after a moment, "Okay. Well, honestly, it hurts. It's mainly my ribs. But, honestly, it's not bad. I'm fine. I'm more confused than anything. I'm not even really sure what happened or how I got here." He's rubbing one of my knuckles with his thumb, soft, gentle circles. "I remember being in the bar with you, being a little drunk—"

"A *little* drunk?" I laugh, teasing him. "You were *wasted*."

He rolls his eyes. "I wasn't *that* drunk. Certainly not blackout drunk, but . . ." He shakes his head slowly. "I remember sitting at the bar with you, and I kissed you, and then things just went black. I don't remember falling over, and I don't think I was so wasted I'd have fallen off a damn chair. But how else could I have blacked out? I had five or six drinks, at the most. That's not anywhere *near* enough to make me black out. But after I kissed you, everything is just a blank. I don't know how I got here, and I *really* don't know what happened to my ribs."

"I think *I* kissed *you*," I say, by way of nudging the conversation away from certain unexplainable events.

Unexplainable to a human, at least.

My free hand is fidgeting with the hem of his gown sleeve, tracing the line of his muscles between bicep and tricep. "I remember that pretty clearly, since

I *was* sober. I definitely kissed you." Talking about the kiss is dangerous, because I want to kiss him again, and I shouldn't, I can't, he's already been hurt enough simply for being seen with me once, but talking about the kiss is the best tactic I can come up with for distracting him from asking questions I can't answer.

And goodness knows Carson has enough unanswered questions in his life.

"I don't know," he says. "I'm pretty sure I kissed you first. You were sort of leaning in a little bit, but I made the move first."

I shake my head, insisting, "No, you were the one leaning in, but I *for sure* kissed you first." I'm so close to kissing him again, and I know I shouldn't.

But I don't think I can lie to him. Not convincingly, at least. He'd know.

"You must have been more drunk than you realized," he says, laughing. "Because you're remembering wrong. I may have had a fair bit to drink, but my memory of that much, at least, is clear as a bell."

We've both leaned forward in imperceptible increments, until we're within kissing distance.

"I *wasn't* drunk," I say, letting my hand drift up from his arm to his shoulder. "I'd had like three sips from my drink, which I had just poured after my shift was over. I wasn't even buzzed. We were sitting a lot like this: close, but not quite . . . there. . . ."

He's raising a skeptical eyebrow, a saucy, sarcastic, unspoken comment. I don't move in any closer, still fighting with myself about letting this happen.

I want him to make the move. I want him to show me how he feels.

But I shouldn't want that. I should leave the hospital right now, before we kiss again, before I get myself deeper in trouble with this all-too-sexy detective. Before the whirling vortex of trouble that is my life pulls him in any further. He's the polar opposite of all that my family, my clan, and even my entire race represents. And not just that; he poses a complication in my life that I can't justify, not when I've already got so many problems to figure out.

But now it's too late: he's closed the distance and has put his lips to mine, a slow, delicate movement, so tender and questing, so sensual coming from such a rugged man. He's big and tough and hard and he's kissing me like he's worried I may shut him down. I *should* shut him down, but I can't. I don't. I won't. Instead of pushing him away and running like a smart girl would do, I slip my hand behind his head, to the close-cropped down-soft hair by his neck, and pull him gently towards me to deepen the kiss.

I am a fool.

Why the hell am I kissing him? The sensible part of my brain is screaming at me. This is the fourth time

I've seen this man, and I don't think he even knows my last name.

This is stupid and foolish, and it'll only lead to heartbreak for both of us.

But I can't stop myself. He tastes like Jell-O and coffee, and his tongue is pushing against mine, his hand is brushing my cheek and burying itself in my hair. Our other hands are still entwined together, fingers tangled and tightening as the kiss goes from innocent to hungry in an instant.

I manage to pull away before it goes too far. Our faces are still mere inches from each other, and his eyes are hunting and searching mine, looking for something, digging into me, asking a thousand silent questions.

I don't have the answers to his questions, and I don't know why I'm so attracted to him.

Sure, he's hot as hell in that tall, dark, and handsome, all-American football player sort of way and, yeah, there's an element of danger to him, a rugged sense of primal, sexual power. But there's more to it than that. It's him, the man, the person. He has a way of shredding my will, a way of communicating how much he wants me with a mere look, or a touch of his fingers. Being wanted for who I am? God help me, I can't resist him. He touches me, looks at me, talks to me, and I know he likes me, or at least, what little he knows of me. I know he desires Leila the woman.

A quiet, insistent voice in my soul asks me a question that douses my hunger: will he still want me when he knows what I am? Will he want me when he knows what my family is? I don't know the answer to those questions. Another problem: I should be asking *if* he knows, not *when*. I don't want him to know. He can't know.

He must sense the conflict in me, for he pulls back and asks, "What's wrong?"

I shake my head. Where do I start? What do I say?

"I obviously shouldn't have kissed you," he guesses, dejection in his voice.

"No!" I say. "That's not it. I kissed you back, didn't I? I wanted you to kiss me."

"Then what? There's something wrong. I can tell there is, so don't try and say there isn't." He's perceptive and insistent, and I know he'll hear the lie in my voice.

I lie anyway. "It's just . . . this is crazy, you know? We don't even know each other."

He hisses in frustration, rolling his eyes. "Maybe it is crazy, but . . . it's also not. And that's not it either."

I know he's right, and he knows I'm evading answering his question. As crazy as it is to be kissing a man I barely know, with Carson it just feels . . . *right*. The problem is that I simply cannot get the truth to come out. All I can do is shake my head, as if that could dislodge the words that would allay his suspicions.

"Leila, what happened at the bar?" There's the question, direct and uncompromising.

I feel panic bolt through me. "I'm not really sure," I say, feeling another lie burning the air between us. "It must have been a robbery, or something. It all happened so fast, and I didn't really get a good look at whoever it was."

Carson is staring at me, and the suspicion and disappointment on his face are almost too much to take. "That's bullshit, Leila. The doors were all locked and we were talking, and then the next thing I remember is . . . being hit on the back of the head? That's the only thing that makes sense. The doctor told me my concussion was caused by blunt force trauma. Sometime later I wake up here, feeling as if a building had fallen on top of me. So don't tell me it was a robbery, and don't tell me you don't know. You weren't hurt, and you didn't report a robbery. I know, I checked. So . . . you must have seen *something*. What the hell happened? You *have to* remember something."

"*Like a building fell on top of me . . .*" Oh god, if only he knew how correct he is. But if he knew what happened in the bar, it'd only lead to more questions, none of which have easy answers.

"I don't know what happened, Carson. I really don't." The lie is searing through me, and it's all I can do to keep from either kissing him again or running from the room.

"Okay, Leila. Fine. Whatever you say." He lets it go for now and I'm thankful, but I'm also really scared. He's not a man who will let this drop.

The silence between us is awkward and thick, freighted with a complex amalgam of desire and lies.

"Listen, I . . . I should go," I say. I have to get out of here. I have to get away from him, away from his sensual, accusing eyes, away from his lips that are drawing me in even now, away from his hands that I want to feel on my skin. Away from the truth that I know he seeks.

He nods, releases my hands, grabs the remote for the TV. I stand up, my purse dangling from one hand. I'm not sure whether I should hug him or just walk away. I lean toward him and wrap my arms around him in a hug, cursing myself for the idiot I am. His arms snake around me and rest on my back, on the nape of my neck, and I like them there. Despite everything I'm enjoying the restrained strength in his touch. As I start to pull away Carson brushes an errant strand of hair away from my face and stares into my eyes, searching me once again. He sees the lies in my eyes as clearly as he sees the nose on my face. I also know he sees my desire, my confusion. I know he sees it all there, for it's roiling just beneath the surface, and I've never been good at hiding my emotions. He kisses me, a quick, hard brush of the lips. There's a familiarity about it, as if he always kisses me before we part.

I hate myself for loving how natural it feels.

"So . . . was this our first date, then?" he asks, changing the subject, but somehow I know his real question is still poised on the tip of his tongue.

"What? What do you mean?"

"I asked you out, remember? We were supposed to go out Tuesday, which is tomorrow. I think. But, I can't exactly take you out tomorrow, so . . ." He trails off, hoping I'll fill in the space.

And I do: "How about we call this a visit, and then you can take me on a real date when you get out of here?"

Why did I just say that? The last thing I should be doing is going out on a date with Detective Carson Hale. If I had any sense I would shut this down right now.

But . . . no. The reckless, impulsive, selfish part of me is telling me that I've already kissed him twice now, so I might as well go for broke by going on a date with him.

"I'd like that," he says, grinning like I've just

made his day.

"Me too," I say, and I'm smiling too, unable to stop myself.

I'm trying to pull away so I can leave, but his hand is still in mine and I want to sit back down and kiss him again. I can see him wanting the same thing. The desire is pulsating from him, evident in the way he's gazing at me, in the way he's still searching my eyes as if trying to glean the truth from me without having to pull it out of me one word at a time.

It takes a few minutes, but I finally manage to get myself out of his hospital room and into the maze of hallways. I'm still thinking about his lips on mine and how much I loved the feel of his hands in my hair, his tongue tip exploring near mine, not quite daring to kiss me deeply.

I know for a fact that if I were to kiss him again, there would be no turning back. He'll push the boundaries of passion, he'll ignite me, and there will be no keeping my hands to myself.

No, I'll exult in his touch.

I am in a world of trouble.

Well . . . *more* trouble, as if I didn't already have enough.

I'm in my car, the radio turned up too loud, as if Bruno Mars could make sense of my imbroglio. Now that I'm away from Carson, reality is catching up to me.

My father has expectations of me, and I know he'll be sending people after me. There is a limit to his indulgence; he as much as told me so the last time I spoke to him. He sees me living on my own in Detroit as a slap in the face, an insult to his Old World sensibilities. He has no problem with the idea of dragging me back to Chicago and forcing me to play his game. He believes it is my duty to return to Chicago and succumb to their will, my needs and dreams and desires be damned.

Duty is everything to my family; I know that all too well. I did my *duty* to them all growing up. I wore the hijab. I maintained good grades. I didn't talk to boys. I attended mosque with Mother. I was obedient and subservient and did everything I was ever told.

And then Father pulled me into his study when I was sixteen and informed me that he had betrothed me to Hassan al-Jabiri.

Betrothed. As in, promised me in marriage to a man I'd never met, to a man whose clan had a long history of feuding with mine. To a *criminal*. A butcher. A maniac.

Marry Hassan? No way. Not in a million years. That's what I told Father, that day in his study. *I don't care how rich or powerful he is. I don't care that he's the heir to the al-Jabiri clan's patriarchy. None of that matters to me. He's a pig, an arrogant, selfish, vicious criminal, and the thought of being his wife . . . I want to vomit just thinking about it.*

I remember Father's words verbatim: *Vomit if you wish, Leila, but when the time comes, you* will *marry Hassan.*

Father never asked me what I want. He never said a word about what he was planning, he just arranged it as if he had the right to marry me off to whomever he wished, as if this was the twelfth century or something. Even Mother knew there was nothing she could do, for she had been betrothed to a man many years her senior whom she neither knew nor loved, and I grew up witnessing the cold and brittle nature of their relationship.

The day we met, Hassan had looked at me with greed and calculation, knowing exactly what he stood to gain when we married. If it had been mere lust in his eyes, I could have dealt with it better, oddly enough. If he had just wanted me for my body, for the sexual consummation of the marriage, I could have understood it, as much as he repulsed me. What made me burn with rage was his greed and cupidity. He didn't—and doesn't—just want me for my body, or for who I am. No, he wants me for my inheritance, for my familial name, and for the fact that Father is the patriarch of one of our race's oldest and most powerful clans.

Then there's Carson. Handsome, sweet Carson, who knows none of this.

Carson is the last person I should be thinking about, yet he is all that I can see in my mind. His eyes, his body, his hands . . . they're hooked into me, and I can't get them out. I don't want to. I want them there, and that's what really worries me.

I pull into my apartment parking lot, thinking of Carson and his lips on mine.

I should have seen the black Mercedes in the parking lot, but I didn't.

CHAPTER 3: THE GATHERING STORM

Carson

EXCEPT FOR A FEW VIVID DETAILS, MY MEMORY IS ALMOST a complete blank. Nothing. Nada. I remember the sweet taste of her lips, cherries, and the feel of something cold, cold like a winter wind. I remember the feel of her body under my hands . . . soft and warm. I remember talking to her, kissing her, and then there's an impression of brief, sharp pain, followed by darkness and silence.

My next memory was waking up in a hospital bed, wearing a tiny hospital gown, my mind in overdrive with questions.

How did I get here? What had happened to me?

As soon as I woke up I called the nurse to try

to get some answers, asking after Leila, and I was assured I had been admitted alone last night—there was no patient in the hospital named Leila. I was brought in alone, the nurse repeated. Dropped off at the door of the ER, and no, no one remembers who brought me. That's the kind of detail a busy metropolitan emergency room nurse has no hope of remembering. She asked me if I wanted her to call a friend or family member, but I shut that down—I have no one to call. Then she told me about my injuries and strongly recommended I get some rest.

I've already spoken to Captain Archer and explained the best I can, and she told me to take whatever time I need to recover, as well as assuring me she would personally look into what happened last night. I need to know what happened at The Old Shillelagh.

I've been going to The Old Shillelagh to drink and think about difficult cases my entire career. It's quiet, out of the way and I never meet anyone I know, so there's never anyone to distract me from my thoughts. I get some of my best thinking done in that place.

And then one day, a few months ago, I was there after work when I looked up and there she was. Five-eight and curvy as sin, thick black hair tied back in a neat ponytail, bright brown eyes glittering with intelligence and curiosity, a hint of a smile on her lips that said she knew something she wasn't telling. Busy hands with short, red-painted nails, no wedding or engagement rings. She was graceful when she moved, light on her feet, drifting, almost as if blown across the room by a secret wind.

She floats, she dances, she twists and flutters.

She's . . . ethereal. That's the word for her. Ethereal.

I was attracted to her from that moment when I first laid eyes on her. Before that, even. I'd heard her voice before I saw her, and something in the way she spoke had resonated within me. It was as if some note in her voice struck a chord in my soul, and that note continues to reverberate every time I look at her.

But mere physical attraction doesn't explain everything. I've been drinking at The Old Shillelagh for years, and there have been plenty other attractive bartenders and waitresses. But none of them have ever made the lasting impression that Leila has. Sure, she makes great conversation, and has this way of making sense of my tangled thoughts. Sure, she's insanely gorgeous and seems to like me as much as I do her. And sure, she's kissed me back, not just once, but twice. She even twisted her fingers in my hair and pulled me close to deepen the kiss.

But it's more than that. More than a physical attraction. More than chemistry. It's something deeper.

I'm *drawn* to her. There's a mystery about her. Her eyes hold secrets that I'm compelled to unearth. Mysteries in the playful winds that always seem to follow her, hidden truths behind the lies she's told even as her eyes and frayed nerves betrayed her.

My fingers are cramping, and I glance down to see I'm twisting the blanket in my hands, squeezing and bunching the fabric until my knuckles turn white. I force myself to release the thin cotton blanket and try to calm myself.

Every time I try to make sense of what happened in the bar my mind is pulled away to Leila, which only deepens the mystery. Every time I close my eyes I see Leila. I see her hips swaying as she dances behind the bar, making the dull closing ritual into a ballet of beautiful motion. I try to think of something else, but my mind keeps coming back to the moment of our first kiss, my hands on her knees and inching toward her hips, an electric tingle running through me at the feel of her body under my palms, the way her hands brush my skin, lighting some long-banked fire in my gut.

I'm trying to categorize what I feel for her, and I can't. I've had more than a few flings, mostly with badge-chasers who warmed my bed for a night or two or three before we both moved on in mutual, unspoken agreement. I'd been attracted to those women on a superficial level, but I hadn't really *known* them. They were just bodies, nothing but flesh and warmth, scratching the proverbial itch. And I haven't been with a woman like that in quite a while. Something about the one-night-stands left me more and more unsatisfied. I felt pissed off with myself and just generally discontent with the way my life was going.

If I'm being honest with myself—and when are you more honest with yourself than when you're stuck in a hospital bed?—those quick sexual encounters never satisfied me. They didn't even completely satisfy the physical urges. And even the couple of fairly serious girlfriends I've had—women I knew fairly well, nice, interesting, good-looking girls from good families—those didn't satisfy either, and never lasted more than six months, a year at most. The job always put an end to those relationships, for one thing. They'd get tired of being stood up, annoyed with the last-minute phone calls canceling dates. Basically, I think they got tired of playing second fiddle to my career.

And . . . in truth I was never very invested in those relationships. I hadn't opened up, hadn't let them see the real Carson Hale. They didn't know much about my job—they hadn't asked and I hadn't told them anything. If I'm being brutally honest, they had been little more than long-term booty calls.

Which may make me a prick, but I never pretended to feel emotions I didn't have, and I was always clear that my career would come first.

What am I trying to say? What do I want to tell myself? I feel myself circling around a core truth that I've been avoiding.

I'm lonely.

There it is.

No amount of casual sex can chase away the loneliness. When they're getting dressed, shrugging their bras back on and sitting on the edge of the bed strapping on fancy heels, that's when I feel the loneliness even more. Sometimes they'd sneak away in the middle of the night, and when I woke up to find them gone I'd feel a combination of relief and guilt . . . along with a whole lot of emptiness.

Casual sex is like eating Pringles when you're hungry; no matter how many you eat or how tasty they may be, you're never satisfied with the empty calories.

Eventually, I stopped bothering, stopped making the effort. I ignored the advances, flirtatious glances, and the bold invitations. I threw myself into work, taking one case after the other and working each of them with relentless ferocity. Work distracted me, sure, but it never filled the underlying emptiness.

Then I met Leila, and without even trying she

managed to fill that black hole, somehow. I don't really know much about her, but she makes me feel less alone, for reasons I can't begin to fathom. It's ridiculous and absurd that I should feel this way about someone I barely know, but it's true. I've been trying to convince myself that I'm only physically attracted to her, but I know it's more than that.

For one thing, I can tell she's not like the women who just want a guy in a uniform. Those girls are happy to let me take them out and wine-and-dine them, but the dates always end up being little more than an excuse to get into bed as quickly as possible. They were after empty sex as much as I was. At least, that's how it *used* to be.

Leila isn't the kind of woman to be tumbling onto her back after the first date. That much I do know, and I appreciate it about her, and not just for the challenge. I like the fact that it's not all about the sex. I want her to make me wait. I want the sex to *mean* something.

I must have drifted off because the next thing I know the captain is entering my hospital room.

Brushing aside the curtain, Captain Archer takes one look at the darkened room and huffs in amusement. "Brooding again, Carson?" She sets a pair of disposable coffee cups on the moveable table, along with a bag of Einstein Brothers bagels.

"Me? Brooding? Never," I say with a grin, reaching for the coffee and a chocolate chip bagel.

Archer laughs and pops the lid off her coffee, taking a careful sip and wincing at the scalding heat. "Carson, I've known you for six years. I know when you're brooding."

I nod. "Yeah, I guess I am," I admit, between bites. "So, what can you tell me? How the hell did I end up here?"

Archer won't meet my eyes, and that's when I know something is amiss. "Well, I'm afraid what little I do know won't answer too many questions."

"I figured." I finished one bagel and reached for another. "Well, out with it already."

Captain Lisa Archer is the closest thing I have to a family. She's a complicated woman, tough as nails yet still feminine, a black woman born and raised in inner-city Detroit. She started her police career at the bottom, as a patrol officer, and clawed her way to the top, fighting sexism, racism, corruption, and fraternalism every step of the way, but she's never forgotten her roots, no matter how high up the ranks she goes.

She sets a manila file folder on my lap and points at a series of photographs. They show what had been a building and was now merely rubble, a pile of toppled brick and twisted metal, charred wood and smashed glass. I flip through the photos quickly at first, then again more slowly, looking for details. One photograph shows an intact brick wall with what looks like a broken length of rebar sticking out from the brickwork. The rebar is embedded into the brick, looking a lot like a steel javelin thrown by a giant. The whole scene looks like the aftermath of a tornado.

"I can't make sense of this, Captain," I grumble. "There's fire damage in a few of these shots, but then it also looks like a tornado hit the building. What is this I'm looking at?"

"That's what's left of The Old Shillelagh," she says. "We can't figure out what the hell happened either. It doesn't make any sense. It does look like a tornado hit it, but there's no damage to any other buildings in the area, and the weather last night was clear and calm. It was a totally quiet July night. No wind, no rain, no thunder, nothing but clear skies. There's a lot of fire and water damage and, thank god, no reported casualties. No other buildings touched. Like, not even a speck of mortar out of place. Yet the Shillelagh? Well, you see the photos. It's totalled. Leveled down to rubble. But then there's you, whacked on the back of the head, and looking like the building fell on top of you."

"What about Leila?"

"Who?"

"The bartender? The one I was—the bartender working when all this happened."

Archer catches my slip. "The one you were what?"

I try to cover, "The one I was talking to, just before whatever happened, happened."

Archer rolls her eyes. "Yeah, 'cause that's what you were gonna say." She shakes her head and waves the subject away with a sweep of her long fingers. "Anyway, we spoke to her, but she claims not to know anything. Says she has no idea how the building was destroyed."

"Do you believe her?" I ask. Connections are forming in the back of my mind, but I refuse to examine them.

Not yet, least.

"Not really," Archer says with a shrug. "But there's no evidence of any kind of a crime. You were with her, and she says it must have been a robbery, but the building is so damaged that it's impossible to tell if anything was stolen. I personally think she's hiding something, but I don't know what, and I got no proof of anything at all, regardless of my feelings. I'm not even sure what I'm looking for. This is one of the more bizarre things I've ever encountered."

I can only nod and sip my coffee. It's all too

strange. Too much like the al-Mansur case in far too many ways, and I have no intention of getting caught up in another case like that one.

Captain Archer is staring at me intently, examining me. "You like her, don't you? The bartender?"

I shrug, not wanting to talk about her.

"Look, Hale," she said. "You're *allowed* to like her. Something weird happened, sure, but there's no conflict of interest that I can see. God knows you need a girlfriend. You're working too hard, you need something to look forward to 'sides one case after another. If you like her, go after her. That's my motherly advice for today."

I wish it were that simple. I've got a feeling it will be anything but.

With instructions to take it easy and to come back to work only when I'm ready, the captain leaves.

Not even an hour after Captain Archer leaves, Leila shows up, looking as toned and fit and sexy as ever. We talk, I resist asking questions, and she avoids providing any answers. The whole time she's here I feel a thousand questions boiling in the back of my head, demanding I ask her about what happened. But before I can do that, through flirting banter, we talk about our first kiss in the bar, and Leila seems to think *she* kissed *me* first, when I know for a fact it was the other way around. Her tongue flicks out to lick her lips, and I can't help but remember how her tongue had tentatively touched mine in that first kiss.

All my questions are buried by her proximity. Her lips are only centimeters from mine now, and I feel a sense of reckless abandon wash through me. I can't help what comes next, and I don't try to stop it. Resistance is pointless. Her lips are so close, her eyes huge and dark and waiting, and her hand is in mine, and it's just a matter of tilting my head just so, and our lips will touch, in the briefest of caresses.

She tastes of cherry lip balm again, and something else now, a slushy maybe, frozen Coke. Her hand drifts up to the back of my head, and there's something so tender, so affectionate and familiar about the gesture. It sets me on fire, makes me crazy with desire for her. Her tongue brushes against mine, a questing touch, and the fire becomes a blaze.

I forget everything except Leila, except her lips and her hands, the silk-soft skin of her face beneath my fingers. Wrapping my arms around her body, I touch her back and the nape of her neck, and she arches into my touch.

And then she tenses and pulls away, although I can tell it took some effort. Her eyes are deep and dark, full of secrets and mysteries. There's so much hidden behind her gaze.

I have trouble tearing my eyes from hers, but the

questions about the explosion—or whatever it was that happened and why I am here, in the hospital— are boiling up inside me, and I know I won't be able to contain them for long. The cop in me is just too strong.

I can see the conflict in her eyes, and I hate the fact that I have no idea what's causing it. There are so many questions, and so few answers. She's with- holding so much from me, and I know it. I can see it in her eyes; can feel the lies emanating from her skin in palpable waves.

When I outright ask her what happened, she lies and says she doesn't know.

After years of questioning witnesses and sus- pects, I can sense evasion and sniff out omission. I know a lie when I hear one, and she's lying through her fucking teeth.

Yet, as much as that pisses me off, I can't bring myself to push the issue. She's keeping secrets, that much is painfully clear. As a detective, my instinct is to pursue the truth with relentless ferocity. But as a man interested in a woman, I'm conflicted; I want to respect her privacy.

How do I reconcile the two?

Her visit is brief, and I wonder if part of the rea- son is she's scared of my questions, scared of telling the truth for reasons beyond my ability to fathom.

When she's gone, I'm torn between equal parts of relief and disappointment: relief from the internal war of the need for truth, the desire to respect her privacy, and the disappointment that she's actually gone, leaving me to my whirling, confused thoughts.

After Leila leaves, I ask the nurse to lower the lights and draw the curtain around my half of the room. I turn the TV to ESPN and put it on mute. There's a lot to think about, and I can't imagine getting any sleep right now.

I slump lower in the hard, uncomfortable bed, scratching at the tubes taped to my forearm, flipping through the pictures again, trying to ignore the increasingly strong feeling that Leila had something to do with the destruction of The Old Shillelagh, that she knows exactly what happened and is just refusing to tell me, for reasons I can't quite figure out.

God, I wish I could re-wind my life by twenty-four hours.

CHAPTER 4: CONSTRICTING COILS

Leila

RETURNING FROM THE HOSPITAL, I ARRIVE HOME AND unlock my door, distracted and flustered by my visit with Carson. It is very difficult to avoid his questions. I can see that he doesn't believe me. I don't want to lie to him, but I have no other option.

Entering, I lock the door behind me and set my keys on the small ledge by the door. An overpowering yet familiar scent hits me in the face . . . what is it? Cologne, a thick miasma. It's then that I notice Hassan lounging on my couch, dirty shoes propped up on my glass coffee table, smearing mud on the clean surface.

Rage washes through me, and I clutch at the core of power always swirling within me. My hair is whipping around my head, a sudden, impossible wind blowing through the cramped one-bedroom apartment, plucking bills and magazines and books into a whorling vortex with me at the center.

Hassan shields his face with his arms, shrinking back against the couch. The wind buffets him, batters at his human form; flickers of flame spurt from his body. His arms and legs flash between being wind-blown flame and human flesh.

"Hey!" he shouts. "What are you doing? Cut it out! I'm just here to talk!"

I pull the winds back into myself, tamping them down and forcing them to quiet, but I keep them coiled just beneath the surface.

"What do you *want*, Hassan?" My voice is cold and hard. I'm disgusted by the fact that he is in my personal living space.

I want nothing so much as to use my powers to throw him through the wall, but I don't. For one thing, I'm not sure I could win a battle of powers between us.

"I just want to talk, Leila. Just listen to me, okay?" He relaxes his defensive posture and stands up, brushing at his Armani suit and adjusting his diamond-studded Rolex. Hassan is tall and handsome and very, very wealthy. He exudes power, authority, and arrogance. His features are Old World, a hawkish nose, deep-set, glittering black eyes, high cheekbones, lips always curled in sneering contempt.

"There's nothing to talk about. I'm not marrying you."

He grins, a sarcastic, snide smile. "Well, now, that's not really up to you, is it?" He crosses the room to stand inches from me; his evil, dark eyes are hard and fixed on me. He stinks of too much cologne, and I'm choking with it. "You know what's at stake, Leila. Are you sure you're willing to sacrifice the well-being of your entire family? I'm not so bad." With a lascivious smirk he adds, "You'll see, once you get to know me. I can be very . . . entertaining."

I push past him, stifling a shudder of revulsion as I pass him, and set my purse on the kitchen counter. He's right about the fact that marrying him is not my decision.

This only angers me all the more. "You're a *pig*, Hassan. I'd rather spend eternity in hell than marry you. My father knows this, but he doesn't listen. Just like you, all he cares about is himself and his business."

"He loves you, Leila. He wants what's best for you. He knows I can take care of you when he's gone." Hassan is picking lint from the sleeves of his suit jacket as he speaks. Always so concerned with his appearance. Vain as a peacock. "He's aging, your father. He's growing aware that the end of his life is near. He wants to ensure you are cared for. He knows I can give you everything you've ever wanted, and more."

I huff out a laugh; as if I'd take anything from him. "There's nothing you have that I want." I whirl to face him, stabbing a finger at him. "Not from you *or* from my father. The only thing either of you care about is money and power. All my life, I've never wanted for anything. I grew up getting whatever I asked for and more, yet I left all that behind . . . *on purpose.* You think I'm living in this tiny apartment because I like it? I pay for this myself, with what I *earn,* something you know nothing about. You inherited your wealth. You've done *nothing* to earn it, except maybe kill people. I don't want your dirty money, I don't want your diamonds or cars or mansions. I don't want *you.* All I want is to be left *alone."*

Hassan isn't the least bit fazed by my outburst. "No one is asking what you want, Princess."

"I KNOW!" I shout. "No one has ever asked what I want! And don't call me *Princess.* That's not who I am anymore."

But Hassan isn't done. "No one is giving you a choice about marrying me. You know what's at stake. If you won't come willingly, I'll drag you, and nothing and no one can stop me."

Hassan's lips curl up in a snarl, and he's suddenly pressed close against me, gripping my arms in a painful vise-like grip. I didn't even see him move. His eyes turn to flickering flames, orange and hungry and hot.

"You're mine . . . *Princess*. There's nothing you can do about it. You belong to *me*. I have *purchased* you, do you understand that? Your existence is *mine*, bought and paid for." His breath is foul, putrid and sour. "So here's what's going to happen: you are coming with me to Chicago, and we are going to be married, whether you like it or not. The alliance will be sealed, and your family's wealth will be mine, as will your body and your future. I *own* you. I own your father, your mother, your cousins. Everyone. Everything. Their lives depend on your actions. So either you go home on your own, or I drag you kicking and screaming back to Chicago. Perhaps I'll tie you up and put you in the trunk of my car. Would you like that? Bound and gagged? Either way, in two weeks you'll sign the fucking contract and you'll speak the fucking words, do you hear me? I will do whatever I must to ensure this is done according to our laws."

"And if I resist you?" I ask with a bravado I don't feel.

Hassan's eyes spark and flare, orange flames glinting with threat.

"I'll make you regret it," he hisses. "I won't harm

a hair on *your* head, oh no. You're too valuable to me intact. But you *will* regret it, let's just put it that way. You understand what I'm saying? No? Then let me spell it out for you—everyone you love, everyone you care about will pay the price for your selfish, stubborn refusal to obey your betters. Your father, your mother, your aunt and uncle, your cousins, all of them will pay the price for your childish stupidity. You wouldn't want anything to . . . *happen* to them, would you?"

I suppress my rage; my father is a fool, and he has indebted himself thrice over to the al-Jabiri clan, and now *I* must pay the price to absolve *his* debt.

"There will be no marriage, Hassan," I say. "Not in two weeks, not ever. You and your gorillas trashed the bar I work at, and now the police are all over me. They suspect it wasn't an accident. I will not be cowed by your threats. It will take time to convince them I had nothing to do with the . . . explosion."

"That's your problem, Princess," Hassan says, his smile sickly sweet. I want to bash in his perfect white teeth. "You should know better than to associate with human men. You are not for them. You are mine. That was . . . just a little warning. To you, and to that human you were rubbing yourself all over. Next time I catch you with him or anyone else, the consequence will be much worse."

"The police—" I begin, but Hassan cuts in over

me.

"Are humans. They will find nothing. They will decide it was a freak occurrence of nature, and move on. And if not . . . ? Well, then there will be a strange outbreak of house fires, mysteriously claiming only the lives of local police officers. Which, of course, will be on your conscience." He grins, pointing a finger at me. "Two weeks, Leila. I'll be back for you in two weeks. If I have to knock you unconscious and cart you back to Chicago in my trunk, I will. This alliance *will* happen, or I will slaughter your family in front of you, one by one. I don't need any of them alive to take control of your clan's assets." His eyes are dead and cold, his fingers dig into my arm, his breath stinks of garlic and cigars and alcohol. "I will tie you to a chair and cut your father's throat. I will rape your mother and your aunt and all your delicious little cousins, and then I'll kill them too. I'll cut them all into pieces and feed them to my dogs. Do you understand what I'm saying to you, Leila Najafi? You wouldn't want all that blood on your hands, would you? That much blood doesn't wash off; trust me on that."

He leans close, whispers in my ear. "You can save them all, Leila. All you have to do is stop this ridiculous rebellion against your fate."

I break away, shove him hard, putting magic and wind into the push. "Get out, you ugly pig."

He flies across the room, slams into the wall beside the front door, and then rights himself. "Watch the way you speak to your betrothed, bitch."

"You're not my betrothed and you will *never* be my husband." I refuse to cower as he stalks back toward me, his shape flickering between human flesh and ifriti flame.

He reaches into a pocket and pulls out a huge folding knife, black-bladed and wickedly sharp. "You *don't* want to antagonize me. You don't want to do this the hard way, Princess. You should know me well enough to know I'm not bluffing." He takes a lock of my hair in his fingers, and before I can stop him, he cuts it off, sniffing it. "And next time I see you, you'd better be more appropriately dressed. My wife will not dress like a human whore." He leaves, sauntering and swaggering, my hair still pressed to his nose.

Creep.

I stay upright until he's gone, then slump to the floor, struggling to suppress a sob. I know he's not bluffing. He will do everything he's threatened, and worse. He'll kill everyone I know. I've heard the stories about him, how bloodthirsty he is, how ruthless in getting what he wants. If even half the rumors about him are true, 'cold-blooded killer' would be the nicest of the applicable terms.

I can't hold back the sobs, and they gush forth,

wave after wave of tears born of anger, frustration and fear. The hardest part is that I know Hassan is right about my father. He *does* love me, and he is doing this because he thinks it's best for me, and for the clan. But that's only part of his reasoning. He owes the al-Jabiri clan. Billions of dollars ride on this alliance; centuries of violent feuding between our clans would be settled by this marriage; my life, my family's lives . . . the future of everyone I care about rests on my willingness to marry Hassan al-Jabiri. But I can't. I just *can't*. The thought of signing the marriage contract and speaking the binding words makes me physically ill, to say nothing of having to have physical relations with him.

I shudder and nearly vomit just thinking about it.

But I don't see a way out.

My father never consulted me on his business deals, obviously. He's old school, Old World. Despite the fact that he has been in America for a long time, the ancient Arabic cultural traditions he adheres to mean my opinion doesn't count, especially not when it comes to men and their business. By listening in on conversations and picking up the odd detail, I know Father has done many deals with Hassan's father over the years in attempts to stop the in-fighting and ally them together against the other clans. One deal followed another, and then another, and then things started to go wrong. A deal went sour, and suddenly Father owed them money for a shipment of cocaine and firearms intercepted by the DEA. To get out of that debt, Father had to do another deal, and another, and suddenly he owed Farouk al-Jabiri hundreds of millions of dollars.

And what was my father's grand scheme to get out from under all that debt?

Marry his one and only daughter off to the al-Jabiri family. Yes, he still believes in dowries and brideprice and all that. He is very old school. Very, *very* old school. He may live in a twenty-first-century mansion and drive an Aston Martin and carry an iPhone, but his beliefs and way of life are set firmly in thirteenth-century Baghdad, and that's no exaggeration.

I don't know what to do and I have no one to turn to. God help me. I can't marry Hassan, I just can't. But I also can't sit by and watch my family get murdered on my account.

And then there's Carson, and I can't even begin to figure out where *he* fits into all of this.

Nowhere, is the correct answer. But my heart and my body don't seem to be getting that message.

I can still taste him on my lips; feel his hand pulling me ever so subtly. All I want is to flee into his arms and pretend he can make my problems go away.

If he knew the truth about my father's "business"

dealings, would he still want me? Would he tip off the feds to my father's illegal activities? This is a very slippery slope.

Or would he protect me from Hassan?

I have no answers, and eventually my sobs subside.

My arms are bruised from Hassan's fingers, and my apartment is trashed from my little display of power. The first thing I do is clean the mud from my coffee table and spray Febreze in the air, trying to erase any evidence of his presence.

The next thing I do is call my father. Next to Hassan, he's the last person on earth I want to talk to right now, but I have to make sure the family is okay.

I dial his number and hold the phone to my ear.

"You have not called in a very long time, daughter," my father's voice rumbles in my ear. "I worry for you, alone in that barbaric city. You must come home. We have much to discuss."

"Father, listen—" I start, but he cuts me off, talking over me.

"I am willing to forgive your disobedience in running away from me, but you must return home. Now, more than ever, I require your obedience. Hassan will escort you."

"There has to be another way—"

"There is not!" He raises his voice, something he

never does. He's always, always calm. Never rushed, never perturbed, never angry. "You *will* marry Hassan! You must. I have made this clear to you, my daughter. I have no male heir. You cannot inherit. There is no other way. There is no one else suitable. No, it must be Hassan, and you must be his wife. It is the only way. You are my daughter, and you will obey. I have allowed you your little . . . *rebellion* . . . for long enough. You have had your tantrum, and now it is enough. I have tolerated you dressing like a heathen and associating with outsiders for too long. It is time for you to come home. *Now.*"

"Father, you don't understand—"

He doesn't let me finish. "There is nothing else you can say, Leila."

I try again to get him to listen. "Father, you have to listen, Hassan was here, and he—"

"Your objections to him have been made clear, and it is my prerogative to override you. Come home, Leila. Immediately."

Silence, then, and I realize he's hung up. I didn't even get to warn him.

CHAPTER 5: TRUTH AND EXPLORATION

Carson

SHE SHOWS UP AT THE HOSPITAL A LITTLE AFTER FIVE IN THE afternoon the next day, wearing cutoff jean shorts and an orange halter top. I have a feeling she'll be cold in the hospital room. Not that I'm arguing. It's mid-July and it's been hitting the mid- to upper-nineties, so the hospital has the A/C cranked so low it's downright frigid in here.

She's got a brown paper bag full of take-out containers, which she sets down on the bed. I can feel the heat emanating from the containers, and the scent of fresh French fries fills the air. My stomach rumbles loudly enough for Leila to hear, and she laughs, a breathy sound accompanied by a flash of white teeth.

Dragging the larger recliner-style chair from across the room with a deafening grating noise, Leila plops herself in it, sitting cross-legged.

I have to force my gaze away from the expanse of tanned, muscular thigh. I shake myself and meet her bright brown eyes, helping her arrange the food on the tray.

"Oh, awesome," I say when I see the juicy burgers and shoestring fries. "Nemo's! I was worried you'd bring some sort of girly vegetarian shit."

Leila laughs. "Do I seem like the broccoli and wheat germ type to you?"

"I don't know," I say around a mouthful of fries. "We've never discussed food before. You've got runner's legs, so you could very well have been a health food nut."

Leila glances at me as she takes a huge bite of her burger, her eyes gleaming with amusement. "I've got runner's legs, huh?" she asks, her mouth half-full.

"Uh-huh." I shrug, going for nonchalance and not quite succeeding.

"What's that mean?" She doesn't look pissed, but it's hard to be sure.

I sip from my can of Coke, trying to figure out how to explain myself without sounding like an asshole. "I don't know. Long and muscular. The muscles are long and lean, though, not bunchy like a soccer player or something."

Leila's staring at me with a raised eyebrow. "I'm not sure whether I should be flattered that you've looked that closely at my legs, or weirded out by the fact that you can classify a woman according to the kind of legs she has." She stretches a leg out in front of her to rest on the bed, pointing her toes and flexing the muscle as if trying to see what I saw.

"You've got nice legs, what can I say?" I murmur, tracing the line of her muscle from calf to knee, and then from knee up to her thigh.

I try to restrain myself from running my hand up her thigh, but I can't. Her skin is soft, the muscles firm under my palm. She's not breathing and neither am I. My fingers slip closer to the frayed hem of her cut-off shorts.

"That tickles," Leila whispers, but she doesn't move her leg away or stop my hand from its upward exploration.

She meets my eyes, takes a slow bite from her burger and shifts her leg to the side. It's a subtle movement, but it sends a clear and intentional message. My heart is pounding crazily, nerves making my fingers tremble slightly, even though I'm doing nothing more than touching her leg. I'm barely halfway up her thigh, but I'm as excited and nervous as a boy copping his first feel.

Centimeter by centimeter, I let my hand slide along the smooth, warm expanse of her skin, electricity thrilling through me at the feel of her flesh. She's watching me intently, her breasts rising and falling with every deep breath, her eyes widening as my fingers reach the white-thread hem of her jean shorts. A few more inches and the moment will shift from being innocently flirtatious to dangerously sexual.

We're both intensely aware of the transitional nature of the moment: if I move my fingers any higher, I'll be crossing a line. A kiss could be discounted, forgotten, ignored. A friendship could be maintained, despite the kisses. But if I continue to explore further up her thigh, it'll constitute a blatant promise of things to come.

I can see the debate in Leila's eyes.

I leave my hand where it is, on the innocent side of the invisible line, waiting for her give me an indication of what she wants. The moment stretches out, and I realize she's not debating or deciding, but is waiting for *me*. She isn't moving away or shifting her position to break the spell, but she's not encouraging me either, as if she wants me to slide my hand further up her thigh, but yet is afraid of what it would mean for both of us if I do.

I don't think; don't stop to wonder if this is a good idea. I set aside my food, lean toward her, and kiss her. The act of leaning in to press my mouth to hers pushes my hand upward, sliding my fingers under the hem of her shorts. My breath catches as she stretches her thigh to one side and pulls me closer, in the process giving me access to what lies beneath the denim.

My fingers slide higher, pressing into soft flesh and firm muscle, and then I feel the crease of her leg where it meets her hip, and I feel her muscles trembling, quivering ever so gently.

My hair stirs, and I feel the sheet across my hips flutter. I feel Leila's hair drifting in a breeze.

I feel myself hardening with desire. I feel the edge of her panties, the soft silk covering her core, and I want to slip my fingers under it and delve in, find her heat. But I don't. Intentionally, I don't. I slide my touch up along her hip and back into relative innocense. It's a conscious choice to delay the moment, and as my fingers move away from her core, I feel Leila relaxing slightly, hear her exhale a breath. She seems both disappointed and relieved. I withdraw my hand entirely and let it rest on her knee.

We finish our food in silence.

"Why'd you stop?" Leila finally asks, when we're both done eating. She won't quite meet my eyes. "You were right there, but you didn't touch me."

"I almost did," I admit. "I wanted to, but I didn't

want to start something I couldn't finish." I feather my fingers into her hair, lean close and whisper my lips over her ear. "And Leila, what I want to do . . . we can't finish it here."

She shivers, and I feel goose bumps ripple across her skin. "Scootch over. I'm cold." Leila shifts out of the chair and perches on the edge of the bed, nudging me over.

I move aside for her, spreading the sheet and the thin blanket over both of us. The bed is narrow enough that we're both nearly hanging off the edge. She's lying partially on her side, partially on her back. It's another instinctive reaction: I slide my arm beneath her neck and pull her to my chest. She scrunches down to fit her head in the crook of my shoulder, resting a knee and thigh over mine.

It's strange, lying in so familiar and intimate a way with a girl I barely know; but it doesn't feel awkward, though, and that's the strangest part about it. It feels totally natural, totally normal.

Comforting.

I rarely just hold a woman like this. If there's a woman in my bed, she's not just lying there. That's part of what sets Leila apart, in my mind.

It's not that I don't want her that way, but I don't want it to be casual. I've had casual, and I'm over it. I'm enjoying this feeling, the closeness, the sense of affection in the way she's resting her head on me. There's a sweetness and an innocent tenderness in the stillness between us, a comfort in the easy silence. Her hair tickles my face, and I smooth it away. I want her, I do, but she's different and, as I've said before, I want to wait for her.

Now that I've managed to get control of my libido, I feel the questions bubbling up again. There's so much about her I want to know, and that in itself is unusual. The other women I've dated before now, the casual-sex acquaintances, even the kind-of-serious girlfriends, are women I've never invested much time in, at least not in a deeply personal way. I got to know their surface interests, facts about their families and a general timeline of their lives. But those things do not define a person.

I find myself wondering oddly specific things about Leila: what she wears to bed, whether she gets along with her parents, what kind of shampoo she uses, what her favorite TV show is . . . the list of questions is seemingly endless. They are the kinds of things I've never known or wanted to know about another person.

And, of course, burning hot and hard beneath everything else is the question of what the hell happened in the bar, and what she's hiding from me. I should be more focused on figuring that out, but it seems so impossible, especially when Leila is sitting right here, tempting and distracting me with her lush beauty.

"Why'd you become a cop?" Leila asks, breaking the silence.

Can she feel the questions burning in my head? Does she really want to know about me, or is she trying to distract me from questioning her?

"Oh, man, *that* is a long story," I say.

"I'm not going anywhere."

"You really want to know?" I twist my position slightly so I can watch her expression and read her reactions.

"I wouldn't have asked if I didn't," Leila says, looking up at me through long lashes.

"What it comes down to is my parents were murdered when I was eighteen. It was random, and brutal. A robbery gone wrong. The killers were never found."

"God, Carson. That's . . . so awful. I'm so sorry." Her musical voice is soft, low, and tender.

"Yeah, it—it was just so sudden, and so senseless, you know? I mean, you hear that phrase all the time: 'senseless violence,' but it doesn't really mean anything to you until someone you love is killed without rhyme or reason." I sigh, rub my forehead with the side of my forefinger. "I was at school, a few days before high school graduation. I had a scholarship to Texas A & M for football. I'd already toured the campus, had even made a few friends. I was looking forward to getting the hell out of Michigan. I was gonna play ball, get a degree, and figure out what the fuck I wanted to do with my life. I had no clue, you know? I was a kid. Sheltered, grew up in the 'burbs, no real problems, nothing remarkable.

"And then I get called down to the office over the PA. That never happens. When your name gets called, last period of the day, it's a big deal. I felt my gut just . . . twist. I don't know how to put it, but I knew something had happened. My dad was an IT guy, worked from home some days, and Mom was a stay-at-home, volunteered at the local elementary for lunches, scrapbooked, had brunches with her friends. So they were both home during the afternoons a lot.

"We lived in a nice neighborhood, but not, like, super upscale. No reason our house would be hit, right? Average TV, average cars, average jewelry. No reason for it. But . . . someone broke in through the back door, shot my mom where she stood in the kitchen. Shot her three times. Guessing my dad heard it, came running, right? He was shot in the doorway, in the hall going from his study to the kitchen. He was shot twice. Some jewelry was missing, the DVD player, my dad's golf clubs, his watch off his fucking wrist. Bunch of random shit. It made no sense.

"So the shots get called in, they find my parents shot to death, blood everywhere. Robbery gone wrong, easy. It was a neighborhood in the middle of the day, should be some witnesses, right? Someone who saw the car, or the shooter?

"Nope. Apparently not. One guy saw a white full-size van, older model, maybe, couldn't be sure. Saw one guy, average height, wearing khakis and a black hoodie. No license plate, no other description. No one else saw anything. No fingerprints were found that matched anyone in the database, no weapon was found so the ballistics meant nothing. No other robberies or murders that could be confidently connected. After a couple months, they closed the case. Sorry, they told me. No leads, no evidence. It's gone cold."

I have to pause. It's still hard to talk about. I blink, sigh, and pick at the fries, eat one.

"Did you have any other family? Anyone? What did you do?"

"I was alone. I mean, I have an uncle, he helped out a bit, sent me some money now and then, but for all intents and purposes . . . I was alone. My grandparents all passed when I was young, my mom was an only child, and my dad just had the one brother, but Uncle Bill has always been kind of reclusive. He helped me out with taking care of the arrangements, but he did it all remotely.

"I . . . started school, played ball, but it was empty. It meant nothing. And when they closed the case, I got angry. I demanded to know what they'd done to find the killers. The detective, he was a nice guy. Jim Wisniewski. Twenty-year veteran of the force. Gave me a kind of crash course in how hard it is to solve a case like that, how you got no leads, no clues, nothing to go on. Sort of piqued my interest, I guess.

"Old Jim bent a few rules, showed me things he shouldn't have. But I needed closure, and he knew it. I needed to know what happened. What was being done. I guess I needed to feel like someone in the world gave half a shit about me, and he was the one who showed me.

"And I realized he was right, there was nothing. You have no witnesses, no camera footage, no physical evidence, no weapon, no suspect or motive. Like someone just walked in, shot them, and took a few random things, then left. Like, the TV was there, a two-thousand-dollar Sony, didn't take that. Didn't take my dad's computer. It all made no sense. Just . . . just a random act of violence.

"Guess that was the impetus, needing to know what happened to my parents. Needing to find them, to catch the assholes who do shit like that. So I got a criminal justice degree, joined the force, got fast-tracked to detective." I laugh, a forced, hollow sound. "Well, now that I've told you *that* happy story . . ."

Leila shook her head. "I'm so sorry, Carson. I don't even know what to say."

"It's old history, at this point. I mean, I'm not sure that's something you ever really just get over totally, but I think I am, as much as I'll ever be. So, yeah. That's why I became a cop." I shrug and look down at Leila. "What about you? Where is your family?"

Leila looks panicked for a split second but recovers quickly. "I—oh, my family isn't that interesting."

"You'd be surprised what would interest me," I tell her. "And you know, that's not the first time you've evaded that question."

"It's not an evasion, Carson—" she starts.

"The hell it isn't." I sound harsh. I sigh and start over. "Leila, look, I'm not asking you to tell me your deepest, darkest secrets or anything like that. Just . . . tell me a little bit about yourself."

She sighs. "Well, I'm Arab-American. My mom and dad moved here from Kuwait long before I was born. My dad is a . . . businessman." She pauses so briefly I almost miss it. "I'm an only child, and my mom is a traditional stay-at-home mom."

"What is the family business?"

"My dad is in . . . transportation. Moving goods around the country, stuff like that. Import, export."

She shrugs, casually dismissive, her tone so persuasive now that I almost believe her. "I was never interested in it, so I never took much notice of it, really. My dad's done really well for himself, though. I grew up in Chicago, I think I told you that before. I went to private schools, got dropped off by limos, vacationed in the south of France every summer, that kind of thing. My parents are really . . . old school. I wore a hijab until I moved here, actually." She makes a motion around her head, indicating a head-covering.

"So you grew up rich, huh?"

"Yeah. My parents are . . . *very* wealthy." She sighs, and it's a sad sound. "But, like I said, they're really, *really* traditional. They had so many expectations of me, you know? They just wanted me to do everything their way. They expected me to marry by the time I was twenty, and have a bunch of kids and live near them and keep quiet, wear the hijab and never shake a man's hand, pray facing Mecca five times a day, and be a dutiful daughter. There's nothing necessarily wrong with that, and a lot of my friends back in Chicago are living that life very happily. But as I got older I realized it was just not for me. I embraced the modern Western culture and I just couldn't do what they wanted. It led to conflict after conflict, and eventually I had to get away. I needed space from them, from their expectations and their disappointment that I couldn't fulfill them, so I moved here a while ago and I haven't looked back."

I can feel the omissions in her story, can sense that she's leaving out more than she's telling. No one leaves their family *that* easily, especially not a wealthy, orthodox Muslim girl.

"You just left? Just like that?" I stare back at her. "Do you miss them?

"Of course I miss them," she says. "They're my family. But I had to do things my way, and they just couldn't accept that. And I can't accept what they want for me. They don't care what I want, they just expect me to obey. To be the dutiful, honorable little female, and that's just . . . not me." Leila stares into the middle distance, distracted and distant.

She's being evasive, leaving out most of the truth. I hold her in silence, debating with myself. I want the truth, but am I willing to hurt her to get it? No. I can sense that if I push the subject, demand the truth from her right now, I might shut her down completely. She's skittish, nervous. She's waiting for me to push the issue, her eyes shifting back and forth, searching mine, and I can feel her silently pleading with me to let it go.

Frustration burns in my chest.

I'm intensely attracted to Leila, but it's more than that. There's a connection unlike anything I've ever experienced, but it's marred by her secrecy, by the lies and the omissions.

What is she hiding?

I shift tactics. "Leila, what really happened at the bar?"

I watch her carefully, assessing her body language, the way her eyes shift away from mine and fix on the ceiling above my shoulder before she speaks.

She closes her eyes briefly. "Carson, I told you everything I know already. I have no clue what happened. One minute we were talking and the next I was standing outside on the pavement."

"Yeah, but what you told me doesn't make sense. My captain looked into it, and there's a lot that just doesn't add up. For one thing, how it is that you're completely fine, not so much as a scratch, while I'm in here? Then there's the bar itself. Captain Archer says it's completely destroyed. The only thing left was a pile of smoking rubble, and forensics can't figure out how it happened. Archer said it looks like both a fire *and* a tornado hit the place, which doesn't make a damn lick of sense. Especially since none of the surrounding buildings were in any way affected, and there was no weather that could have produced a tornado."

Leila stands and paces. I can feel her shutting down. I can feel the lies bubbling up in her.

"Carson . . . please. I know there are things that . . . don't add up, okay? I know." Leila crosses back to my side, standing over me. Her deep brown eyes are pleading, begging me to understand. "But there are things I just can't explain to you. Not right now, not ever. I'm sorry, I just—I *can't*. For my sake and . . . for yours. Just . . . just let it go. Please?"

"I can't, Leila. I'm not wired that way." I shift forward, wincing at the twinge in my ribs. "Plus, I'm a cop. Was it a robbery? Was it a terrorist attack? I was injured, fairly seriously, on my own turf. I can't just let it go, professionally I can't."

"You just *have* to know the truth? What if the truth is ugly? What if the truth is something you can't handle? What then? What if the truth led you into another case like the one you were telling me about, if not worse? What if the truth meant you and I couldn't . . ." She trails off, biting her lip, squeezing her eyes closed.

"Couldn't what? Be together? What secrets could you possibly have that would keep us apart? I've seen damn near everything in this job, Leila. I've dealt with the worst humanity has to offer. So trust me when I say there's nothing you could say to me that would shock me." She's shaking her head, but I ignore it and keep going, letting the truth spill out of me. "I like you, okay. A lot. I think that's pretty well clear at this point, but it goes deeper than that. A *lot* deeper. I like you in a way I've never liked anyone. Why can't you just trust me? What do you think I'm gonna do when you tell me the truth? Especially after the way I handled things with Miriam."

"It's not that I don't trust you, Carson. Please believe that." The sorrow in her eyes is a knife to my chest. "But it's complicated. Really, really complicated. It's not just me, it's my family. Running away was bad enough in their eyes. If they found out I was messing around with an *outsider* . . ."

"An outsider? What the hell does that mean?"

Leila looks ready to cry from frustration. "I didn't mean outsider, I just meant . . . I am a Muslim and my family expects me to remain that way. I may not be dressed that way right now, but that's a minor rebellion in comparison to getting involved with someone . . . with someone who lives outside of our ways. Can you please stop asking me questions? Please!" She turns away and buries her face in her hands, sucking in deep shuddering breaths.

I take a deep breath and expel it slowly. I reach for Leila and pull her over to me. She resists at first, but the closer she gets, the more her resistance melts. I pull her down to the bed and tug her onto my lap, ignoring the ache in my ribs. She curls her body in against mine on the tiny hospital bed.

"Listen," I whisper, "I'm sorry I pushed it. I'm just hard-wired to demand the truth. I know there're things you're hiding, and, yeah, that bugs me. But I care about you, okay? I won't ask any more questions right now. Just promise me you'll tell me when you're ready?"

Leila shakes her head. "What if I were to say I couldn't ever tell you everything? What then?"

"I don't know. I want to be with you. I want you to trust me. If you can't trust me, then where do we go from here?"

I feel her tears on the shoulder of my hospital gown.

"I don't know." The words are almost inaudible. "I don't know if I *can* be with you, no matter how much I want to."

"What's stopping you?" I ask.

Leila is silent for a long moment, and I wait for her answer.

"My father, for one thing. And other . . . factors. More of what I just can't explain."

"You mean *won't* explain." I sound bitter, even to myself.

"No, Carson. That's not it. And it's not just about me. If they found out about you it'd be bad, not just for me, but for you, too. If it was just about me, I'd tell you everything in an instant, but there are things that have to do with my family, and my . . . culture."

She freights that last word with an enormous wealth of meaning. "I don't understand," I say, after a long moment.

"I know," she says. "And I'm really, really sorry for that. I just can't. I can't do this. It's too hard on me, and it's not fair to you."

Leila gets up abruptly, snatching her purse from the floor. She stops in the doorway, turning to face me with tearful eyes. "I'm sorry, Carson. Goodbye." There's a sense of finality to her words, a glint of farewell in her eyes.

Leila walks away. I don't expect her to come back.

Chapter 6: Father's Words

Leila

I choke back sobs as I walk away from Carson.

I tell myself I'm doing the right thing. I can't get Carson involved in my problems. If he got wind of my father's real business, he'd be compelled to do something about it. Call the DEA or FBI or something. How could a cop date the daughter of a drug cartel kingpin? But that's not even the craziest part.

He doesn't have a clue as to who . . . as to *what* I really am. He's totally clueless. He had such a hard time with that case, and that girl, Miriam. She sounds like a djinni, from what he told me. He just couldn't accept the truth of what really happened to her, of what she is, so how would he react if he knew I was like her?

How do you even broach the subject? "Oh, by the way, Carson, I'm an ifrit princess. So, how about Greektown for dinner?" Yeah, that'd go over well.

I can barely see where I'm going, but I make it to my car and slump into the seat, letting the sobs out. My body shakes and shudders, and I can't seem to stop it. He knew I was saying goodbye, I saw it on his face just before I turned away.

I can't let him into my life, and I can't let myself trust him, even though I want to so desperately.

It's impossible to get Carson out of my head. Even as I sit and cry my eyes out, his face is running through my mind. His lips on mine, his hands on me, his arms wrapped around me, making me feel safe and protected. He lights me on fire, and he calms me, all at once. I want him, and I need him, and I can't have him.

I remember the way his hand felt on my thigh, inching upward, how I'd trembled with anticipation, how I'd wanted him to keep touching me, to dare to go upward, to make me feel, make me forget.

My phone trills in my purse, and I pull it out, rubbing at my eyes with the heel of my palm. It's a text from Hassan.

Two weeks, Leila. Ready or not, here I come.

I throw the phone down on the seat next to me,

cursing Hassan under my breath. He is relentless. I'll hear from him every day. He'll haunt my every waking moment.

And if he gets even so much as a whiff of Carson, things will get even worse. I have no doubt that Hassan would kill him in a heartbeat. Hassan wouldn't even blink, even though Carson is a police officer.

When I've calmed myself enough to drive, I head back to my apartment, my mind running in overdrive, trying to come up with a way out of this that will let me be with Carson without anyone getting hurt.

The trouble is, I don't see a way out of this without *someone* getting hurt. The situation is impossible. I may not feel a filial duty to my family, but I cannot let them suffer at Hassan's hands. I'll marry him if I have to, and it will be a living hell, but I don't see any other way to protect them. I've never considered suicide in my life, but the thought of Hassan's hands and lips and body . . .

I'd rather die.

Remembering Hassan's last visit, I check the parking lot, but there is no sign of the black Mercedes. I double-check that the front door is still locked before I go in. I go over every inch of my apartment before I allow myself to relax. Once I've confirmed for myself that I'm alone, I need to do something to unwind, so I run a bath. I pour a glass of wine, strip my clothes off, and slip into the steaming water.

I try not to imagine Carson in the bath with me. If I close my eyes, I can almost see his body, smooth and hard and corded with heavy muscle. I can almost feel his hands on me, swirling through the water to caress my skin.

I'm lost in the image, and I feel, distantly, the warm rush of magic opening up inside me. I shut the daydream down before the magic runs awry and brings Carson to me. I've never had the best control over that aspect of the powers that are my birthright, and it's tempting to let the magic have its way, but I manage to control it. There's nothing I'd like more than having Carson Hale wet and naked in my apartment.

He'd be confused at first, but I can think of any number of ways of distracting him . . .

Power is rumbling in my belly, whirling at the core of me. I slow my breathing and push it down, gentling the raging winds of desire and magic.

I want him, but not that way. I want him to know what he's getting into. I want him to know he'd be tangling with a hurricane if he were to be with me.

I distract myself before I let the magic unfurl.

I think of my father, sitting in his office at the

huge cherrywood desk with the blotter calendar and little lamp with the green shade, a fountain pen in one hand, silver-black hair perfectly combed and oiled. His beard is carefully trimmed to a point beneath his chin, and his eyes are like chips of obsidian. He stares at me, glares at me, disappointment rife in his gaze. I could never please him, as a girl. The best grades weren't good enough. My school friends weren't good enough, because they weren't *of the blood*. Only girls from other ifrit clans were allowed over, and only if my father approved of them. They had to wear a hijab, and it had to be traditional white, no fancy new bright colors like some girls wore.

He meant well, I know that. He loves me; he just had no other way of showing it. Now, his fate rests on my decision, on my willingness to marry that demonic pig, Hassan.

A wind kicks up in the bathroom as my thoughts turn to Hassan. The bathwater is tossed by the out-of-control winds, sending sudsy water flying, soaking the floors and walls. My powers rage out of my control. In my mind I hear Hassan's threats, and I can't stop the anger from rushing through me.

I shoot to my feet, standing in the tub, surrounded by a vortex of howling wind and spraying water, the shower curtain ripped off the hooks and flapping above my head, towels whipping around me. I close my eyes and push the memory of Hassan away. I force him from my mind, force the rage away, and force the hatred down, force the winds to die down.

Carson.

His intelligent, vivid blue eyes fill my mind, and I focus on the memory of the feeling of his hand on my skin. I manage to calm myself before real damage is done to the bathroom, pulling the winds back in. I dry myself off, wrap the towel around my torso, and then get a stack of clean towels to mop up the water, which is inch-deep on the floor. I re-hang the shower curtain. When the bathroom is back in order I lie on my bed, trying to further calm my frayed nerves and figure out what to do next.

And then my phone rings. It's Father. I consider hitting "Ignore," but I know I can't. "Hello, Father."

"Leila. You still haven't returned home. I am growing displeased."

"I'm not *going to,* Father. You don't understand me, and you won't listen to anything I have to say. I *won't* marry Hassan, Father. I will not."

"You will. This is for the good of the clan, and the family. I am sorry you find Hassan so distasteful. I wish I could find another way to seal this alliance, but there is no other way. You must do your duty, Leila."

"My *duty,*" I spit. "What about what I want?"

"What you want must be surrendered for the

good of the clan. I expect you to obey me, or there will consequences."

"I *will not* marry Hassan, Father. You know what he said to me? He showed up at my home and told me he'd rape Mother in front of me if I didn't marry him. He told me he'd kill you, Aunt Talia. Everyone." I pause to let that sink in. "And you know as well as I do that he's perfectly capable of actually doing it. He's vile and disgusting and I would rather die than marry him."

My father is silent, if only briefly. "All the more reason to obey," he finally says, with a sigh. "I am sorry, child, but it is decided. He will be your husband. I will send your cousin Amad to retrieve you, rather than Hassan, if you wish."

"Leave Amad out of this. He's a moron who worships the ground Hassan walks on." My voice is shaking with rage. "Hassan is *evil,* Father. He threatened to kill all of you, and this is the man you expect me to marry?"

Father is silent again, and then clears his throat in dismissal. "Hassan was merely making a point to get you to come home."

"He was serious and you know it. You know his reputation, you've heard all the rumors about him. They're true, all of them. He is a demon. A monster of the worst sort."

"You don't know the price of refusal, Leila. There is more than just this family's honor at stake, and even that much should be more than enough reason for you. The clan has deemed this union, not just me. It is the ifrit way, Leila. You *must*. Our clans have warred for thousands of years, and this marriage can end that. You know this."

"What other reasons are there, Father? I know there are things you're not telling me."

"You are a woman. Business is none of your concern."

I want to scream, but I don't. "Women are running businesses," I say, as calmly as I can, "and they have been for decades."

"I don't care what heathen practices this foul nation caters to. We are ifrits of the oldest blood, and we will uphold tradition."

Anger burns through me at his condescension. "You are so backwards, and so damn *arrogant*. I don't owe you obedience, *Father*. This isn't the Moorish Empire; this is America, and I'll do what I want."

"I wish it *were* the Moorish Empire. *They* knew how to rule." He pauses. "That was a pleasurable time."

"But it isn't," I say. "I can't marry Hassan. I won't. He's evil."

His voice softens, and I know he is going to try to

convince me now. This should be interesting. "Hassan is not so bad, girl. He is heir to a great fortune, and he will rule the clans well. You will be a *queen*, Leila. His kingdom will be vast, and the powers he will control will be mighty. You would rather slave away in smelly, dirty kitchens, serving alcohol to lecherous *outsiders?*"

"Oh my god," I groan in frustration. "Stop acting so grandiose, Father. No one talks that way anymore."

"*I* speak this way," he says, his voice icy. "You will show respect to your father."

"It is *decided.*" His voice is hard, and I know the conversation is over; my father is unmovable once he's made up his mind. "You will be here in Chicago by the fourteenth. Too much rides on this alliance. I can't give in to you, Leila. I simply cannot, no matter what you and I may *both* wish. Our family, the entire clan . . . we're depending on you to do your duty."

"I hate you!" I end the call and toss the phone aside, fighting tears.

Father had almost sounded afraid, there at the end.

The fear in his voice, more than anything, is what convinces me I have no choice. If Ibrahim Najafi is afraid of Hassan, the situation must be even more dire than I knew.

CHAPTER 7: TEN DIGITS

Carson

I LEAVE THE HOSPITAL THE NEXT MORNING, STROLLING OUT into the sunshine and taking a deep breath of summer air.

I'm an active, energetic person, so being essentially strapped into a hospital bed for two days was sheer torture. The doctor warned me to go easy on the workouts for a few weeks, but that's going to be impossible for me: strenuous exercise is how I focus on a problem.

Captain Archer is waiting for me in an unmarked car. She had offered to pick me up and drive me home from the hospital. "They finally cut you loose, huh?"

"Yeah, thank god. I was going crazy in there." I

slam the door closed, and Archer guides the cruiser out into traffic. I glance at Archer. "So, any progress on the case?"

She shrugs, and I can tell she's irritated. "Not really. There's just nothing to go on. It really does seem like a bizarre natural accident. That's what forensics says, at least. My instincts tell me different, but without evidence to back it up . . ." She trails off, knowing she doesn't have to spell it out: without evidence, it doesn't matter what your gut tells you.

A few minutes later we pull up in front of my condo building. "Well," I say, "thanks for the ride. I guess I'll see you tomorrow." I get out and shut the door, not waiting for a reply.

My condo stinks from being closed up during the heat of the past few days—an old, empty smell. There are dishes in the sink, half a pot of coffee still in the glass carafe, and a Styrofoam take-out container on the coffee table with week-old food in it that looks as if it has developed its own ecology.

I curse it all and get out the cleaning supplies. I get to work, needing something to do to get my mind working. I scrub the dishes by hand before running them through the dishwasher, gather several bags of garbage and carry them out to the dumpster, then I vacuum the tiny living room.

While I clean, my mind is whirling, questions

burning through my brain. Why is Leila lying to me? What is it she's so afraid of? What doesn't she want me to find out? Every instinct I have is telling me that she's not just lying to me. I think she's withholding some major information, something about herself, or her past, or her family. And whatever her secret is, it was enough to make her walk away from me, despite the obvious attraction between us.

The look in her eyes when she said goodbye is something I will never forget. There was a finality there, a sense of permanent farewell. And behind the sadness was the terror—a bone-deep fear of doing something she really, deeply did not want to do.

The memory of the fear in her gorgeous brown eyes sends my urge to protect her into overdrive. I want to hunt her down and take this on for her. Or, barring that, at least be there with her to help in any way I can.

But I can't. It's not my place to protect her. She's not my girlfriend, and it's looking like she never will be. If she wanted my help, she'd have told me the truth.

Cleaning my apartment only takes an hour, and the need to distract myself wins out over prudence. I walk to the gym—just a few blocks away—and start a workout that is harder than is probably advisable. My still-mending ribs scream, but I ignore them and pound out rep after rep, until I'm shaking with exhaustion. Finally, the pain forces me to step away from the weight machine and slump over, chest heaving, muscles aching. I try to clear my mind and focus on the burning of my muscles, but Leila is all I can think about.

I fantasize about sliding my hands under those tiny shorts, picture what it would feel like to pull them down around her thighs, pushing them away until they drop to the floor, leaving her skin bare to my touch. I imagine her wrapping those long tan legs around my waist and kissing me like she can't get enough. I can hear her moaning, a breathless whimper of ragged desire.

I close my eyes and I can almost see her right now, naked and wet, just out of the bath, maybe. Her hair is thick and dripping wet, her skin beaded with droplets of water. I can almost taste her skin, can almost feel the heavy weight of her breasts in my hands.

I growl and lift the bar off the hooks, lower it to my chest and then slowly push it up, holding it until my arms tremble, and then lower it again. Rep after rep, until my arms are jelly, and then I move to the leg press and pound out set after set until I can barely walk, my abused muscles on fire.

The pain is my friend, though. It gives me something to think about besides Leila. When I'm done punishing my body I go back home and order take-out and watch TV and try not to think about her.

I dream of her, though, and they aren't innocent dreams.

I go into work the next day and begin sorting through the piled-up paperwork.

Captain Archer swings by my desk. "Hale, my office," she barks, and I follow her down the hall. She leans back in her chair and sighs. "Listen, Carson, I think you need to take some time off."

I stare at her. "You're taking me off the case? What do you mean?"

"No," Archer shakes her head. "I'm sending you on vacation, because there *is* no case."

"Wait," I say. "Are we talking about the al-Mansour case?"

Archer shakes her head. "Unless you came up with something new that I don't know about yet, then that case is dead." She eyes me, waiting.

The moment of truth. I consider for a moment, but I know there's nothing else to say. "No. There was nothing. It went nowhere."

She nods. "All right then. That's closed."

"Then what case am I off of?"

She shrugs. "I'm not taking you off a case, Carson, because there's no case to take you off of. I put Jackson and Roberts on it, and they came up with nothing. No signs of anything that would make me think it was foul play. So officially, whatever happened at that bar was a freak accident. I can't afford to waste any more manpower on it. We've got too many other cases that *do* have leads to follow."

"But that doesn't make any sense! I saw the photographs—"

"It's *closed*, Hale," Archer interrupts. "You're on vacation for two weeks, as of this moment. You don't have a choice. You haven't taken a single day off in four years, and you were just injured. You need a vacation. Go to California and learn how to surf. Sit in your apartment alone and get drunk. I don't care. What you do with your time is up to you, but I don't want to see you back here for two weeks, you hear me?"

I nod. "Yes, ma'am."

She leans forward and jabs at me with a pen. "And you better not try to investigate it on your own, either."

Shit, well, there goes that idea. "Take all the fun out of vacation, why don't you." I try to make it a joke, but the captain just stares at me impassively.

"Go on, now. Git. Try and relax, Hale. Find yourself a girl or something." Archer waves a hand and turns to her computer screen, dismissing me.

Find a girl? Now there's an idea.

There's not much in the way of paperwork on the Old Shillelagh case, but there is Leila's statement, along with her contact information. I copy her phone number and address into my phone, and then leave the precinct.

Ten digits.

Call her? Text her? Just show up at her front door?

I'm off the case, or rather, there *is* no case to be off of, so there's no conflict of interest, professionally.

But personally?

I don't even know.

I end up perched on a bar stool, a drink in hand, watching baseball highlights and trying not to think about Leila.

That lasts for all of two innings.

By the time I'm crunching the ice at the bottom of my glass, my phone is out and I'm staring at her number. All I have to do is press the call button.

What am I going to say? She seemed pretty final in the way she'd said goodbye; maybe she really doesn't want to see me. Maybe I'm imagining a connection between us that isn't really there.

But no. She kissed me back, not just once, but

twice. She wouldn't have done that if she didn't want me, on some level at least.

The fear I'd seen in her eyes gives me pause. What is she afraid of? Me? The possibility of us? Herself? Someone else?

There's only one way to find out.

I touch the green button.

Chapter 8: Maelstrom

Leila

I'M GOING CRAZY.

Hassan is calling me nonstop, leaving threatening voicemails. Classic Hassan. It's his way of intimidating me. Hassan is an extremely powerful fire-elemental and has consummate control over his powers. As if that's not enough, he's the heir to one of the most powerful ifrit clans in the world, which gives him access to essentially unlimited funds and somehow endless ranks of both mortal and ifrit henchmen. And, oh yeah, he's a bloodthirsty sociopath with zero compunction about killing anyone who gets in his way.

And I'm supposed to marry him? If it weren't so serious, it would be laughable.

Then there's my father. He sounded frightened at the end of my conversation with him. My father is not an easy man to frighten. He's thousands of years old and immensely powerful. He's watched empires rise and fall. But now he's going on the defensive because of Hassan al-Jabiri? Something is wrong, but I can't figure out what. Sure, a deal might have gone wrong, but it was just one of hundreds of deals. Surely it can't mean *that* much to my father. Hassan must have some kind of chokehold on my father's business; it's got to be something like that. There's no other way he'd let an arrogant, evil excuse for a man like Hassan threaten his family without severe retaliation.

But my father will never tell me what's going on, not in a thousand years. I'm a woman, and his daughter, and men do not discuss business with mere *females,* not in his chauvinistic, patriarchal world.

I don't know what to do about Hassan, or about Father, so I push them out of my head . . . and, of course, my thoughts turn back to Carson. I never gave him my phone number or address, but I keep hoping he'll show up. I glance at my phone every five minutes, and find myself listening for the doorbell. He's a cop; he can find me if he really wants to.

I want him to come after me; I can admit that much to myself. I'd tell him everything, if he were to show up right now.

I would risk my family's wrath to be with him. The strange thing is, though, I have a feeling he'd protect them, if he were to know the truth. There's a sense of restrained power about him, a kind of primal strength that's part of the reason he makes my knees weak when I'm around him. It's impossible, though. Even as much as Carson can undoubtedly take care of himself, Hassan would torch him to a crisp without breaking a sweat.

I can't help remembering the way he touched me in the hospital. I wanted so badly for him to slide his fingers inside me; my legs were shaking as he moved his touch from knee to thigh to groin, and I had to tense all my muscles to keep them from quivering like some virginal schoolgirl. Quivering . . . I was actually quivering.

It would've been embarrassing, but I could see very clearly how it affected Carson. It took even more self-control to keep my hands under the blanket, to restrain myself from touching the source of his desire. In that moment, I was willing to let him do whatever he wanted; I'm not a public-display-of-affection kind of girl, but something about Carson Hale destroys my inhibitions. We were in a hospital room with the privacy curtain open, his fingers less than an inch away from my core.

The memory has me hot all over again. If he

showed up right now, I'd jump him. Literally, I'd dive-tackle him and tear off his clothes, kiss every inch of his muscular body and beg him to take me, right here on the living room floor.

And I realize something even more frightening: if Carson doesn't at least call me before Hassan drags me back to Chicago, I'll be heartbroken.

Which tells me how far this has gone between us: he's a cop, and I'm falling head over heels for him.

Me, the daughter of Ibrahim Najafi, ifrit patriarch and underworld crime boss. Falling in love with a human cop.

I chew on the thought; I'm in love with Carson Hale.

God, I'm in so much trouble.

I'm falling in love, but I'm supposed to marry a sociopathic ifrit killer?

What do I do?

I retreat to the kitchen and make tea, hoping it will calm me down, but I'm so distracted and upset that I leave the silverware drawer open. When I notice it, I can't be bothered to close it. I lean back against the island and sip at the scalding liquid, thinking about Carson and hating Hassan and resenting my father. I don't even feel the power leaking out at first. I'm so lost in the tangled mess of my life that the vortex whirling around me doesn't register until a steak knife flies past my face to impale itself into the drywall be-side the fridge, leaving a stinging scratch on my cheek where the blade grazed my face. My powers have gone haywire. A tornado is howling around my head, catching silverware from the drawer and tangling my hair in a wind-tossed halo. Knives, forks, spoons, chopsticks, all hurtle around me in gale-force winds, tearing the tiny kitchen apart. Cabinets are ripped off their hinges, drawers are pulled free and thrown across the room, bottles of spices smash against the walls, sending cardamom and cinnamon and garlic and salt and pepper and paprika into the tornado. A stream of plates hurtles across the kitchen, smashing against the wall and cracking the drywall one after the other in a ceramic hailstorm.

I close my eyes and focus on calming the rag-ing hurricane of emotion within me, on bottling my powers before I destroy the entire building. When the winds are quiet once more, I open my eyes and curse weakly. The walls and ceiling and floor around me are peppered with silverware, dishes lay smashed in piles all over the floor, herbs and spices float to the floor in a choking, scented cloud, cabinet doors are cracked and hanging loose . . . there's a plate lodged in the ceiling tiles, somehow still intact.

The scene would be comical if it didn't mean losing my damage deposit and possibly even being evicted. I spend an hour and a half cleaning, sweeping up broken flatware and spices, dislodging silverware from the ceiling and the walls, closing the cabinet doors that will close and removing the ones too broken to close. I haul a garbage bag full of smashed plates and bent silverware and broken cabinet doors to the dumpster, and then slump onto the couch, sweaty and irritated.

Just then, my phone rings.

"Hello?"

"Leila." Carson's deep voice washes over me, and I feel a rush of joy. "I hope I'm not interrupting anything."

"No, not at all. It's just—I didn't think I'd given you my number. I meant to, but . . ."

"Oh, I got it from the case file. I hope that's okay." He hesitates, and I take the moment to gather frazzled nerves and inject some strength into my voice. "I just wanted to talk to you. Are you busy?"

If he asks me out, I know I won't be able to say no. I should, but I won't.

"No," I say. "I'm not doing much. Just . . . cleaning up a bit, you could say."

"I thought maybe you'd like to meet somewhere for dinner."

Suddenly, I'm ravenous. "Sure! That sounds great. Where should I meet you?" I hate how eager

I sound.

"Xochimilco's, maybe? Somewhere like that?" I can hear excitement and relief in his voice.

"Okay." My heart is hammering in my chest.

I know I shouldn't do this. If Hassan finds out, it would be bad for me and worse for Carson. I know it, but I can't stop myself. The words are tumbling out before I can stop them, like my heart is acting without my brain, like my heart is in control and my common sense is left out entirely.

"We'll meet outside Xochimilco's, then"

"I'll be there in . . . maybe half an hour? I need to get ready."

"That's fine."

"See you soon," I say.

"Sounds good. Bye." He hangs up, and I'm relieved.

I shower and get dressed faster than I ever have before, my heart hammering with excitement and my stomach twisting and lurching. Unsurprisingly, I hesitate over what to wear. Eventually I decide on a summery orange sundress, not too slinky or revealing but still sexy. I'm nervous. I haven't been on a date in a long time. And this *is* a date, no mistake about it.

I try not to wonder how far things will go tonight. I'm not very successful, because as I drive to meet Carson, my thoughts keep running back to the image I had of him in my bathtub, long limbs wrapped around me, muscular arms drawing me close to his hard body . . .

God, I'm in so much trouble. I've had that thought so many times now, and every time the amount of trouble I'm in where he's concerned has increased.

My earlier thought flits unbidden through my mind: *I'm in love with Carson Hale.* I just have to hope I can keep that thought under control tonight, especially my impulse to tell him everything.

CHAPTER 9: WIND-BORNE

Carson

I STAND OUTSIDE XOCHIMILCO'S, WAITING FOR LEILA.

I'm already attached, and it feels good, even if she isn't telling me everything.

I shove the questions away. I can't worry about any of that; either she'll tell me, or she won't. It's her choice, and I have no right to demand the truth from her, no matter how much I need to know, no matter how much dishonesty pisses me off.

Then she's here, swaying toward me in a short orange dress, the hem brushing an inch above her knees. It's not super low-cut or immodest, but the way it drapes her body shows off her curves in a way that makes my breath catch. Her thick black hair is loose around her shoulders, blown by the slight breeze drifting between the buildings in downtown Detroit.

I stay where I am as she approaches, trying to cover my sudden rush of nerves; this girl affects me in strange ways. She reaches me, hesitates a moment, and then presses up against me in a long, soft embrace. Her arms are around my neck, her lips against my cheek and now on my lips tasting, as always, of cherry lip balm. Her full breasts are crushed against my chest, and my hands skim down her back to curl around her backside.

She pulls her face away to look at me, smirking in coy amusement. "Oh really?"

"What?" I ask, feigning innocence.

Leila shakes her head, laughing, but doesn't move my hands. My heart is hammering in my chest. I hadn't meant to put my hands there, but when I felt her body pressed against me, I just couldn't help myself.

She doesn't seem to mind, though, and even pushes back into my hands for a moment before backing away from me.

"Dinner?" Leila asks. "As much as I wouldn't mind making out all night with your hands on me, I *am* hungry."

I reluctantly step away and dig my hand into my pocket so I don't grab her lush ass again. "Do you want to go into Xochimilco's, or find somewhere else?"

"Oh, this is fine," Leila says, pointing to the restaurant behind us. "I've never been here before."

We go in and are seated after a short wait. I order us some chips and salsa and a pitcher of sangria. We spend a few minutes perusing the menu, even though I know it by heart at this point. I'm careful to keep the conversation light and innocent, keep it away from anything that might lead to awkward questions I know she won't answer.

Despite the small talk and the good food I can sense that she's . . . distant? I'm not sure if that's the right word. It feels like she's not entirely here with me, as if part of her is somewhere else, focused on another problem. I recognize the behavior, as it's something I myself do all too frequently.

When I'm working a case, it tends to overwhelm my entire being, even when I'm off-duty. I'll be talking to someone and, on the surface, I'll be listening and paying attention, eyes making full contact, nodding and agreeing and responding in all the right places, but I would never be completely *there.* Part of me is always locked away and working, examining facts and evidence and problems. Leila is in that mode. She listens to me talk about some of my less morbid cases and funny stories from my days as a patrol officer, but

I can tell her mind is elsewhere.

I stop in the middle of a story and change tracks. "Is there anything wrong? You just seem like you've got something bothering you."

Leila shakes her head. "No, no, I'm fine. I'm sorry."

I reach across the table and take her hand. "Look, Leila . . . I know there are things you can't or won't talk to me about, and I've promised both of us that I won't pry. But I can tell you've got something heavy going on in that pretty head of yours. If you don't want to talk about it, fine, but just . . . whatever it is, know that I won't pass judgment, and I'll do my best to help you if you'll let me. All I'm saying is, you don't have to put on a game face for me, okay?"

Leila smiles at me, and squeezes my hand. "I know I've been kind of . . . I don't know . . . evasive, or whatever. It's not that I'm trying to keep secrets from you, it's just that there are things I simply can't talk about. With anyone, not just with you. I know that probably only makes the curiosity worse, and I'm sorry."

"So there's nothing bothering you? For real?" I can't stop the question from popping out.

Leila sighs, exasperated. "There is something, yes. I'm not going to lie to you about that. You're a cop; you're trained to read people. But can you just

. . . just let it go, for now? I promise, I'll explain it all when I can. *If* I can. I just want to be here with you, have a good time, and try not to think about it. Okay? Please?"

I sense a desperation hidden in her words, and don't know what to make of it. On one hand, she's only made my curiosity worse, but on the other hand, I can clearly see she can't talk about whatever is eating at her. I take a deep breath and let it out slowly, trying to push away all the questions yet again.

The evasions are putting up a wall between us, and I want to break it down, but I just don't know how. I have to let it go, try to push it all away and simply enjoy the time I have with her.

"Okay." I reach out and take her hand. "I hear you loud and clear. No more questions, no more pushing. The last thing I'll say is this: you're not alone, in whatever you're going through. At least, you don't have to be. I'm here, and if you need *anything,* all you have to do is ask. I'll be there, and I'll do whatever is in my power to do, okay?"

Leila nods, visibly fighting emotion. "Thank you, Carson. You don't—you don't know what it means to me to hear that."

"I've been on my own my entire adult life," I tell her. "So I think I kind of do, at least a little."

She forces a smile. "So. How 'bout them Tigers,

huh?"

I laugh. "Nice try. I thought you might want to know, I officially closed Miriam's case."

A more genuine smile, this time. "Good. I think, personally speaking, that you made the right decision. I'm not in your shoes, obviously, but from everything you told me . . . I'm not sure you'd ever get the answers you're looking for, at least not that you could take anywhere official. If you've had this hard a time believing the evidence you've seen with your own eyes, imagine how hard it'd be to make a case for people who have only your word on everything?"

I nod. "Exactly. I *saw* it, with my own eyes. I saw what Miriam could do, and I still have a hard time believing it. My captain is by-the-books, show-me-hard-evidence-or-you've-got-nothing. I'd never convince her of the case I'd have to make with the evidence I do have."

Leila moves the subject after that to the latest summer blockbuster movies, and I let her, all too willing to put that case behind me. Leila seems grateful that I'm willing to let the subject be changed, and she makes an obvious effort to focus on me rather than her internal debate.

When we finish eating, I pay the bill and we leave the restaurant, strolling out into the warm evening. My car isn't far away, so I drive us across the city and find a parking space off of West Jefferson Avenue, then tangle my hand in Leila's and lead her across the busy street and past the huge metal fist of Joe Louis to the river's edge. We lean side by side on the railing, watching boats ply the wide river, the lights of Windsor bright in the lowering dark of night, now just two people lost in the summer crowd of a beautiful Detroit evening.

Leila seems content to simply stand next to me and hold my hand, and I'm not inclined to break the silence either. After a while, Leila turns and puts her back against the railing, pulling me to face her, her hands on my shoulders.

"Carson, look. I'm not being fair to you. I know I'm not. It's ridiculous of me to have all these secrets, and tell you they're there, but not tell you about them. Especially with you being the kind of man you are—"

"What kind of man am I?" I ask.

"Well, you're a detective. You have this drive to know the truth. Like Miriam's case? You were obsessed with it. Every time you came into the bar, you were brooding over it. You couldn't let it go." Leila pulls me closer and I slide my hands around her waist, nodding for her to continue.

"So here's something I *can* tell you: My dad . . . sometimes his business isn't entirely . . . legal, okay? Don't ask me to elaborate, but that's part of why I'm hesitant to talk about my past."

"I guessed as much when you told me he was a 'businessman,'" I say, making air quotes with my fingers.

"Okay, so that's part of it, and it makes it tough on me. I don't really want anything to do with his business, legitimate or otherwise. Plus, I'm still a woman, and according to his beliefs, women have no place in business. Yet he has all these expectations of me, and I . . . I can't meet them. I just . . . can't. Except if I don't, I'll end up alienating my whole family, and they're all I have. They're already close to disowning me for moving here, you know, for leaving them and for not being . . . '*traditional.*'" She says that word with bitterness. "Plus, my dad is having trouble with his business, with the . . . the not-so-legal side of things, if you know what I mean? So I'm worried for him on top of everything else because, as I'm sure you're aware, criminals aren't exactly . . . forgiving."

I nod, absorbing and processing what she said. It has the ring of truth, but it still leaves me with more questions than answers; Leila is obviously trying to put my curiosity at ease without revealing anything too compromising.

"Listen, I don't care what your dad does. It's out of my jurisdiction, for one thing. I'm a small-time Detroit detective, okay? I'm not DEA or FBI or anything, so there's nothing I can do anyway. Even if I wanted to make a claim or a report, I'd need evidence to get them to make a move. And I've got enough on my plate going on in Detroit that I just don't have the attention to spare to look into some drug dealer in Chicago, or whatever it is he does. But all of that aside, I understand if you can't talk about it, even though I suspected as much anyway. But—" I hesitate, and then go for broke, speaking the deep-down truth.

I rub the stubble on my cheek, then return my hand to her waist. "That's not what's really bothering me, Leila. It's that you don't trust me. I know we've only known each other a short time, and I have no right to demand every little secret and detail about you and your life, but . . . I *want* them. That's the honest truth, Leila. I *want* all the details, and I want the secrets. I want you to trust me." I grip her waist tightly, pin her with my eyes, let her see into me. "The other part of what I'm feeling here is that I *know* there's more to it than just your dad's occupation, legal or otherwise. That's another evasion, a half-truth, or a truth meant to distract me from the deeper reality. There's something else, something major that you're holding back."

Leila tries to speak, but I hold up a hand. "Just wait a second, please. Just let me say this. I like you, Leila. I like you a lot. God, that sounds so juvenile, like we're in grade school or some shit. 'Do you like me, check yes or no.' You know? But I . . . I want to *be* with you." The words stick in my throat, not wanting to come out, but I force them out, push them past the lump of nerves. "You're not like anyone I've ever known in my life, and I'm crazy attracted to you, on every level. But, if you have these secrets, I'm honestly not sure where this can go. If you have issues to resolve, or whatever, I can wait. I can give you time, if that's what you need."

Leila's features crumple with emotion. She seems on the verge of tears, and I can't decipher whether she's happy that I told her how I feel, or upset because she doesn't feel the same, or if it's something else entirely.

She takes several deep breaths. "Carson, god . . . You don't know how happy it makes me to hear that. You really don't. I want to be with you too . . ."

"But?"

"But I'm not sure it's possible, no matter what I want. And the 'why' of it is all tied up in the rest of what I can't talk about. The deeper reality that I can't explain to you."

I shake my head, not quite able to accept that. "So you want to be with me, but you're not sure you can, but you can't tell me why you can't?"

Leila just nods, not meeting my eyes, head lowered, face in her hands. Her shoulders start to shake, and I realize she's crying. Not just crying, but sobbing. I'm completely at a loss for a moment, then I do the only thing I know to do: I lift her face to mine and kiss her. She pulls away at first, but I follow her, putting a hand on her cheek, fingers splayed across her jaw, my thumb brushing away her hot tears.

She hiccups, laughing and sobbing, and pulls back slightly, not out of my embrace but enough so she can catch her breath. She meets my eyes, hers sparkling with tears and a thousand emotions I have no words for.

I rest my forehead against hers, our lips not quite touching. "You are so beautiful, Leila," I whisper.

I wish I could express what I'm feeling for her, but I simply can't summon the right words.

I decide to give her an easy out. "You don't have to tell me anything, okay? I don't need to know. If you can't be with me, I'll understand, and I'll respect that." I start to pull away, but Leila puts her hand behind my head, tangling her fingers in my hair, and tugs me back toward her into another kiss.

She kisses me with a passion that seems desperate, as if she needs me and can't get enough, as if to get as much of me as she can while she has the chance. I close the gap between us so our hips are pressed together, kissing her back with the same fierce need.

It feels like she's saying goodbye yet again, an all-too familiar sensation now, and the sense of desperation I'm getting from her is contagious, washing through me in palpable waves.

A breeze kicks up from the river, blowing over us and ruffling our hair, rippling our clothes. It's a warm, steady wind at first, the kind of breeze I'd expect from a summer night on the Detroit River. But as our kiss deepens, tongues flicking out and exploring tentatively, hands wandering and caressing, the wind starts to pick up, blowing harder and hotter, buffeting us from all directions, skirling around us in wild eddies. It feels like we're standing in a river of wind, like we're caught in a jetstream. I'm blown against her so we're pressed against the railing with enough force that I put a hand on the railing to steady us. People around us are beginning to flee, huddling together, shrieking as hats and purses are plucked away and tossed by the wind, now blowing violently.

Leila pulls away to break the kiss, looking around at the now-empty river walk, which only moments before had been teeming with people. The wind is playing with her hair, blowing it around her in black waves that never seem to tangle. She meets my gaze, her eyes steady but fraught with emotion.

The river behind us is wild with white-capped waves, the clouds above shredded and blown apart.

Trees are bent sideways, and the few people still making their way out of Hart Plaza lean forward into the wind, shielding their eyes from the dust and dirt and grit lacing the gale-force winds. I look back to Leila, and what I see now makes me question my own sanity: the wind isn't buffeting against her as it is me; she's not being knocked around by the constantly shifting gusts of battering wind. It's as if the wind is blowing *through* her, as if she's not quite solid, somehow. The wind gusts and pushes against her without moving her, and the edges of her form dim and turn translucent, as if she could fade away and become part of the sudden storm. When the wind changes direction, the edges of her form dissolve into nothingness, flickering and fluttering and fading away in the same direction.

She *is* the wind.

Through all of this, her gaze never wavers from mine. Her dark eyes have been replaced by blinding, brilliant white orbs, their substance whirling and moving and shifting with each gust. She's showing me something, I realize. She wants me to see this, to see the wind curling and skirling around her like a living, visible thing, her body disappearing into the substance of the gale, her eyes white as cumulus clouds lit by the sun.

Then she kisses me again, and when our lips touch, the wind howls around us with renewed hurricane force. I hear a scrape and a crash, glancing out of the corner of my eye to see a big orange-and-white construction pylon tumbling away like a plastic bag caught in a breeze. I taste wind on her breath, taste the dust of a thousand faraway places, taste the green glow of sunlight on leaves, taste trees bending in storm winds, taste ocean salt and clean cool rain.

Around us, the howling wind reaches a crescendo, roaring around us to block out the world, pushing away problems and questions. All I know, now, is her, Leila, a soft mass of curves caught up in my arms, her body blown away by the wind into near invisibility yet somehow still solid and soft and real in my hands. I can feel her heart beating against my chest, can feel the heat of her body radiating against mine, the soft skin of her arms wrapped around my neck. I let my hands explore downward to lift the hem of her skirt, the soft silk of her thighs under my palms changing to the firm muscle of her taut ass. She pushes back against me, and I know she's feeling the hardness of my desire crushed between us. The roaring winds tug at us, push and pull us, and I suddenly feel weightless, my stomach dropping away, feel myself borne up by the constant rush of air beneath my feet, pushing me skyward.

I open my eyes and break the kiss, glance to one side and see the earth falling away beneath us, Hart

Plaza and the fist sculpture and the river all visible through a vortex of dust and newspaper and leaves and lost articles of clothing. I'm standing on air somehow, clutching Leila to my chest, standing at the center of a massive tornado a hundred and fifty feet above the ground.

Leila touches my jaw to turn my face back to hers, a small smile on her lips, her alien all-white eyes still somehow familiar. She kisses my jaw, my neck, nudges aside the collar of my button-down shirt to kiss my chest, and my breath catches at the tender affection of her lips on my skin. Her hands on my back slide down to slip under the waistband of my pants and my underwear to clutch my skin, kissing, kissing, kissing me as if she can't ever get enough.

All this as we are unexplainably, impossibly airborne.

Somewhere inside my head, I'm freaking out, my mind screaming questions, but I shove them away. I know what's happening is impossible, but I don't care. I know I should be terrified, I know I should be asking how this is happening, but I don't ask. I know Leila is making this happen somehow, and that scares me, but I ignore that, too.

Her lips on me, her hands unbuttoning my jeans, her breasts and her breath, this is all I know.

Then, abruptly, she jerks her hands away from

me, only moments from having me in her hand. I'm left gasping, aching, trembling, but I know from the look in her now-human eyes that the craziness of the situation is impinging on her consciousness.

The winds slow and lower us gently to the ground once more.

Leila falls against me, sobbing. "I can't—I can't . . . I want you, but I just can't. It's not fair to you, and—god, I'm so sorry . . ." and then her words fail her and she succumbs to the tears.

I wrap my arms around her shoulders, holding her in an embrace, not speaking, just holding her until the storm of tears slows.

"Why? Why can't you? Please tell me," I murmur.

She shakes her head. "Please, *please* . . . don't ask that. It's too painful." She looks up at me, her mascara running. "Don't you see, though? Do you see what I can't say?"

"Yes," I answer. "I see. But I also see that there's *still* something huge keeping you from me. I saw what Miriam was capable of. I see what you're capable of. I can accept it, I can believe it. It may take some time to adjust and come to grips with the truth, but I can accept who . . . and *what* . . . you are. But that's not the problem. Not really. If I knew the real, true obstacle keeping us apart, I might be able to figure out a way to solve it."

She shakes her head. "No, you couldn't. It's . . . impossible."

"Why?"

Leila groans, bumping her forehead against my chest. "Don't ask that. Don't make me lie. I can't tell you. It's for your own protection as much as anything."

That only irritates me more, and I let the irritation show in my voice. "I don't need protection, Leila. I can take care of myself."

"Oh, yeah?" Leila shoots back, an edge to her voice, waving at the overturned cars, street signs ripped out of concrete. "You saw what I just did. Can you defend yourself against that? I had you a hundred and fifty feet in the air, held up only with my power. Now imagine if I was an enemy, someone out to kill you . . . remember Miriam? What you told me she could do?"

I try to imagine that kind of power but directed against me. My mind boggles, and resists, refuses to capitulate to the truth. "Maybe . . . maybe it was just a coincidence. I mean, it could have been a freak windstorm or—"

"*Carson,*" Leila interrupts. "Don't play stupid, all right? You saw that, you felt it, and you *know* it was me. You wanted me to trust you and I did, at great risk to myself, I should add. I shouldn't have done that, I shouldn't have shown you that. It goes against the oldest and most basic laws of my people, so don't insult me by pretending it was some freak coincidence. If you can't handle the truth, don't ask for it." She jerks away from me, walking out of the plaza, straightening her clothes and running her fingers through her hair.

I adjust my own clothes and jog after her, catching at her arm.

"Leila," I say, spinning her to face me.

"No, Carson. Just *don't*. If you can't believe the truth when it's right in front of you, this won't work. And nothing has changed—you have to understand that. I'm still bound by—" Leila stops and starts over, facing away from me, watching the cars rush down Jefferson Avenue. "I can't be with you, whether you believe what you just experienced or not. So I guess it doesn't matter. This is out of my hands, and certainly out of yours."

My mind and heart are at war with each other: my mind is telling me that what I'd seen and felt was impossible, but my heart is telling me it doesn't matter; I love her whether she's some weird tornado-woman or not.

I love her? That thought takes me by surprise, shocking me into stillness.

Then what she's just said filters through to my

awareness.

"You can't be with me? I thought you just weren't sure?"

"Carson, why can't you just stop asking me so many questions?" She claws her fingers through her long, loose black hair, tips her head back and growls under her breath. "The truth is I've *never* been free to be with you, not from the very beginning. I've been trying to convince myself I could find a way around it, but . . . I can't. I *can't.* I've gone in circles about this so many times, wishing, hoping, fighting against the facts, and . . . there's just nothing I can do." Leila finally meets my eyes, and I see a sadness in her gaze, a resignation laced with anger. "I . . . I care more for you than I should, Carson, and the worst part is I'll never be able to be with you. Not ever. I never should have kissed you. I never should have even let whatever this is between us get started, and I *really* shouldn't have let things go this far. It's not fair to you, and it only makes what I have to do all the more painful for me, because now I know what it feels like—what could have—" She breaks off, fighting tears, pain rife in her gaze.

I try to summon a response, but no words come out. I want to kiss her again, I want to take her to my apartment and make love to her until we're both exhausted and sated, and most of all I want to whisper

the three little words I've never said to anyone before
. . .

Maybe she sees this in my eyes, or maybe she has other powers that allow her to read my thoughts. I don't know.

She shakes her head, puts her finger to my lips. "Please don't," she whispers, "*please* don't make this harder than it has to be. I *can't*, Carson. No matter what I feel for you, I can't do anything about it. I'm sorry. I'm so sorry." She backs away, gaze fixed on me.

"Goodbye, Carson." Her voice trembles, her shoulders shake, and a tear tracks down her cheek.

She turns on her heel and jogs away.

I let her go, feeling something crack inside me.

Chapter 10: Soliloquy

Leila

I MANAGE TO GET AROUND THE CORNER BEFORE I BREAK down in hysterics. I can't believe I let that happen. I should never have indulged in any of this, and that's exactly what this has been: indulgence. Carson has never been for me and never will be.

I slump down against a brick wall, my back against the cold surface of a building, sobbing. I can feel my makeup running, but that's the last thing I care about. I've done the right thing, telling Carson goodbye, but that doesn't stop the pain inside. It feels like my heart has been cracked into a million pieces, and I know for a fact I'll never be whole again.

Not without Carson Hale.

There's no other choice, though, I know that much. I may not want anything to do with my father's criminal activities, but I can't let my family get hurt simply because I don't like Hassan. It's more complicated than that, of course. It's *marriage*, for god's sake. It's permanent. Forever. Once Hassan has me, he'll never let me go, and the ifrit marriage rites are magically binding anyway.

But what if I just told Carson everything . . . ?

But I can't do that. I just can't.

But why not? I've already shown him what I can do. He may not know the terms and the history and all the details, but he knows now that I'm not just an ordinary girl. He's come to some sort of acceptance in regards to Miriam, for one thing, and closed her case despite what might be termed an ethical objection. He's trying to be open-minded. He's learning to accept the impossible. So what if I ran away with him?

I can't stop myself from reliving those moments when the two of us were standing by the river. God, his hands felt *so* good, exploring my body, skimming across my curves. His lips set me to trembling. I wanted so badly to take his hard length in my hands and caress him until he exploded, but I knew if I'd done that, there would be no return. It's taking every last shred of my will power to stop myself from running back to him. I know he's still standing back at the railing by the river, watching the waves glint in the moonlight, trying to figure out what the hell just happened.

The way he looks at me, I swear, it turns me to Jell-O. I shouldn't torture myself like this, but I can't help thinking he feels about me the way I do about him. I could swear he was moments from telling me he loves me. Which is stupid and impossible and ridiculous, because we've known each other for a matter of weeks, two months at the most, but there it is. It's in his eyes and the way he kisses me and the way he touches me. Greedy, but with restraint. He wants me, but not just for the sake of sex. He could've had that already, and he knows it. If he were to push me over the edge, I wouldn't stop him. I couldn't. I would've made love to him right there in the vortex, a hundred and fifty feet off the ground in the middle of downtown Detroit.

I open my eyes and force myself to pull it together, make my legs take one step after another, away from Carson. With every step, my heart cracks further, splits away from the rest of me. My heart is with Carson, and I'm walking away.

I can't see him again. That was the last time. I repeat the promise to myself: the last time.

Halfway to my car, I hear the sound of footsteps behind me. Harsh whispers break through my wall of self-pity. I turn my head enough to glance behind me: three young men, two white, one Hispanic, dressed in shorts that sag halfway down to their ankles, T-shirts about ten sizes too big, flat-brimmed ball caps turned not-quite sideways, hands at their crotches, holding up their shorts. It doesn't take much imagination to realize what their intentions are.

They think I'm easy prey, a pretty young girl alone, downtown, in a little sundress and flats, a clutch purse. Easy, right?

I pity them.

I slow down, letting them draw closer, while wrapping strands of elemental power around me. If they could see my face, they'd see my eyes glowing blinding white. I'm sure they feel the wind that suddenly howls down the street, but they pay no mind. All they see is me—or rather, all they see is my ass in the orange dress, more likely. I sway a bit, taunting them. I can hear them laughing, slapping each other, howling like wolves, jogging quickly to catch up.

I stop and turn around. The smile I give them probably seems seductive. They don't see the rage boiling behind it. If they could, they'd run screaming. In this moment, I have enough anger and pent-up sexual frustration that I don't have much ability to control what's about to happen.

They close in, mere feet away, now. The wind is skirling around me, hurricane-serpents.

"Hey sweetheart," one of them says, clutching himself and thrusting his crotch at me. "Come on, baby. Make this easy on us."

"Yeah, sexy," another one pipes up. "Don't make us hurt you, 'kay?"

The one who hasn't spoken reaches behind his back, for a gun most likely, and that's when I make my move. Three fists of wind smash into their chests, hurling them twenty feet away. I could let it go at that, but it'd be too easy. They've picked the wrong day to mess with me.

I walk forward as they're picking themselves up, obviously wondering what happened. I send a trickle of magic out, just a little illusion to make the winds visible. Now they can see the power rushing around me, illuminated by skeins of red flame. The fire is the illusion, cold and harmless, but they don't know that. I lash out again, wrap the wind around them, crushing their arms to their sides. I lift them up, letting them see the white glow of magic in my eyes.

I smell urine: one of them has a wet spot on his pants leg. I laugh, and the sound echoes like thunder from the buildings around me. They're pleading with me to let them go, not to hurt them, that they were just joking. I don't answer. At least, not with words.

I throw them, hard. They smash into a building across the street, fall to the sidewalk in a shower of broken glass, crumbling concrete and droplets of blood. I let the winds turn me ethereal and blow me across the intervening space to stand over them.

I feel no remorse as I look down at them. Blood trickles from their mouths and noses and ears. They cough, and gobbets of dark red bubble from their lips. And they are terrified.

They won't last the night.

I'm sure I'll feel a few pangs of guilt later but, for now, I feel relieved. The pressure has been lifted, a little. It felt good to have someone to lash out at. They would've killed me, I'm sure.

I make it home and fall fully clothed into bed. I can't stop the tears from flooding through me once again. I wonder what Carson is thinking. I wonder if he'll believe what he experienced, or if he'll try to block it out. He has a hard time believing in anything other than hard facts.

It's strange, though: I've never taken my ifrit powers too seriously. I've learned to control them, of course, because every ifrit child has to learn the basics to survive in the human world without giving themselves away. But I've never used them for much of anything, and besides, girls are only taught the basics. Not like boys, who are tutored and trained until they can wield their powers as second nature. When Hassan showed up and threatened me the other day, that was the first time I'd used my powers in several years. And then again, tonight, with Carson. They seem to be flying out of control. Whenever Carson kissed me, they flared up, and tonight, at the river walk . . . it was all I could do to keep them contained. I couldn't have stopped that if I'd wanted to. And, honestly, I didn't want to. It was a way to let Carson see some of the truth I couldn't spell out for him.

None of the other boyfriends I've had have ever made my powers flare up like that. Granted, there haven't been many, but the ones there have been were lackluster and boring compared to Carson. I knew it when I dated them, but I think I wanted it like that. I wanted to use them more to rebel against my father's conservative, Old-World prudishness than for any real desire for the boys themselves. They were boys, too, not men. Yuppy Chicago boys, all of them. I'd parade them in front of my father's study, knowing he dare not show his anger in front of humans. The boys would be in awe of all the marble and the Aston Martin out front, and the grand, curving staircase . . . all bought by drug money, some of it paid for in blood.

Those poor, clueless boys.

It wasn't until I moved out that I let one of them take me past "second base," as they called it. It was quick and awkward and not entirely pleasant.

Jeff Yardley, his name was. Barely twenty-one, worked at a gas station. Attended community college and had no clue what to do with his life. He was cute, in a puppyish sort of way. He was completely inno-cent. I don't think he'd ever been in a fist fight. White bread, my friend Tameka called him. Tameka was an ifrit too, of Moorish descent. She is an Almoravid, I think, but we never discussed our lineage. We both wanted to get away from all that. Tameka wanted me to find someone "worth my while," not an awkward boy like Jeff, but all I cared about was spiting Father.

Eventually I got tired of Jeff and stopped answer-ing his calls. He got the point after I let Father throw him out.

Carson . . . is unlike anyone I've ever known. He makes me feel like a woman, sultry and sexy. He's a man. He's dangerous, in his own way. He's both seen and experienced violence. He's shed blood; I can see it in his eyes. There's a hardness there, not terribly unlike the hardness in Hassan's eyes, but with Car-son, it's counterbalanced by kindness, goodness, and compassion.

I'm torturing myself yet again. My body is re-membering the feel of his hands, squeezing and caressing so gently, and I want that again. I want him here, in this bed. I want to feel him peel off my dress, inch by inch. I want to feel him above me, his strong arms around me, pulling me against him as our passions rise.

I know I've promised myself I won't see him again, but deep down, I know I will. It's inevitable.

CHAPTER 11: DREAMS AND VISIONS

Carson

I'M UPSET. I'M CONFUSED. I'M ANGRY. I'M HURT. I'M A turbulent, potent mix of emotions, and I don't know what to do with any of them, so I go to the shooting range with a box of shells, riddle paper targets with holes while my thoughts wander in circles.

Why do I care about Leila so much? She's just a girl, and girls come and go. I've dated a shitload of girls, and none of them have ever meant anything to me. But Leila has wormed her way into my every waking thought after just a few weeks. It's not just her looks—although god knows she makes my mouth go dry and my breath catch and my cock go iron hard. Even now, with the acrid smell of gunpowder in my nose, the crashing of pistols from down range, and the pinging of spent shells, all I can think of is the way she curled into me, the way she wordlessly encouraged me to kiss her more deeply, to touch her, to hold her . . .

Of course, that leads to thoughts of her skin under my hands and the wind blowing around us, the way her dress was molded to her curves . . .

The wind. I can't deny what happened by the river; I've tried to pretend it didn't happen, but that only worked for about five seconds. The truth is undeniable: a windstorm kicked up, gale-force winds strong enough to hurl vehicles across the street and uproot street signs from the concrete. That same wind somehow formed a tornado around us and lifted us off the ground, gently and carefully.

I know without a doubt that it was Leila's doing. She was showing me something; she wanted me to see who she really is. Maybe that business with the wind is her secret, maybe she's worried I'd be scared off by her crazy powers.

It's a little scary, yeah, I don't mind admitting. If she can do that, lift us off the ground and throw a Taurus across Jefferson Avenue, then there's no telling what else she can do. That would certainly explain the strange tornado damage at The Old Shillelagh . . . but it doesn't explain the fire.

My mind goes back to Miriam. She killed a man in self-defense, and she did it with fire. *I'm a djinni,* she told me. I remember sitting in an interview room at the precinct, watching a candle flame waltz across the table and hop onto my hand. Unexplainable, but real. Miriam's boyfriend Jack saw the flame too; I saw his reaction to the little flame-figure.

I'm pragmatic enough to admit that what I experienced with that flame was real, and that what happened tonight with the maelstrom was real, too. What did it mean? Was Leila . . . what? Something other than human? A djinni, like Miriam? What's a djinni? A genetic mutation, like the X-Men? Miriam and Leila are similar, in some way. Their . . . abilities, for lack of a better term, use different elements, but seem to function in the same basic away. When Miriam summoned the flame, her eyes changed, turned to flame. That, combined with Betsy Willis's report of a glowing woman, leads me to believe Miriam could . . . become flame entirely, somehow. I don't even know how to think about it, but that seems right. The little flame was a miniscule portion of her powers. Snapping her fingers, just to prove her point, essentially.

So how does this relate to Leila? Miriam was a fire-woman, which makes Leila a wind-woman. Where the powers come from is irrelevant, although a facscinating question. The real issue is what Leila's other-than-human nature means for me, for any pos-sibility of an *us*. She showed me her powers, showed me, at risk to herself and to me, she claimed, who and/or what she is. So the truth of her nature isn't the obstacle keeping her from being with me. She ran away from home, so it's not her parents or religion or whatever. It's something else. Something significant. Some . . . duty, or . . . I don't know. I can only conjec-ture at this point. She walked away from me again, claimed once more that she just couldn't explain any-thing to me. For my protection, and her own.

What a mess.

I pop off the last few rounds in the clip, then set the pistol down, removing the sound-baffling ear pro-tectors.

When she walked away from me today, it was painfully obvious she was saying goodbye permanent-ly, and the thought of never seeing her again makes my heart clench. This is not an option I'm willing to consider. I don't care what I have to do.

But what can I do? She wants to be with me too. She feels the same way I do, yet she still walked away before anything could happen between us.

So what can I do to change her mind?

I go over it all again, try to focus in on details. There's obviously something else going on with her that she can't or won't tell me, and it's keeping her from being with me. She wants me, I'm absolutely positive of that. She cares for me, too, beyond physical attraction: I saw the pain in her eyes as she walked away,

Maybe it's her father? She'd said her dad is old-school . . . maybe he'd disown her if she dated the wrong person, someone not Arabic, or someone not from "her people," someone without wind-powers or whatever? But if that was the case then why had she moved away from her family? Plus, I don't think she'd let that stop her if she really cared for me the way I think she does. Not if she'd already run away from home in the pursuit of freedom to live her life her way. She must have a much stronger motivation than familial disapproval.

If this were an investigation, I'd say I've hit the wall, reached a point where the case can't progress any further without new evidence.

I leave the range and go home. Sleep is slow in coming, and when it does I dream of her. In my dream, she stands in the doorway of my bedroom, wearing the sexy orange dress she wore on our date, but in the dream she watches me with those eerie white-glowing eyes, a sultry smile on her lips, slowly peeling the dress up over her head, revealing black lace panties and a matching bra. In my dream, she walks toward me, body swaying seductively, hair blowing in a perpetual breeze despite the closed window, and then she straddles me, rides me. . . .

In my dream, she reaches up behind her back and unclasps her bra, but I wake up before the cups fall away from her breasts, and I'm left uncomfortably hard, sweating profusely, feeling lonely and sad.

I pour myself a finger of gin, drink it warm and straight up, and follow it with another, a third, and then I force myself to put the bottle away and return to my bedroom.

When I finally fall back asleep, Leila is waiting for me in my doorway, wearing that orange dress and the sexy smile, and she straddles me, reaches for her bra clasp again . . .

I wake up again, just before her bra falls away.

Days pass, and I dream of Leila every single night. I manage to keep my drinking to a minimum, just enough to fall asleep at night and stay asleep, but without work to distract me, it gets increasingly difficult. I stay home, watch TV shows I've never heard of, go to the gym and work out until I can barely move. I lace on my running shoes and run the city streets until my lungs burn and my legs tremble. These two weeks of vacation are a total waste of time; I could be working, solving cases.

Nothing helps. I nearly dial her number a thousand times, but the farewell I saw in her eyes stops me every time. Maybe I misinterpreted things, maybe she'd just been physically attracted to me and decided she didn't want to get involved with someone who didn't have the same powers, or maybe she wasn't even attracted to me at all. The more time passes, the more tangled and distorted my memories become, making me doubt what I saw, making me doubt what I felt for her in the first place.

Finally, at the start of the second week, I show up at the precinct, intending to beg the captain to let me go back to work. I don't even get past the front desk. Archer is there as I walk through the front doors, telling me in no uncertain terms to get lost.

I've got another week before I can go back to work; I'll be bat-shit crazy by then, no doubt. So I run, go to the practice range, and bench more weight than is safe . . .

And Leila teases me in my dreams, peeling that orange dress over her head, lips centimeters from mine but never meeting, secrets abounding in her dark eyes, breasts swaying and moments from being bared to me.

Every gust of wind smells of her, shampoo and cherry lip balm and jasmine. Every gust of wind makes me turn around and look for her. I hear her voice, echoing just around the corner.

She's in the wind, slipping through my fingers.

I honestly can't explain how, today, I happen to be standing outside this particular door. It's crazy, but here I am, at the end of my rope, about to knock on the door of a virtual stranger.

I lift my hand and rap on the door, hear a gruff voice say, "Just a minute, hold your horses then, I'm comin.'"

Sean Byrne opens the door, iron-gray hair ruffled, a red cardigan hanging off his shoulders despite the late July heat. "Detective Hale, yeah?" Sean says.

"Yes, Mr. Byrne. It's Detective Hale." I feel stupid, standing here bothering an old man I met once.

But I've got no one else to talk to, nowhere else to turn, and for some reason, Sean Byrne seems like a possible answer. He's Jack Byrne's father, and he's old Irish. In the course of investigating Miriam, I spent an interesting afternoon talking to Sean, who claims to have what he calls the "Second Sight," which, as far as I can tell, is some kind of ability to see the future. When old Sean Byrne made that claim then, I'd dismissed him out of hand as crazy, just another old coot suffering from dementia or something. But now, after what I've experienced regarding both Miriam and Leila, I'm having second thoughts.

And honestly, what do I have to lose? If he claims to be able to see the future, maybe he won't be as quick to dismiss my craziness as I was his.

"Well boy-o, come on in. No sense air-conditionin' the outdoors, yeah?" Sean pulls me inside and closes the door, waving for me to follow him through a formal living room to a bright kitchen painted a powder blue.

Sean waves me toward a stool at the island in the center of the kitchen. "So," he says. "What is it you want, then? Why're you here, Detective? Hmmm? It's not for work, I know that much. You've settled the investigation into Miriam, she's told me as much."

"I . . . I'm honestly not sure, Mr. Byrne."

"Och, call me Sean. So, you're here, but you don't know why. Well, start at the beginning and mebbe we can figure it out." Sean goes to a cupboard above the stainless steel refrigerator and grabs a bottle of Johnnie Walker. "Care for a whiskey? You look like you could use one, if you don't mind my saying so."

"Sure. I'm off duty." I accept the tumbler of amber liquid, but I sip at it sparingly.

Sean nods, peering at me with piercing eyes. "Listen, son, I don't know why you're here exactly, but I'd best make one thing clear to you right now: I can't see the future on command. It doesn't work that way."

I shake my head. "It's not that. I mean, if you *could* see the future, that might help, but . . . like I said, I'm not sure why I'm here. I've got a lot on my mind right now, and I wasn't sure who to talk to . . . and for some reason, you came to mind. I hope I'm not bothering you. It's totally out of the blue, I know."

Sean waves a hand. "No way, lad. I'm a bored old man. You'll be the most interesting thing to happen all week." Sean grabs my hand and squeezes it, a grandfatherly gesture that somehow makes me feel immediately calmer. "Just start at the beginning, yeah?"

I draw a breath and begin my story, hesitantly at first. I tell Sean about the case with Miriam and how it turned out, how I met Leila, and then I explain my reservations and doubts and questions, though the oddness of doing so to a complete stranger isn't lost on me. Through it all Sean merely nods now and then, giving away nothing of what he thinks.

When I finish telling Sean about my latest encounter with Leila, he's silent and thoughtful for a long moment.

"Look, I've got no Sight on this, lad. I'm sorry." Sean shrugs apologetically. "But I can tell you this, and it don't take no visions, only the wisdom of age and the experience with heartbreak: the girl loves you. You love her back, and that's a fact. But if she's got secrets, it's for a reason. But in my experience, I can tell you that secrets will out, in time. Don't force 'em from her, lad. That's the surest way to make sure she bolts, and then you won't never get her back. Take that from one who knows." Sean's eyes cloud, staring beyond me and into the past.

I sigh; I know Sean's right, but I'd come to the same conclusion already, and I'm still wondering what I'm doing here. Just as I'm about to thank Sean and make my exit, the side door to the kitchen opens.

Jack Byrne strolls in, keys in one hand, cell phone in the other. "Hey, Gramps. I'm home," he calls out, not looking up from his phone.

He stops in the entryway, the screen door not quite closed, distracted in that peculiar way people have when typing a text message. He sends the message and looks up, freezing when he sees me sitting at the table.

"Did I miss something?" Jack asked. "Is everything okay? It can't be Miriam, I just talked with her a second ago . . ."

"Relax, boy-o," Sean says, waving a hand in a 'calm down' motion. "He's here on personal business, not as a copper."

"Gramps, no one calls them 'coppers' anymore," Jack says, shaking his head. "And I'm pretty sure that's rude."

I laugh. "No, it's fine. It's funny actually. But your

grandfather is right, Jack. I'm not here as part of an investigation. Sorry if I startled you."

Jack pulls out a chair between the two men and sits down, leaning back on the chair's hind legs. "What possible personal business could you have with Gramps?" he asks, his voice openly suspicious.

Before I can respond, Sean reaches out and grabs his grandson's hand, fixing him with a hard, piercing gaze. "Why don't you ask him that yourself, son? Take a look."

Jack shifts in his chair and lets the front legs touch back down. "He wants a Sight? Is that why he's here? How does he even know about that?" Jack sounds exasperated. "You can't go telling everyone you see that you have the Second Sight, Gramps, I've told you this. Not everyone will understand."

Gramps huffs scornfully. "Jackie, son, I'm almost ninety years old. I've had the Second Sight since I was knee-high to a grasshopper, and I believe I know who to tell and who not to. You forget who you're talkin' to sometimes, boy-o. Try not to." Sean's voice is hard as iron, and Jack looks chagrined.

"Sorry, Gramps."

"Eh, don't mention it, son. Now, do as I say. Look, and See."

Jack sighs, nodding. He reaches out and takes my hand in his, which has me shifting uncomfortably, but

Jack squeezes hard, not letting me draw away.

"It's necessary, boy," Gramps tells me. "Just let it be."

I'm not sure what to expect, especially after the unbelievable things I've experienced with both Miriam and Leila. What happens when someone has a Sight? Flashes of light? Mental probing? Levitation? And what is the Second Sight, anyway?

Jack is silent for several awkward minutes, eyes closed, hand clamped down like a vise on mine. The silence drags on so long that I'm about to jerk myself free, but then Jack's eyes flick open and I'm pinned in place by the odd and unnatural light there. His brown irises seem to flicker and flare with a distant flame, and I feel a wave of heat wash over me, traveling up from my hand to my arm, then blazing through my whole body, setting every hair on my body on end. My heart palpitates wildly, each second drawing out and lengthening into lifetimes.

Jack's eyes stare away into the middle distance, seeing something not physically present, and I note idly how much like his grandfather Jack looks. When he speaks, Jack's voice is preternaturally deep and echoes off the walls with impossible volume, reverberating in my chest.

"She's about to run," Jack says, still gazing into nothingness over my shoulder. "You can't let her go.

The window of opportunity is short, and you have to seize it or all will be lost. You are called to greater things than you know, but Leila's secrets will change you. You can only achieve your destiny if she is with you. Your mind is closed to the truth, Detective. You must open it, and not fear what you do not understand." Jack's words are oddly formal and out of character, and the inherent accuracy of them chills me to the marrow of my bones. There is no way Jack Byrne could possibly know what's going on, as he hadn't been home when I told my story to Sean. There's just no way. I shake my head, pushing backward in my chair, scraping it on the floor tiles.

"How can you . . ." I stand up too fast, knocking the chair over. "You can't . . ."

Sean rises as well, takes me by the shoulders, shaking me. "You came looking for this, boy-o. Don't panic on me, now. He had a Sight, and a true one. Can't get much clearer than that, lad, let me tell you. Sometimes these Sights only cloud the issue, but you got lucky."

Jack seems exhausted, slumping forward on the table. He glances up at me. "Well? Don't just stand here, dumbass! Go! Find her, before it's too late."

I head toward the door, but Sean stops me. "You don't want to believe, at first," he says. "You want to think it's your imagination, or a coincidence. You'll want to run off and do things your own way, and I'd advise you against that. The only answers you'll find, looking into it your way, will be answers you won't like. Just remember, when the moment comes, what you heard here. You'll be faced with a choice, and it won't be an easy one. When that moment comes, trust your heart and your instincts, not your mind."

I feel the words hammer into me, driving down deep and resonating; I know Sean is right.

The moment I'm out of this house, away from Sean and Jack, I know my mind will start to play tricks on me. I'll replay our conversations mentally, over and over again, and I'll look for flaws and try to convince myself it's all impossible.

And I'm right: as soon as I feel the freeway humming under my tires, the doubts begin. I fight them, but they seep in anyway. All the lies and evasions Leila has fed me are rearing up into insurmountable obstacles, and her strange, frightening powers are laced throughout it all, painting everything with broad strokes of implausibility.

The dreams, recurring and tempting, those too are part of the picture. Is she feeding me the dreams, somehow? Sending me dreams of herself for some nefarious purpose? Is she using me, twisting and brainwashing me for her own purposes? She seems so genuine when I'm with her, yet so conflicted by desire and fear.

But what if all that is a game?

By the time I'm back at my apartment, my head is spinning with a million questions, a million doubts and a million theories, and through it all I keep seeing her as she had been in the vortex, her black hair haloed around her, her eyes white and her hands bold, dress pressed to her lush body by the raging winds turning the edges of her form invisible.

I lie in my bed, still fully clothed, every muscle tense, refusing to allow myself to move, forcing all thoughts from my mind. Eventually sleep claims me, but even in sleep I can't escape Leila, because the dreams are waiting.

Chapter 12: The Calculus of a Moment

Leila

I'm tempted to not answer the door when I hear the knock. It can't be anything good. Right now, with the way I'm feeling, I'd like nothing more than to just disappear, leaving behind Carson and Hassan and my father and everything, but I know that won't solve a thing.

I open the door. The woman standing in front of me is about my height but a little heavier and a little curvier, thick black hair pulled up into a loose, sloppy knot. She radiates power, but not ifrit power . . . I nearly stumble backward when I realize she's a djinni, and an immensely powerful one at that. My hackles rise, my defenses slamming into place. Djinn are the natural, polar opposite of my people. The two races are mortal enemies, even though we are much the same; ours is an age-old feud, rooted in the beginnings of time itself.

The woman is examining me, looking into me, assessing me. "You're Leila," she says, pushing past me into my apartment uninvited.

"Yes. Who are you, and what are you doing here?" I'm coiling my power, ready to hurl it at her if she makes a move I don't like.

"Don't do that," she warns. "I know our kinds don't usually get along, but I'm not here for a fight. I wouldn't have knocked on your door if I was."

"What do you want?" My nerves are on edge, and my powers automatically ignite, causing winds to skirl around us, fluttering our clothes and hair.

The sense of raw power I'm getting from her is nerve-wracking, and she's not even holding her powers at the ready, as I am. I force myself to relax, letting the winds abate. She's not posing a threat, and I've done enough damage to my apartment as it is. I just spent a bunch of money I didn't really have to spend on getting the kitchen fixed.

When the energy subsides within me and the winds die down, the woman visibly loosens. "That's better. Now, how about a drink?"

"A drink? It's ten in the morning." Despite my

protestations, I'm pulling a pair of Michelob Lights from the fridge and opening them.

The woman takes hers and drains a quarter of it immediately. She sits down on my couch, crossing thick, muscular legs. I notice for the first time how scantily she's dressed: she's wearing a pair of black nylons, an embarrassingly low-cut shirt and a skirt that barely deserves the name. She's wearing an apron with a pad of paper and straws peeking out from the pocket. She stinks of cigarettes and alcohol. I assume that she's a waitress, probably at a nightclub or one of the casinos, more likely. If she's dressed like that at ten in the morning, she's probably coming off of a midnight shift.

"Thanks," she says. "My name is Nadira Nasri. As you seem to have guessed, I'm a djinni."

It's odd to be drinking beer this early in the morning, but this whole thing is strange, and the beer helps calm my nerves. "What do you want, Nadira? And how do you know me?" I sit down on the loveseat kitty corner to her.

"That's complicated. Here's the short version: you're in love with Carson Hale, right?" I nod and try to contain my shock; no sense in denying it when it's stated so baldly. She continues: "Carson was part of an investigation recently into a rather unusual death at the MGM. Do you know anything about this?"

I nod again. "Yeah, I know a little about it. It had something to do with a girl named Miriam, I think. She was a djinni, I'm pretty sure. A fire elemental, I know that much, at least. The whole case really threw him for a loop."

Nadira takes a long drink, uncrossing her legs and leans forward. "You're correct: Miriam is a djinni, a fire elemental. And what's more, she was raised not knowing what she was. Anyway, Miriam is dating a guy named Jack, and Jack has what's called the Second Sight. It's the ability to see the future, but more like prophecy than clairvoyance. Don't worry if you've never heard of it; what's relevant to you is that Carson met with Jack and his grandpa, and your name came up. I know this doesn't make any sense, so just listen. Jack had a Sight about the two of you—you and Carson—but he didn't tell Carson everything he saw in that vision. Okay? It wouldn't've made any sense to him, because Carson doesn't know a damn thing about our world and Jack knew that."

My head is spinning. Carson talked to Miriam's boyfriend? Second Sight? "What the *hell* are you talking about?" I'm up and pacing, and I can't quite keep the winds from leaking out to gust around me like a cape trailing behind me.

Nadira stays seated, watching me pace. "Like I said, I know this sounds crazy. You don't know Miriam, or Jack, or me. But you're involved with us. Or at least, you *will* be." I pass by her, and Nadira latches on to my wrist and pulls me to a stop, her eyes intense. "The point is that a war is brewing. Djinn and ifrits have feuded for millennia. You know this. And although we've had a sort of tenuous peace for the last few hundred years, that's going to come to an end, and *soon*. People like your *betrothed*—" she puts an emphasis on that word, making it sound almost like a curseword, "are causing trouble. Hassan is out of control, making public scenes, drawing attention to himself, and thus to all of us. For thousands of years, our kind have attempted to blend in, stay hidden, keep our powers contained and out of human sight. But lately, the ifrits, led by the likes of Hassan al-Jabiri, have been making problems for everyone. I know *you* may not have anything to do with this, but if you're not careful, you'll get drawn in to what's coming. You don't want to be on the wrong side when open war comes."

She's right about the treaty between the djinn and ifrits, and about Hassan; I can't deny that. Hassan and his ilk use their powers far too publicly, and I've always worried it would cause problems. The djinn have always been more prone to staying hidden. They're the careful ones. If things like good and evil exist, then the djinn are more innately good than my people. Hassan and my father are prime examples of this.

Her final statement sinks in. "Are you threatening me?" I can feel the coil of magic tightening within me as I speak.

Nadira lifts her hands to show innocence. "No! That's not . . . that came out wrong. I'm just saying, you seem like a nice girl, okay? I know who you are, and I know who your father is, and I know who Hassan is. I don't want to see you get caught on the wrong side when things go down, okay? I really don't."

"How do you know all this?" I ask.

She doesn't quite meet my eyes when she says, "That's complicated. Just call it . . . part of my job."

"Part of your job as a cocktail waitress?"

She rolls her eyes. "People *do* work more than one job, you know." Nadira waves her hand to dismiss that subject.

She moves so she's sitting next to me, suddenly coming across as girly, as if we're best friends, taking my hands in hers. I try to withdraw, but she's stronger than she looks.

"Listen, Leila," she says. "I've been where you are, okay? I know what you're going through. I was betrothed to a real asshole too, once upon a time, and I also was in love with a human."

"I'm not in love with him," I protest. It's a lie, a

last-ditch attempt to convince myself.

"Don't bullshit a bullshitter, sweetheart," Nadira says. "I know what you're trying to do, and it won't work. Your father got himself into this mess, okay? You don't owe it to him to get him out of it. Especially not when it means marriage to a slimy little fuck like Hassan al-Jabiri."

"You don't understand," I tell her. "You don't know the situation. You don't know what he'll do if don't—"

She interrupts me. "The *hell* I don't. I know exactly what Hassan is capable of. Probably better than you do."

"So then you know why I have to do what he says. I'm not doing it to get my father out of his mess. If it was just business, if it meant Father lost money, that'd be one thing. I wouldn't give it half a thought. But Hassan said he'd—"

"I'm sure he did. He said he'd do all sorts of nasty things to everyone you care about. But remember what I said about a war brewing? Hassan is at the forefront of that. Things are happening, and when shit gets messy, Hassan will be the first target my people go after. Your father will be next in line, too, but we're more inclined to give him a chance to fix things. He's always tried to follow the rules."

"Your people?"

"I can't tell you much more than that, and you'll find out soon enough anyway." She releases my hands. "My advice to you is to come clean to Carson. Tell him everything. *Everything.* He can handle it. You guys need each other, and you know it."

"This is all crazy," I say. "You can't just . . . just barge into my house . . . a perfect stranger . . . and try to feed me this kind of craziness."

The idea of telling Carson everything is so very tempting. I want to. I *want* to let everything work itself out. I *want* to believe this djinni woman. And . . . the idea of a war between djinn and ifrits is more believable than I'd like to admit, which scares me senseless. A war like that has the potential to get really ugly, really fast. The last time that happened, we had the Moors and their quest to build an empire to hide behind: so many people were dying already, a few thousand more didn't get noticed. But nowadays? The idea is terrifying.

"I know," Nadira says, clearly reading my thoughts from my expression. "It's a scary thought, but it's already happening. You don't belong on the ifrit side, Leila. You know that. You have to believe me. This isn't just about organized crime, either. It's about the feud between our people. Tensions have been building for hundreds of years, and it's all coming to a head."

She's right. God help me, she's right. I've seen it, sensed it, heard about it.

"Please don't make the same mistake I did," Nadira urges. "Don't let Carson get away. You'll regret it the rest of your life. I know you don't know me, and I know this has to be the craziest conversation you've ever had, but please, try to believe me. You know I'm right." She hands me a business card with only her name and a phone number on it.

"Call me, any time, okay? You have a friend, as unlikely as it seems." Nadira finishes her beer and goes to the door. "Don't wait till it's too late, Leila." Then she's gone and I'm alone with my thoughts, which are buzzing in my head, angry and stinging like a hive of hornets.

I try to calm myself, but everything Nadira told me is howling through me, and I can't take it anymore. I put on a pair of spandex running shorts, a sports bra and my Nikes, strapping my iPod Nano to my arm. I slip my house key into my bra and set out, not bothering to stretch out first. I know I'll regret that later, but right now all I care about is motion.

My pace is hellish, driving.

It's a cloudy, windy morning, and I'm too lost in my thoughts, the wind is pushing me along at a frantic pace. I'm flying, almost, running as if chased, fleeing the pursuit of my father, Hassan, even Carson.

They all want me for different reasons, and they're all pulling me in different directions. I want so badly to listen to Nadira's advice, because it just seems so logical, it all fits so perfectly.

The other ifrit clans I've encountered are just like Hassan's: they've been letting their powers show openly in recent years, chasing power and money and influence, brutally using their powers to get whatever they want, whenever they want it. Displays like Hassan's at The Old Shillelagh are becoming more frequent, and I know the humans are starting to ask questions. I've faced that already with Carson's investigation into Miriam, and the questions about what happened at both the MGM and at The Old Shillelagh. There will come a time when the investigations won't just be abandoned, when the truth will be hunted down until it comes out, and when that does . . .

The djinn have threatened for centuries to crack down on ifrit recklessness in order to protect the safety of our species as a whole; my father often complained that the djinn saw themselves as some kind of enforcers, as if they were in charge of making sure our secret didn't get outed. If Father is right and the djinn were to get fed up with ifrit carelessness, they might very well go on the offensive, and people like Hassan would be the first to be targeted in an attempt to make an example of the worst offender.

In which case, being Hassan's wife—however un-willingly—would be a rather precarious position for me to be in.

If I was with Carson, however, and I kept my powers hidden, I might be able to stay out of it. Let *them* fight it out, I don't want any part in a djinni-ifrit war. I just want to be left alone to live *my* life *my* way.

That won't happen, though, no matter how much I may want it; if a war is brewing, I'll end up being involved.

Which leads me back to Nadira's question: which side do I want to be on?

Not Hassan's, that's for damn sure. Father's? That answer is slower in coming, but it comes, none-theless. I feel like a traitor for the answer that emerges from within: my people are wrong, and the djinn are right. If I was forced to choose, I wouldn't side with the ifrits; yet at the same time, I couldn't ever face off against my father. It's untenable.

The thought of having to choose, of being forced into marriage to Hassan, brings the rage boiling back to the surface. My legs burn with renewed energy, pushing me along the concrete of the sidewalk, past people strolling in groups, and homeless people with shopping carts, ignoring the whistles and leers and the stares of awe as the winds push me and magic blazes through me until I'm running faster than a normal human ever could.

They think they can just decide what I'm going to do, and with whom? They think they can drag *me* into their stupid business deals and use me like some kind of pawn in their idiotic games of chess?

I *don't* think so. I want no part of their drug deals and their stolen cars and their laundered money and their crates of guns. I'm done with them and their archaic, outmoded, chauvinistic, patriarchal way of ruling everything. They won't control me. I will not allow it. I won't be dragged into a war, either.

The wind is carrying me away and my rage is clouding my sight, so I don't see him emerging from a doorway. I slam into him and we go rolling along the ground in a tangle of sweaty limbs.

Carson ends up beneath me, and his eyes are wide and glittering with emotion as they bore into me. I can feel his heart beating, and I can smell him. He's as sweaty as I am, and I realize he's emerged from a gym. His hair is mussed and wet and sticking up in all directions, his limbs are slick, and his muscles are hot and swollen. He's shirtless, and his muscular torso is hard beneath me; I can't seem to stop my hands from running along the lines of his abs to his chest, and I feel his heat radiating into me, the smell of male sweat hot in my nostrils.

His hands are on my lower back and edging

downward, his lips inches from mine. I can feel the effect I'm having on him. He's hardening and lengthening beneath me, pressing into my belly, and before I can shut it away the thought is blowing through me: I want him inside me. My body is a traitor, my desire for him howling inside me, turning me liquid, leaving me helpless in a puddle on top of him. His hands are cupping my ass hungrily now, squeezing and kneading and pushing and pulling, grinding me into him. My thighs are shaking, and my breath is coming in ragged gasps against his mouth.

We still haven't said a word. Our eyes are locked on each other, his ocean eyes swallowing me and subsuming me in their emotive depths.

I haven't seen this man in over a week, and it's like I never left him. All my thoughts of duty and family, djinni and ifrit, all of it is blown away by the way he's looking at me in this moment. My decision whether or not to return home no longer exists. Hassan, my father, Nadira, none of them exist. There's nothing but Carson, his hard body, his lips on mine, his hands on my flesh.

I force myself to slide off him, but arousal makes even that into a sensual slither of skin against skin. He shudders as my hands run along his belly to his thighs and rest there, longer than they should. Finally I manage to get to my feet, but my legs won't hold me up.

Carson rises to his feet, much more gracefully than I did, and he's careful to leave a gap of several inches between us. I'm grateful for that space, as I don't trust myself not to attack him just yet, but I hate the distance separating us. I want so badly to push myself against him, tell him to take me home, take me to bed.

The silence continues, awkward, full of a million unspoken sentiments.

God, I want you.

He's thinking it, I'm thinking it. His fingers are curling into fists, clenching and unclenching in a constant rhythm as if willing his heart to slow to a normal pace. I'm still breathing hard, panting and heaving, but it's not entirely from the run. I can feel my breasts swelling in my sports bra with each breath, and I don't mind Carson's wandering gaze. I'd strip the bra off and show him all of me, if we weren't in the middle of a sidewalk in downtown Detroit.

"Hi." He breaks the silence, finally.

"Hi." The weeklong avoidance looms between us, and I sense his questions trying to break free from him, but he contains them.

"I missed you," he blurts, and then shuts his eyes briefly, embarrassed.

"I missed you, too," I tell him, as much to relieve his embarrassment as anything else; although god knows it's the truth.

"You did?" The hope in his voice is palpable, and it sets my heart to thudding again.

"More than I should've. I mean, it's only been a week." A bead of sweat rolls down my neck to disappear between my breasts, and Carson's eyes follow its path before jumping back up to meet mine, searching.

"Felt like a year," he says. "It's been rough."

"It wasn't easy for me either, Carson. You have to know that. I didn't want to . . ." I trail off.

"Didn't want to what? Walk away? Leave me with more questions than answers? Leave me wondering if I'd ever see you again?" Carson's voice is thick and tense.

He's upset, and I don't blame him. I'm glad he's at least showing me what he's feeling.

"Yeah, that too—" I start, but he cuts me off.

"You did, though. The way you said goodbye, it sounded like you meant forever. Like you weren't intending to see me again." It sounds almost like an accusation.

"Yeah, that was the idea. I didn't . . . I mean—" The explanations stick in my throat, acidic and rotten. They'd be lies, or half-truths, and I can't feed him those anymore. All I have left is either the truth, or more evasions. Or running away.

"Don't *fucking* lie to me anymore, Leila!" His eyes

blaze anger, the words hissed, so vitriolic I flinch at their force. "Tell me the truth. *Please.* Or just . . . just go and stay gone! No more evasions, no half-truths. Either tell me the *goddamned* truth—and *all* of the truth—or stay away from me. I love—" The word is out before he can choke it back down, and my heart is pounding in my chest, exploding with a hurricane of emotions: love, fear, sadness, excitement, disbelief. "Shit," he whispers, more to himself than to me.

He looks up at me, eyes suddenly intense with something akin to fury. It's the look I imagine is in his eyes when he breaks a door down to chase a fugitive.

"Fuck it," he growls. "I said it, I may as well own it. I'm in love with you. It's crazy, it's stupid, it's *way* too soon, and it's bound to get my heart broken because you obviously can't and won't trust me with the truth, but there it is."

He's suddenly wavering in my vision, blurring and splintering, and I realize I'm crying. Adrenaline, anger, and desire have been propping me up thus far, but now all that is knocked aside by his admission. Thumbs wipe away my tears, strong, gentle, and callused, brushing the loose tendrils of hair back behind my ear. Sobs are stuck in my throat, collecting and damming and overflowing.

I will *not* break down. Not here. Not in front of him, not now. I breathe deeply, close my eyes, force the shuddering breaths to steady. But then his arms pull me close, and his wet, sweat-slick chest is against my cheek, and his tender strength and man-smell and heat all gang up on me and break down the dam to let the flood of tears out. A sob escapes, and my legs give out. He catches me, scoops me up into his brawny arms. His car must be nearby because he helps me into the passenger seat. I slump into the seat, kicking aside Mountain Dew bottles and empty Styrofoam coffee cups.

I'm wracked with sobs, unable to stop or slow them, and I'm not even sure why I'm like this, but it doesn't matter because I just can't get hold of my raging emotions. His hand is wrapped around mine, and he's not saying anything, not telling me it's okay, not telling me not to cry. He's just holding my hand and letting me sob. I'm distantly aware that he's driving, and I don't care where he's taking me. Minutes pass, and the storm of tears isn't subsiding. It's not just him, not just his sudden and horribly timed declaration of love—it's everything. Father, Hassan, the threats against my family, being alone here for so many months . . . it seems like everything is conspiring to make me completely lose it. I've pushed all my problems and emotions down into a tiny, fragile bottle, and now it's all pressurized and exploding out of me.

Wind batters at the windows, leaking out of me to lift bottles and cups and wrappers up off the floor of the vehicle, sending it all swirling in mini-tornadoes at my feet, bottles racketing off the windows and the ceiling, smacking me in the face, knocking against my calves. I can't stop the leak of power right now . . . all I can do is try to contain it, keep it manageable, keep it from spiraling out of control.

Eventually Carson stops the car and helps me out, and I see my apartment building through my tears. The fact that he knows where I live is not a surprise. I try to fish my key out of my bra, but fumble and drop it back down between my cleavage. His fingers are hot against the skin of my breast, and he's gentle and careful in the way he finds the key, not erotic at all, which only makes me cry harder. He more than half-carries me into the living room, sits on the couch with me on his lap as if I were a child. He reaches for the box of Kleenex and presses a handful to me. I dab at my nose and collapse against him.

I hate myself for doing this. I have to get a grip on myself. I try to wiggle free, but he holds me in place.

"Don't," he says. "It's okay. To cry, I mean. I don't know what's going on with you, and you don't have to tell me. We'll get to that. I'm here, okay? I'm here for you. Don't fight it. You don't have to be strong all the time."

I make a sound in protest, trying to speak, trying to tell him . . . I don't know what. He shushes me, rubbing my back and kissing my temple. Which *really* helps my attempts to stop crying, of course. Right. His tender affection is making it even worse.

He loves me. I speak the words in my mind: *Carson Hale loves me.* They echo in my head, reverberate through my heart. He shouldn't, he doesn't even know me. But then . . . he does, though, doesn't he? He's seen my powers, felt them, experienced them, and he's still here, comforting me. He's suspected at least some of the truth regarding Father being a criminal, and he's put up with my constant lies and evasions.

Yet here he is in my living room, holding me as I bawl like baby when he doesn't even know why, and he isn't asking, just holding me and kissing my cheek and my jaw and my forehead and shushing me and caressing my arms and somehow making it all seem bearable.

At some point my sobbing slows and I'm able to wipe the tears away and clean my dripping nose. My breathing evens out, and I sit up straighter on his lap. I'm a tall girl, and I'm in shape, but he makes me feel small, his muscular presence surrounding me like a blanket.

I can finally look at him, meet his eyes. Yes, they

burn with questions, curiosity, the drive to know, but they also burn with passion, desire, and love. Seeing love in his eyes as he looks at me, that makes my breath hitch again, makes hope well up inside me, and I'm quick to stomp it down. He reaches up and pulls the band from my hair, carefully, slowly, brushing through my thick black tresses with his fingers.

That's all it takes.

I'm lost, now, buried beneath an avalanche of my own need. The intensity I see in him is matched within me, and I can't fight it, I can't push it away or pretend it's something else.

Our eyes are connected by a thread of tension, and I can feel the magic skirling up within me, bubbling up out of my core where it comes to seep out of my skin through my pores, and the wind is blowing, gentle and steady and warm. The magic is crawling on my skin, coating me with glowing gold like specks of light, pinpricks of sun on my flesh. I'm watching Carson's eyes, and I know he sees it releasing from me. He doesn't flinch away when the magic latches onto him and coils around his hands, sliding onto his wrists and forearms and biceps, seeping into his pores, in the reverse of how it emerged from me. His breathing stops and his eyes widen as he feels the slippery heat of the magic binding to his cells, to his blood and muscles.

When it works by itself like this, there's no telling what the magic will do, since my control over the magical aspect of my powers is rudimentary at best. I never got—never *deserved*—the training my male cousins got. I worry for a moment, but nothing happens, other than the continuous flow of sunlight particles from me to Carson and the thrum of power inside me. I have to fight to keep the storm under control, keep the winds from blowing this place apart.

Carson opens his eyes, and I can see the question.

"Ask me, Carson," I whisper.

"What *are* you?" Wonder is in his voice, and a little fear.

"I'm an ifrit," I say, knowing the word likely won't mean anything to him.

"A what?" Confusion wrinkles his forehead.

"Ifrit," I say again. "Like a djinni, but on the opposite end of the spectrum, so to speak." He shakes his head and shrugs, and I sigh. "You'd call it Arabic mythology. Djinn and ifrits are beings of magic and elemental power. The word 'genie' comes from the word 'djinni.'"

"Like genie in a bottle? Aladdin and all that?"

I can't help but laughing. "That's the popular American version, yes, although it bears no resemblance to my people whatsoever. The genie in the bottle is as close to what we are as the Hollywood version of cowboys and Indians is to the historical truth."

"And you're an . . . *eef*-rit?" He butchers the word, and I roll my eyes at him.

"Ih-*freet*," I correct him. "Ih-*freet*."

He nods. "Ifrit. Got it." I can see him thinking, and I know what's coming next. "So then Miriam is like you?"

"Well, she's a djinni," I say, careful to enunciate the last word so it sounds like *gin-ee.* "But yes. I'm not going to get into the details right now, but we're very similar in some ways, and completely opposite in others."

I'm still sitting on his lap, and somehow my arms are around his neck, and it feels familiar and intimate and comfortable. He's looking at me like he's never seen me before, and the fear is largely gone. I don't move to get off him, and I don't think he'd let me if I tried. I expected more resistance from him than this, and it worries me, somehow.

There's silence again, and I don't know what it means.

"What?" I ask. "I finally tell you the truth about what I am, and you don't say anything."

"What do you want me to say? I don't know how to respond. You're some kind of magical wind-girl from Arabic mythology. I knew you were something other than a normal human girl, especially after what happened at the park. Now I have a name for it. Did you expect me to go all crazy? Freak out?"

I laugh, nodding my head. "Yeah, I did, I guess."

"What the hell do you think I've been doing this past week?" He laughs. "I've been freaking out, trying to come to grips with the reality of making out with you in the middle of a fucking tornado in Hart Plaza."

I'm remembering that moment, and I can tell he is too. His hand stops its slow circling on my back, freezes on the skin between bra and shorts.

"Yeah, sorry about that," I say. "My powers don't usually get away from me like that. There's something about you that makes me lose control."

Carson shakes his head, brushing my hair aside with his other hand. "Don't apologize. That was incredible. Kind of scary, but incredible." He's moving toward me, centimeter by centimeter as he speaks, and I don't pull away. "Kind of like you. A little scary because, shit, if you can do that, what else can you do? But you're also incredible. So beautiful, so amazing."

His lips are moving against mine as he speaks, his breath warming my face. I'm spinning, dizzy, lost in his eyes, lost in the depth of emotion he's showing me. He's baring himself to me; letting me see his heart, see the inside of his soul. How can I reject that? How can I deny the effect he has on me, physically, mentally, and emotionally? I can't, and I no longer want to try.

"So, knowing what I am, you don't . . . you're not
. . ." I'm not sure what I'm asking, and I trail off.

"Afraid of you? As in going to run away? No. I'm
more afraid of how strongly I feel for you than I am
of who or what you are." He smiles, and the next
three words come easier than they did the first time:
"I love you."

He's testing them out, tasting them, watching
me to see how they affect me. He's said it twice now,
and he needs to know my response.

Terror is hounding me suddenly, gripping me. I
can't—I can't. If I say that . . . if I speak those words
to him . . . all is lost. I'll be abandoning my family to
Hassan's mercy—a quality he does not possess.

Then, I realize a dark and terrifying truth: I've
already abandoned them to him. I can't be Hassan's
wife, and I *won't* be.

The answer hits me like a flash:

I can take on Hassan. I'd rather die fighting him
and just maybe win than offer myself up to him as a
peace offering. There will be no peace, regardless of
what I do. If I go along with this stupid betrothal, I'll
just get dragged into the wrong side of a war. Hassan
is powerful and dangerous, but I *could* take him, under the right circumstances. If I got him alone, away
from his men . . . it's possible.

Carson is waiting, watching me think this through.

The decision is made, and I let myself go. Whatever happens next, I can at least enjoy this moment.

A smile curls across my lips, and my pulse picks up until it's thundering in my ears. "I love you, Carson." The words are whispered, almost inaudible, almost snatched away by the nearly imperceptible breeze in the room.

My words spark a fire.

He stands up easily, lifting me in his arms. I dissolve into giggles, which is just completely ridiculous. I never giggle. It's embarrassing.

"What? What's so funny?"

I take a deep breath and let it out. "This, the way you're holding me, it's just . . . so cheesy. Like a romance book. You're gonna carry me across the threshold into my room, and lay me down and kiss me . . . and it's just so classic, and it's funny for some reason." Carson just shakes his head and starts to put me down, but I clutch his neck to stop him. "I didn't say I didn't like it."

He laughs, kissing my throat, and the giggles are gone now, replaced by butterflies fluttering in my stomach. My bedroom door is open, my bed unmade, clothes on the floor; I'm not the neatest girl in the world. Carson either doesn't notice, or doesn't care.

He sets me down on the bed, slowly, so slowly, a sexy smile on his lips. He's showing off, demonstrating his strength, posturing. It's so cute, so sweet, and so silly that I almost lose myself to giggling again, but then he kisses me.

It's just a brush of lips against lips at first, a nudge, his arms planted on either side of me, one of his knees on the bed between my legs, the other foot on the floor. He's still holding back, I realize, giving me an opportunity to pull away, to stop him, to tell him I don't want this.

I hesitate for a split second: it's now or never.

But I know I've made my choice. I lift up to deepen the kiss, start the fire raging with my palms on his sides, running up the ridged muscles to his back, gripping his shoulder blades and pulling him down to me. He moans low in his throat, but it's not just a moan, it's a growl, deep and primal, feral, lupine. He pulls back, and the magic has insinuated itself into him, I can see it glowing on his skin, golden specks floating behind his eyes, as if his irises and pupils were curtains and the magic was a storm of light raging in his skull.

Through the magic connecting us I can feel the question before he even speaks it. "I'll tell you everything, I promise," I say. "I promise. But don't make me wait any more. I need this. Make love to me. *Please.*"

I need this. I need him.

He growls again, the sound rumbling in his chest buzzing into me, until I feel it as much as hear it. The ferocity and intensity I see in his eyes and feel in his trembling muscles sets me loose, and I know restraint is no longer an option.

I don't use my magic often, preferring to live as normally as possible—which has also contributed to my overall lack of control over my natural abilities—but now I cast two spells, both for protection. The first is one of the most basic uses of magic, a spell that every ifrit child is taught while they're still learning to walk and talk and run and speak, a spell I should use far more often than I do: a burst of magic sends a cocoon of energy around us to contain the winds that will inevitably blow out of control. The second burst goes within, flowing through my blood and tissue down to my womb, forming a wall around my cervix, protecting us from the impetuosity of this moment. I remember my aunt teaching me this trick when I turned sixteen, warning me against using it, telling me it's not infallible, just like any other form of birth control, but that it will work in emergencies. I thank her silently, and then all thoughts are washed away by his lips on my neck, by his hands on my belly, by his weight hovering above me.

I kiss his shoulder, his clavicle, his neck, his jaw, the side of his mouth, feeling the hooks of love dig themselves deeper into my heart every time my lips touch his skin. I'm abandoned to the reckless foolishness of this act, fully aware of the heartbreak that will be engendered when reality catches up. I love him, fully and completely, and this moment might be all I have to show him, might be the only moment I will ever feel such love.

My nails claw down his back, eliciting a hiss from him. He's kissing my breastbone, his lips shooting electric thrills through me, magical in their stinging pleasure. His hands are slipping and sliding on the skin beneath my bra, and I arch my back and thrust my chest against his, encouraging him to take it off. His forefinger slides under the elastic of the sports bra, and then another, brushing the side of my left breast with a fingernail. He knows how much I want him to touch my breasts, but he's teasing me, touching his lips to my breasts above the fabric and then down between my breasts and back up to my lips.

A growl escapes my lips, and he huffs laughter against my neck. He likes the control, likes knowing he's driving me crazy. I tug at his shorts, but they're tied too tightly to just come off. I find the drawstrings and fumble at the loose knot, feeling a wicked desperation. I need to feel him bare against me, I can't wait any longer. I've dreamed of this, fantasized about this, seen it waking and asleep, and now here he is, *finally* in my bed, and I can't get his stupid shorts off. It's almost comical.

Finally the knot is free and I slide my hands under the waistband and along the skin of his tight, muscular ass, cool and smooth under my palms. I leave them there momentarily, stopped mid-motion as he finally rolls my bra up over my breasts and lifts it free over my head, tossing it aside. I can't even breathe as he moves his mouth from my ribcage up to between my breasts, one hand supporting himself on the bed, the other roaming with sadistic slowness along my side, tracing a tickling line along my underarm to elicit a rebellious giggle and shiver from me. His mouth is hovering over my breast, and I put a hand to the back of his head and arch my back, thrusting my boob against his mouth. He sucks at my nipple, pulling a whimper of satisfaction from me, and then he draws it out of his mouth, then uses two fingers to pinch and roll my other nipple, and I finally remember that I too have hands and a mouth.

I yank the shorts down but they snag on his erection. I tug them free and slide them down, rolling my weight into him and push him down onto his back. He tries to lift up and retake control, but I give a wicked smile and release the torrent of magic and elemental fury that has been building up within me all these minutes that have felt like a lifetime.

The field of protection directs the winds back at us, forcing them in a circle, as the bubble of protection forms a globe around us. The winds buffet us, slip beneath us and lift us from the bed in a stomach-dropping rush. The wind forms a cushion beneath us, holds us firmly aloft in a bed of down-soft, skin-warm air. Carson looks to either side, shifting his body to test the solidity of this magical bed, laughs a little nervously, and then returns his gaze to me, all thoughts of wind or magic lost.

I draw his shorts the rest of the way off first, teasing both myself and him, leaving his tight red boxer-briefs mostly on, pulled down on one side to reveal his hipbone. Straddling his knees, I look down at him for a moment, just delighting in the beauty of his form. He rubs his hands on my thighs, slips them under the spandex of my running shorts and back out. He wants them off, but I'm determined to draw this out as long as possible, to make both of us wait until we're crazed with need.

I lean forward and rest my tits on his chest, tangle my fingers in his hair, kiss his forehead and his cheekbones and the tip of his nose. His hands run the length of my spine and back down, curl around my ass and tug at my shorts. I let him pull them partway down, let his hands feel my bare skin, then I draw away, kissing my way down his chest as I go, and he makes a frustrated growling sound in the back of his throat that is so pathetic I can't help but laugh. I pull the winds back into myself, dropping us to the bed, letting them howl around us but not touch us. He's tangling his hands in my hair and arching his back, reaching for me, but I continue my downward journey.

I come to his boxers and pause, looking up at him, locking eyes with him, then curl my fingers under the waistband and gently, slowly pull them down, kissing his belly just above his erection, sliding a hand underneath the hard length of his cock as I push his boxers the rest of the way off with my feet. My fingers wrap of their own accord around his velvety thickness, and my pulse hammers in my veins with excitement and desire and passion and delight at the feel of him, so much more perfect than I'd ever imagined.

He lifts forward and pulls me up, draws me toward him, rips my shorts off and drops them to the side. He rolls with me so we're lying side by side, and now he leans into me and kisses me, and if I thought his kisses before were intense, I had simply no idea what I was in for. He kisses me with a desperation I didn't think possible, as if he'd been drowning and I was his oxygen. His hands are clutching my face with a delicacy that makes my heart leap, and his tongue pushes between my lips to touch mine, probing and searching for my response. I don't hold back, but rather put everything I feel into kissing him back. I delve into him and drown everything I am into the connection of our bodies and our mouths and my magic flowing out of me and into him, letting him feel even my fear and the forlorn realization that I might very well lose him soon. I let it all go, push it out of me and into the kiss.

The magic responds, filling us both, coiling around us, raging within us, pushing us closer than ever, leaping from my soul to his. I know he feels it, because he melts into me, pushing our bodies together so every inch of us is touching. For a wild, disorienting moment I see myself from the outside, through his eyes. But it's not just physical, it's emotional as well. I feel his love for me like a freshly lit inferno, a fire he hadn't known he possessed, hadn't known was possible. The fury of it is shocking to him, and to me, and I know he'd do anything to protect me. I can't go there, though, can't allow myself to think of all the reasons I need protecting. All I want in this moment is to revel in the pure, unadulterated wonder of it all.

I open my eyes and meet his gaze, and I know he experienced the same mental transportation, the same juxtaposition, and I know how deeply and desperately I love him. I know he also felt the fear, the terror, the grim determination to free myself from the many bonds tied to me. He felt the fear of it, but can't see the reason behind it.

"I'll explain it all, I promise," I say again.

He only nods and kisses me again. I roll over and drape myself on top of him, not breaking the kiss, leaning forward to deepen it and spread my legs to straddle him. I lift up, take his thick, throbbing cock in my hands and guide him toward me, but he pulls away, tenses, and I sink back, wondering why he's holding back *now*, of all times.

"What about protection? I don't have anything with me."

"It's okay. I'm protected." He still hesitates, and I rest a palm on his cheek and gaze down at him. "It's okay. I swear." His eyes search mine, find what they're looking for, and he relaxes, assuming I mean I'm on birth control, and that's close enough. I'll tell him all about it . . . later.

The only thought in my head is for him, for the final culmination of what has seemed like an eternity of restraint, of keeping myself away, of telling myself no. In this moment, the answer is yes, and that fills me, overtakes me, and rules me. I lift up again, one hand propping myself up, the other holding the hot, hard, trembling length of him in my hands. Our eyes remain locked on each other as I push the tip of him against my cleft, gasping at the pressure. I

sink down slowly, millimeter by millimeter, swallowing him inside me, my gasp of pleasure turning to a
moan as I collapse forward to kiss him, clumsily and
hungrily. He tries to thrust up, but I match his motion by pulling back. He grunts in protest, and I kiss
him, put my hands in the pillow beside his face, and
pull him almost out of me. The pure ecstasy of feeling him inside me is rocketing and raging within me,
and I drink in every nanosecond of it, quivering with
the sensation. Then I plunge my hips down to take
him all the way in, and I can tell he's nearly there already, about to explode. I hold us there, him buried so
deep our hip bones are pressed together. My lips are
against his neck, our breathing is synched, the winds
rage around us with typhoon violence, the magic billowing through us like a floodtide of golden glowing
particles of power, and I am caught up in momentary
flashes of sight through his eyes, feeling what he feels.

I latch onto that fleeting sensation that I know is
his: it's alien, strange and disconcerting, but also intensely erotic, a feeling of maleness in my mind, the
sensation of bulky muscles tensed to hold back, feeling the soft wet press of lips on my neck, but it's not
my neck, it's *his,* and I'm him now, completely—

*My hands are rough and big, touching her back so
gently, cupping her ass and wanting to pull her closer but
holding still at the same time. I'm trying to hold back the*

whirling tidepool of my near-climax, stroking her spine and tangling my fingers in her hair, every muscle in my body flexed in the effort to hold back. I'm so hard, so deep inside her and I'm about to explode, not just come, but literally explode and she's holding me back, keeping me just this side of the edge, holding perfectly still, barely even breathing and holy lord fuck I've never ever experienced anything like this in my life. I want to rock myself into her, drive into her, but she's not there yet, I want it to be together—

I withdraw, momentarily so disoriented I would fall over except for Carson holding me in place. His eyes are boring into mine, seeking, asking.

"I don't know . . ." I breathe, shake my head, as shocked and confused as he is. "I've never . . . never . . . I don't know."

I've drawn it out as long as I can, and now it's his turn. I pull my hips up so he slips out of me, and I see him go rigid all over, his jaw clenching. I lie down on my back, pulling him toward me.

His gaze is hooded with need, every muscle in his body still tense and trembling, and I know he'll explode the moment he's back inside me and that's exactly what I want. I've never known desire like this before, never known such primal need. This is pure heaven, here with him, every single second of ecstasy a moment I will remember for as long as I live.

He crawls with predator grace, his knees nudging

between mine, pushing them apart, his mouth kissing my thighs, my pubic bone, my belly, my chest. Now his teeth graze my nipple, nipping gently and suddenly so I squeal softly. His hand wraps around my other breast and kneads it, then switches. His hand drops away from my breast and moves downward, between my legs, touching me gently, then he pushes a single finger into me, moving in a circle, then another finger and he's moving them together and scissoring them, looking for just the right spot, finding it unerringly. I'm already wet with arousal, but when he finds that spot and presses his fingers to it so tenderly, so carefully, and circles it, I gush even more, thrusting my hips into his hand as he moves in slow-fast-slow-fast rhythm, taking me higher and bringing me back down, and then back up, and I realize I've forgotten my intention.

I meant to draw him into me and make him explode, but he distracted me, and now he's doing it again and I can't think, can't breathe for the pulsating rocking series of miniature explosions that erupt deep inside me. I need him, all of him, now, now, god now. I reach down and grasp him, pull him to me, brush his hand away.

"Take me," I whisper in his ear. It's a plea. "I need you inside me!"

He covers my mouth with his, smothering my

words. He's throbbing in my hands, and he pushes his hips towards mine.

Yes, yes, yes.

I'm not sure if the words are mine or his, whispered or thought, but it doesn't matter. I release him and put my hands on his ass, pulling him closer, exactly as I'd seen in his thoughts.

It's a whisper at first, the pressure of him pushing inside, a bare breath against me. A nudge, the tenderest of touches. I pull him again, urging him, whispering his name, murmuring please with a stuttering tongue, but he resists, going at his own pace. He looks down at me, smirking, and I know he's getting me back for all the teasing I did to him.

He breaches the entrance, slipping slowly inside, and I moan low in my throat, thrust against him, but he mimics my action from earlier, pulling away. I whimper, and he kisses me, moves his torso aside enough to take my nipple in his fingers again, and now I can't and don't try to hold in the fully voiced cry as he drives himself in at the same moment he takes my breast in his mouth.

But then he's back out, nearly all the way, and I rake my nails down his back, biting his shoulder. "Please, *please*," I beg him.

I earned this teasing, I love it, but I can't take it anymore. He moves in again, slowly sliding up my body until our bones knock together, and when he's there he moves in rhythmic fluttering thrusts. I feel the explosions begin again, deep in my belly, trembling outward to rock my whole body with shuddering pulsations of pure joy. The trembling doesn't subside, though, and he pulls out just slightly and drives back in, stays there, repeating the same fluttering motion. God, god, god, what is he doing to me? I'm being ripped apart from the inside out now; with every motion the detonations increase their intensity. The maelstrom of ecstasy is tearing through him; I can feel his body quivering as he attempts to keep control.

I don't want control anymore. I want abandonment.

I wrap my legs around him and clutch him close, deep inside, snake my arms around his neck and pull him down to me.

His eyes meet mine, mere inches away. "I love you, Carson," I say, and those four words drive him over the edge.

He rocks against me and I match his motions, we sync our rhythms. The tempo is slow at first, then we increase our pace exponentially. We're frantic, suddenly, wild and panting. I moan in his ear, and he says my name, a breath on the winds that are whirling around us, lifting us up once more off the bed to float in mid-air, held aloft by powers run wild. When he says my name, whispers it to the winds, my soul clenches, draws in all the love he's pouring forth. I try to match his outpouring, try to push into him with all the pent-up love I have, knowing it can never be enough to truly express everything I feel.

Time stops, stutters, and I can feel the magic all around us, but all I have eyes for is him, for his gleaming cerulean gaze locked on mine, and now all falls away so there is no bedroom, no bed, no past or future, only his eyes on me, only his soul braided around mine.

All this time, a matter of perhaps a minute, my body has been wracked with tremors and convulsions as we near completion together, and now, now I feel him bury his head in the hollow between my shoulder and neck as he moves his body on mine with a desperation that only increases as I feel the tremors grow into explosions, small at first. Oh god, oh god, now he's going wild and all I can do is whimper his name and match his frenzy with my own, which of course only urges him even more, and my entire body is going nova, going supernova, and I hear him groaning in my ear, growling the wolf-growl, saying my name in a guttural stutter as his body clenches and releases in a hot flood, and I know I'm screaming, ululating—

I disappear, he disappears—she disappears, and I do—there is no distinction between he and she, between

I and I. Vision tangles and twines and coruscates so that male and female body and mind are mixed and split and merged until Carson and Leila are not names or identities or anything at all but words snatched away by the furious coriolis wind scouring their souls clean of all but each other, each other that is I, one being knowing her thoughts of how can I give this up *and his thoughts of* where has she been all my life *and each of the united souls know all the secrets and demons and fears and hopes and dreams of the other but it's all in a flood carrying skeins of images and fear bobbing in the gush of notions and memories until individual ideas are lost in the pointillist whole and this shared river of self is called LOVE—*

. . . and I'm clutching him, curled around him, each limb tangled until there is no knowing where I begin and he ends. The winds still hold us aloft, and I have no control over them and the magic.

I have no idea what just happened, but I know I could never ever make love to another man again for as long as I live, because now Carson is so fully enmeshed with my identity that I am unable to close my eyes without seeing him in my mind. I close my eyes and relax into Carson's embrace, but with my eyes closed all I see is the nexus of identity that was us in a timeless instant of orgasmic self-coalescing love.

I know only one thing, before sleep claims me: I will never be the same.

Chapter 13: Hunting for Truth

Carson

I'M PROPPED UP ON AN ELBOW, WATCHING LEILA SLEEP. HER lovely features are relaxed, one hand curled next to her face. She's still naked, the blanket bunched by her hips, leaving her upper torso bare. I can't help touching her, letting my fingers trace the line of her ribs as they expand and contract with each breath, her full breasts pulled by gravity to each side, flattening them slightly. Her skin is dusky, tan and taut, her navel a perfect round dip in her flat stomach, her hair splayed in a halo around her head, covering the pillow with a curtain of fine black strands.

My heart seems to swell as I look at her. I've come to accept that I'm in love with her, especially now that

I know she loves me back. What I haven't been able to come to grips with entirely is how potent that feeling is. It seems to fill every molecule of my being, setting my blood on fire with a fierce, protective urge to wrap her up in my arms and never let go, not for anything. It struck so suddenly, growing somehow from attraction to affection to desire to overpowering love, and the emotions and the need to protect are still unfurling, unspooling further and further with each breath, with each time I look at her.

I've faced a lot of frightening situations in the line of duty. Detroit is a dangerous place, though not quite the war-zone the media makes it out to be. As a officer of the law serving my city I've been shot, stabbed, punched, kicked, and was nearly run over by a car once. I was afraid, of course. Only the suicidal or crazy don't feel fear. I just don't let myself freeze up when the fear hits. I've learned to rely on my training, learned how to swallow the fear and push it down, cram it into the smallest corner of myself and refuse to let it out until the danger is past. And then, when I'm alone and it's safe to do so, only then do I let it out, let it run through me.

Now, with Leila sleeping next to me, so vulnerable and so beautiful, and *mine* . . . now I feel fear. Paralyzing, soul-shaking fear. The kind of terror that makes the blood sluggish, and the muscles unresponsive. I'm not afraid of *her,* or of her power or her family or the fact that she's not exactly human; no, I'm afraid of losing her. I'm afraid of letting her down, of not being man enough to take care of her, to be what she needs. I caught glimpses while we made love of what she's facing—although making love doesn't seem to be a strong enough phrase for what we experienced. It was joining, merging, truly becoming one in a way I still don't quite comprehend.

She needs me. I know it, sense it, smell it, but I also know she's not quite ready to admit that she needs me or why any more than I'm ready to admit that I need her.

It's all so crazy, so sudden, so unlikely and impossible. Is this all real? Can I really feel this for her, so much and so soon? Or is it just a bizarre form of lust, an obsession, an infatuation? God knows I want her body badly enough, but I can't deny that it goes way beyond that. Since I've stopped drinking I've forced myself to ask the hard questions and to answer them without flinching.

It's not just lust; I knew I was falling in love with her *before* we made love; what we just experienced only made it all that much more potent. No, my emotions are involved in this, not just my dick. I've spent long enough thinking with that particular part of my anatomy to know, but I need to be sure. I can't go any further with her until I'm sure this is a real thing, a true relationship rather than mere sex.

I try to imagine a relationship with her *without* sex: the fact that I can visualize spending day after day with her both in bed and out of it tells me I'm probably on the right track. I like talking to her, I like sitting with her and telling her about my job; I trust her, even though I probably shouldn't since she's clearly keeping a whole slew of things from me. Something tells me she has a good reason for withholding whatever it is she's hiding, though, and she *did* promise to tell me everything. I in turn have to listen with an open mind and not pass any judgment before I have the facts.

One thing still bothers me, though: I feel as if she's planning something, like this has all been part of her goodbye to me, like she doesn't plan to come back. There's no way in hell I'm gonna let that happen. My finely-tuned instincts tell me she's getting ready to do something she doesn't want to, something altruistic and stupid.

"I'll follow you to the ends of the earth," I whisper to her, "and I'll save you from whatever it is you're planning to do. I just found you and I'm not going to let you go."

She hears me, stirs, and rolls over to face me. "Hmmm? D'you say something?" she mumbles, a muzzy, contented smile on her face.

I lie down next to her, put a hand on the swell of her ass, caress the length of her body from calf to breast and back down, kiss her lips with all the tenderness I can summon, trying to impart all the love I feel into that gentle meeting of lips. Her eyes are still half-closed but she kisses me back, stretching languorously, cat-like, a slight moan escaping from the back of her throat as she arches her back and curls her toes, every muscle tensed and quivering. As the stretch ends she wraps her arms around my neck and pulls me closer to her. There's something at once cute and erotic in the way she stretches, the motion languid and lazy, sexy and sweet, stirring both my heart and my dick at once.

We pull apart at the same moment, my body not quite on top of hers.

Leila brushes errant locks of hair away from her eyes. "So what were you saying?"

"Sorry, I didn't mean to wake you," I say, not quite ready to tell her what I'd really said. "I was just talking to myself."

She wrinkles her nose, irritated. "Uh-huh. Fine, be that way. Don't tell me."

I sigh, shaking my head. "You really want to know?" She nods, and I take a deep breath. "What I said was, 'I'll follow you to the ends of the earth, and I'll save you from whatever it is you're planning to do.

I just found you and I'm not letting you go.' That's what I said."

My heart is thudding in my chest and I'm suddenly nervous, although I can't pinpoint exactly why. Leila is frozen, her dark eyes wide and frightened. A tear trickles slowly down one cheek, and I brush it away with the edge of my thumb.

"Why does that make you cry?" I ask.

"Because you can't," she says in a hoarse whisper.

She turns away, pulling the thin fleece blanket up to her shoulder. I follow her so my chest is to her back and put my chin on her arm.

"Why not? What is it you're hiding from me? What is it that has you so scared? Is it me? Is it us?" I tug at her gently, but she resists.

"No, it's not you, and it's not us." Her eyes go to mine. "You promised you weren't going to ask."

"You made me a promise too." It's quiet, a reminder.

I push my forehead against her arm, frustrated that I've trapped myself with my own promise. "Yeah, you're right. I did promise that, but I just—I wish you'd tell me. You won't scare me away. I can help you. Whatever it is, I can help you. We can do it together."

Leila laughs, but there's no humor or amusement in the sound. "Not this, you can't. No one can."

Silence hangs still and heavy between us.

Leila rolls into me, her dark gaze intense and sad. "I know I did, Carson. It's just . . . it's impossible to explain. And if I tell you everything, you'll want to be all manly and try to fix it, but there's no way to do that. There just isn't."

"You don't know that. I'm a cop, I have resources you may not have considered."

"This isn't a situation any amount of resources can fix, Carson." Leila scooches up, pulling the blanket up with her, tucking it under her arms.

"Okay, maybe . . . maybe I can't fix anything, and you're right, I *will* want to do something about it— that's just how I'm built. But even if I can't do anything, I still want to know. And . . ." I blink slowly, hesitating to say what I'm thinking.

"And what?" Leila asks.

I let out a breath. "Whether or not I can do anything to fix your problem or not, I'm falling in love with you, Leila, and I think I deserve to know the truth."

Leila's eyes slide closed, pain on her beautiful features. She just breathes for a moment, and her expression hardens, tenses. "God, Carson. You're right. You do deserve the truth. You deserved the truth a long time ago." She reaches out and touches my cheek with shaky fingers. "I haven't kept it from you because I don't think you deserve it, or because I don't care for you, or—I mean, I . . . I kept it from you to protect you. But you deserve the truth, so here it is: I'm betrothed."

The word hangs in the air between us, almost visible. "Betrothed?" I can't quite manage a full breath. "Like . . . engaged to be married?"

"Sort of, but not quite. It means I'm supposed to be getting married, yes, but . . . engaged is—it's something you agree to, voluntarily. Like, if you asked me to marry you, and I said yes, we'd be engaged." Leila won't look at me when she says that last part. "Betrothed is different. My family is old-fashioned, I guess you could say. Djinn and ifrits, since we're not really human, we don't age the same way. We still age, as in we're not completely immortal, we just live a lot longer. So my father . . . when I say he's old-fashioned, I mean it's because he's lived in the human world for several centuries, and he just doesn't care to change with the rest of the world. He's stuck in the thirteenth century, and I mean that *very* literally. He believes in betrothal, as in *arranged* marriages, and he believes in marriage for political alliance rather than love."

I don't even know where to start. "So . . . who are you betrothed to?" I'm choking, suffocating, pain constricting around my chest like a steel band.

A thought crosses my mind: *if her father is stuck in*

the thirteenth century, then how old is Leila? But that's a line of thought I just don't have the mental werewithal to pursue yet.

"I am betrothed to an ifrit prince named Hassan al-Jabiri." Leila frowns, thinking. "Well, 'prince' isn't really the right word, but there isn't one in English that fits. In ifrit culture, we don't really have family units as you would think of them. We have clans in the traditional sense—groups of families spanning several generations, ruled by a patriarch, the most powerful male of the family. But since we live so long, a clan usually comprises hundreds of people. And we're not just a family, we're . . . an entity. Politically, in a sense. Like a city-state. Historically, a clan would usually rule an entire village, or even a city if the clan is big and powerful enough. And the patriarch controls the clan's wealth, makes strategic decisions, arranges marriages, alliances, things like that. My race, ifrit, we have a tendency toward violence, both internally and externally. Clan fighting clan, that kind of thing, trying to claim territory, assets, whatever. In my family, the Najafi clan, my father is the patriarch. Hassan is the heir to his clan's patriarchy. There's a lot more to it, but that's it. And my clan and Hassan's are both very wealthy and very powerful. Each one controls huge amounts of wealth and wields influence on many aspects of human society, controlling local politics in some cases and organized crime in others—although the two aren't necessarily mutually exclusive, obviously. An alliance between the Najafi and al-Jabiri clans would be a huge, *huge* deal. Like a multi-billion-dollar merger between corporations, essentially. And it all hinges on me marrying Hassan."

I'm not sure what to say. "So . . . this Hassan . . . is he a good man? Do you love him?"

I'm trying to pull myself back together, trying to gather the pieces of my breaking heart.

She's *betrothed?* What the fuck?

"No! Carson, you're not understanding." She snuggles closer to me, puts her hand to my face and kisses me. "It's not like that. I *hate* Hassan. He's a pig . . . he's an evil, violent sociopath. Hassan is . . . he's a criminal of the worst kind, a killer and a drug dealer and a thug. I . . . I *hate* him. My father arranged the be-trothal against my will, and he and Hassan are trying to force me to go along with it."

"Force you how?" A gleam of hope pierces through the cloud of darkness descending on me; hope, along with a growing rage.

Leila doesn't answer right away, and I can tell she's trying to gauge how much to tell me.

"Don't," I growl. "Don't give me any more par-tial-truths. Don't hold anything back and don't lie to me. I *love* you, Leila, and I'm not going to just sit around and do nothing, but I can't make the right move if you don't trust me."

Everything she's told me so far seems unbelievable at best, and impossible at worst, but her eyes shine with truth. I have to accept what she's telling me, even if it seems ridiculous.

"Okay, Carson. All right." A weight seems to lift from her shoulders, and she draws a deep breath, letting it out slowly. "If I don't marry Hassan, he'll hurt the rest of my family. He's . . . powerful. Not just in terms of wealth or influence or whatever, but in terms of ifrit powers. He's dangerous. He's got the backing of his entire clan, hundreds of other ifrits at his disposal. And my father, *my* clan . . . we used to be a force to be reckoned with. We used to be one of the most powerful clans in the world, but my father has . . . how do I put it? His hold has slipped, and Hassan's father is cunning and tricky. He roped my father into business deals that went bad, tricked Father into owing him a debt. I don't know how or what, I just know Father has had to do other deals to absolve *that* debt, and it just keeps piling on, one thing after another, and he finally had to figure out a way to get rid of it all. I have no brother, so Father has no heir to take over the patriarchy. I'm a woman, so I don't really count.

"And on top of all *that* there's been a feud between our clans that goes back a thousand years. We've fought the same stupid battles over and over again over the centuries. Father's brother died in one of those fights, and I've lost cousins here and there, too. Our clans have both been significantly lessened because of the feud, and they've tried again and again to make a truce, but it's never lasted. Someone always kills someone else and the truce is off."

"So they see this marriage as a way of ending the feud once and for all?" I ask.

"Yeah. If I marry him and we have a baby, the clans will be related by blood, and the fighting will *have* to stop. And it *has* to stop, because the djinn are threatening to start a war, and that's a war no one will win, especially not your kind."

I'm trying to absorb what she's telling me. "A war? About what?"

"Does that really matter?"

"No, not really, I guess," I say. "I'm just trying to understand the situation."

"It would take a lifetime for you to understand it all, and I don't say that to sound condescending, it's just that there are so many layers to all this, the ifrit-djinni enmity as a whole on top of the feud between my clan and Hassan's, and then there's my family's position within our clan, plus our clan's position among the other ifrits, and then there's Farouk al-Jabiri's hold over my father . . ."

"No, you're right. I don't need to know all that stuff. You can explain it to me another time. The important thing is figuring a way out, for you."

"There *isn't* a way out, Carson. I've got less than a *week*. Hassan is going to come for me, and he'll drag me back to Chicago one way or another. If I put up a fight, he'll kill everyone I care about, you included."

My blood is boiling, my heart thudding with rage, my vision going red. "Not if I have anything to say about it."

"Carson," Leila pleads, "you *don't know* him. You don't understand what he's capable of."

"And you don't know what *I'm* capable of," I growl. "I'll deal with this Hassan jackass, and I'll deal with his pals. Trust me."

Her eyes are fixed on mine. She looks like she wants to believe me but can't quite bring herself to do so. "Please, Carson, please don't. I can't watch you get hurt. You're . . . you're not an ifrit, Carson, you're a *human*. You've never seen an elemental battle . . . Hassan is a fire elemental like Miriam, except he's spent his entire life knowing what he is and being trained to control his powers. He's got dozens of armed men under his command, and each of them is an ifrit. This isn't a Rambo movie, Carson. You can't just go in guns blazing and hope it all works out."

"So what? I'm supposed to just go 'oh well' and let you marry this sick douchebag?"

She won't quite look at me. "You'll get killed trying to stop him, and I couldn't handle that."

"So what was your plan? Make love to me and then . . . what? Just disappear in the morning? Go off and marry this asshole and let him do whatever he wants to you?"

Leila shakes her head. "I'll fight him. I'd rather die than marry him." The unspoken implication is that she'd lose the fight.

"I'm not okay with that."

"It's not your choice!" Leila shouts. "This is *my* life, *my* family, *my* problem, not yours!"

"What if I make it my problem? What if I tell you I'm not going to let you leave?"

Leila rolls out of the bed, clutching the sheet to her chest, eyes blazing now. "I'm so *sick* of men thinking they can control my life! This isn't your choice, Carson! I'm in love with you, yes, but I have a duty to my family too. I just . . . I can't let Hassan hurt them because of me. I don't expect you to understand, but you can't make this choice for me, and you can't tell me what to do."

"That's not—I didn't mean it like that, Leila. I just meant . . . god, this is not how I expected this morning to go." I stand up and round the bed, take her by the arms and pull her against my chest. She resists at first, stiff and unmoving, but I wrap my arms around her anyway, kissing the top of her head.

"You don't have to do this alone, Leila," I whisper. "I'm sorry. I didn't mean to tell you what to do. That wasn't what I intended. I just meant that I have a choice in this too, and I won't sit idly by while you marry some crazy thug or ifrit king or whatever just to protect your family . . . who're the reason you're in this mess to begin with, I might add. If I want to risk my life to help you, that's *my* choice. If you try to run off, I'll follow you and I'll find a way to fix this mess you're in or I'll die trying."

She melts a little, tilting her head up to look at me. "Why? Why would you do that for me?"

"It's how I'm built; it's in my nature to protect. It's why I became a cop, why I wear the badge. But more importantly . . . I love you." It's getting easier to say those three words. "I'm not going to let you go. Not without a fight."

"You barely know me."

"Stop playing devil's advocate. I know enough. I know you're sweet and caring, and I know you're stubborn and smart and athletic, and I know you're an ifrit princess, and that you control the winds and that you control my heart. I know you're sexy as hell and that you can turn me on just by looking at me.

I may not have known you for very long, but I feel like I've known you forever, and I can't picture my life without you in it." Leila lets go of the sheet and wraps her arms around my neck as I speak, playing with the hair at the back of my neck, the pressure of our bodies holding the sheet in place. "I will do anything I have to—*anything*—to keep you in my life, and to protect you."

Leila's lips part, but no words come out. She wipes at her face, at the tears that track down her cheeks. "How did we get to this place?" she whispers. "How can you know that?"

"I just do. I . . . as stupid as this may sound, I feel like I've been waiting for you my whole life." I shake my head, laughing at myself. "God, listen to me. I sound like some stupid romance movie. But you know what? It's true, however cliché and cheesy it may be."

Leila lets the sheet fall away, crawls onto the bed and presses her naked body against mine. She gasps as my cock nudges between her folds, she moans as I sink into her, sighs against my neck as I slide deep into her wet warmth. I kiss her peaked nipples and urge her to move, cup her lush taut ass with both hands and grind her body down against my thrusts, and I relish the bite of her nails as they claw down my chest, exult in the slippery slide of our bodies and the rush of heat and the wet sucking of her pussy as I drive up into her soft slickness. She rides me with wild abandon, her hips rolling without slowing or pausing, gasping and groaning and growling low in her throat, fingers digging into my chest, clawing and scraping, hair flying as she thrashes on top of me. I feel her hot tight pussy clench tighter as the climax rushes over her, and I lean up to lap at her thick, rigid nipples as she comes, and when she's limp and leaning over me and trying to stay upright, I roll over and pin her beneath me, cup her beautiful face with my palm and pulse into her, thrusting slowly and gently to my own climax, which explodes in me like wildfire, but I keep my eyes on hers and let her see into me. I move slowly, trembling and silent, letting her see my love, letting her feel it as I fill her.

The winds are silent as we come, but the flood of magic skirls between us, twining our selves into an oblivion of unity.

Eventually, Leila makes me go home to shower and get clean clothes. I refuse to leave until I've gotten a promise from her that she won't do anything until we've had a chance to talk more. I hate leaving her even for an hour, but a part of me knows I need some time alone to process everything I've learned since

Leila crashed into me outside the gym.

I end up back at the gym, lying beneath the free weights bench, pressing the loaded bar with a furious intensity, but it's not desperation driving me this time. I'm flushed with a kid-like excitement at the prospect of being with Leila, happier than I've ever been. I still smell of her, feel her skin against mine, remember the look of love in her eyes as we came together, and that drives me to pushing the bar harder and harder until my arms quiver with exhaustion, and yet still I lift and lower again and again.

I know I shouldn't be lifting free weights without a spotter, especially with the kind of weight I've got on the bar, but the gym is empty and I need the challenge to get my thoughts in gear. I push the bar back up on the hooks and rest for a few moments between sets, thinking.

The situation Leila describes definitely presents a few problems, certainly, but strangely I feel no fear. Maybe I should, since even the small glimpse I've gotten of her powers shook me to the core, and by her account, this Hassan is even more powerful than either Miriam or Leila. And now that I'm thinking about it, Hassan does sound like a kind of hopped-up Mafia kingpin with X-Men powers, and honestly that *does* worry me. What if bullets don't work on ifrits?

I really don't have much of a plan beyond driving down to Chicago and confronting Hassan and Leila's father. As much as I hate to admit it, the idea of that confrontation does send a thrill of fear down my spine; I've seen first-hand what Miriam's fire-powers can do to a body, and I've seen Leila's powers toss automobiles around like confetti. I sure as hell don't have a death wish, but I'm not willing to stay out of it either.

I need to do some research; if I've learned anything as a detective, it's that all problems are better handled with more information. I know a few people down in Chicago; maybe I can make few calls, see what I can find out about this Hassan al-Jabiri, and Leila's father, as well.

With a grunt, I push the weight bar free again and lower it to my chest, lift it up and tighten my grip when my sweaty palms shift on the metal. I growl, heave, and get it up, then go for one more, my arms trembling now. I lower the bar to an inch above my chest, but this time it feels like more of a barely-controlled fall. I strain and push, but the bar lowers the last inch and comes to rest on my chest. Three hundred pounds are crushing my sternum, and I'm pushing, pushing, gasping and straining, but I can't quite get it up far enough, and I can't breathe, spots blinking in my vision as a lack of oxygen begins to sap my strength. I feel a fleeting burst of panic as my vision blurs and my lungs burn, the bones in my chest cracking. I'm moments from blacking out, succumbing to the pain, and then a pair of huge black hands grabs the bar and lifts it free easily and suddenly I can breathe again.

"Easy now . . ." The voice accompanying the hands is deep and smooth. "You all right, Carson?"

I'm still gasping for breath and unable to move, trembling with the after-effects of panic and adrenaline. I force my breathing to slow, and my vision eventually stops swimming enough for me to make out the features of Wallace Dixon, who goes by the nickname "Juice." One of the personal trainers at the gym, Juice is *enormous,* standing six-foot-six with arms bigger than my thighs, legs like tree trunks, and scars and tats on his ebony skin that speak of time behind bars. I work out with Juice all the time, since we're both here nearly every day, and I consider the burly but quiet ex-convict a friend, despite his mysterious past.

"Yeah, yeah, I'm fine now," I say. "Thanks. I don't know what happened."

Juice chuckles, a low rumble like boulders colliding. "What happened is you was thinkin' instead of lifting."

"Yeah, I suppose you're right," I agree.

Juice is a complex man, I've come to realize. Our

many conversations over the years spent side by side, pushing weights, have shown me that Juice possesses a quick mind and a penchant for philosophy belied by his heavily muscled and thickly scarred exterior. Juice has lived a rough life, I suspect, although he always avoids any discussions of his past. I've never pushed him to talk about it and never will, but I've seen an enormous amount of long-buried pain in his eyes, in the hard-earned wisdom he displays when he does talk.

"Care to talk about it?" Juice asks in his slow, musical voice.

I hesitate: there's a lot I can't talk about, a lot that Juice probably wouldn't even believe if I did tell him, since I'm having a hard time believing it all myself.

"It's complicated, you know?" I don't want to offend my friend, but it's best if I just don't get into it.

Juice nods, his eyes narrowing. "'It's complicated' always means a woman's involved, in my experience. They got a way of complicating things."

I laugh, nodding. "Yeah, they do. Especially this one."

Juice sits down on the weight bench opposite me, a fifty-pound free weight held in each hand, lifting them in a one-two rhythm, slowly and methodically. "Is she worth the complications?"

I nod immediately. "Yeah, she really is. It's just . . .

there's a lot that could keep us apart, and I'm not sure where to start trying to fix things, or if I even can."

Juice doesn't answer right away, focusing on finishing his set first. Then he rests his elbows on his knees. "Well, I can tell you don't wanna get into specifics, which is fine. When shit gets overwhelming, I've learned to pick the biggest problem and fix that one first. Everything else will seem simple by comparison. If she's worth it, you'll get through it, one way or another."

"It's not that I don't trust you, it's just—"

"Hey, it ain't none of my business," Juice interrupts. "You don't owe me an explanation. I'm just offering my two cents."

"Thanks, Juice." I stand up and put the weights away, wipe down the bench I used. "I'm gonna get out of here. I'll talk to you later."

Juice nods, shakes my hand and returns to his weights.

Driving back to my apartment for a shower, I review the situation again, this time isolating the biggest problem: Hassan.

After a shower, I sit down with my cell phone and my laptop and do some research. One phone call leads to two, which leads to four, which leads to a Google search and a printed set of directions to a particular address in Chicago.

I'm in detective mode; the lover, the worried protector, he's buried for now, set aside to make way for the relentless hunter.

A buddy in the FBI emails me a file containing a few pages of basic profile information, a couple photographs, and a list of crimes Hassan al-Jabiri is thought to be connected to. It's extensive: drug deals, murders, assault and battery, breaking and entering, rape, money laundering, kidnapping, assault on a police officer, bribery of a public official . . . the list goes on, and my stomach rebels against the idea of Leila ever being touched by the man these files portray.

The file is marked "Do not apprehend" in bold letters; a small-time badge from Detroit has no business going after a guy like Hassan, the warning implies. But the fact that Rob even sent the file means he knows I won't listen, and that I might as well know what I'm getting into.

If Rob only knew.

A few more searches turn up another name: Ibrahim Najafi. There's significantly less information on him, but what there is reveals a shrewd and cunning businessman, successful and well respected. There are suspicions of illicit dealings on the side, but nothing concrete.

I eventually close the laptop, roll up a few changes of clothes and stuff them in a backpack, then put my personal firearm at the small of my back and swing into my car.

It's time to pay a visit to one Ibrahim Najafi.

CHAPTER 14: SITTING IN THE ASHES

Leila

AFTER CARSON LEAVES TO HIT THE GYM AND CHANGE, I dress for a run and strap my iPod to my arm, enjoying the slight soreness in certain places on my body, smiling at the memory of how I got to be that sore. Running cools my head, gets my thoughts pushing through the fog of day-to-day life. It helps me think. Now, sex-sated and love-saturated and knowing Carson is coming back to me soon, I run with the wind, a bit careless in the way I let it blow me along, letting it fade my edges into invisibility. It's a brilliant, sunny day and I finally feel *alive*, finally feel like something might be going right.

I make some decisions while I run:

I'll go back to Chicago, talk to Father, and tell him I simply will not marry Hassan. There *has* to be another way. Father has to have some back door to all this mess he's gotten himself into.

And if not . . . I'll face Hassan, come what may.

I take a long, scalding-hot shower when I get back, and I daydream again, wishing Carson were in here with me. I feel insatiable, now that I've had a taste of him.

When I get out of the shower and dry off, though, something in my apartment feels . . . off. I wrap myself in my towel, suddenly sure of what I'll find when I emerge from the bathroom.

I open the door and steam billows out past me. My skin tightens, my heart thunders in my chest, and my fists curl, the magic pooled and ready, and the winds skirling around me, tossing my loose wet hair against my cheeks.

Hassan is sitting on the edge of my bed, a pillow in his hand. He looks at me, eyes flickering fire.

"Who was here, Leila?" he demands. "Who was in your bed?"

He stands up, tosses the pillow aside. His other hand is at his side, and I see a black pistol gripped in his fist.

"Who have you been *fucking*, you *whore?*" His voice is a hiss, low and deadly.

He lifts the pistol and points it at me, and suddenly he's in front of me, gripping my hair in one hand, the cold metal mouth pressed to my cheekbone. Fear is not rushing through me as it should be. I'm angry. Furious. Full of venom and rage. I don't answer him, clutching the towel tightly to my chest.

I send a current of magic up from my belly and spread it between my body and his in a thin, hard skin of armor. I hesitate for a beat, watching his eyes, the orbs of flame dead and cold and lifeless despite the fire. I move between one heartbeat and the next, ripping myself from his grasp, tearing my hair from his fist and ignoring the agony as it's ripped out at the roots. I whip my fist around, using a ball of wind to accelerate my blow, turning my hand into a hammer. His face is bashed to the side, blood spurting from his nose, a tooth cracking free and spittle flying. I try to knock the gun aside, but he's already recovered and back-pedaling, the gun still in his hand. Fear begins to eat at me, but I deny it.

"Bitch," he says, dabbing at his nose, prodding the gap where his tooth had been. "You'll regret that."

I don't answer; he doesn't deserve a response. I spit in his face, and when he flinches in shock I lash out with my foot, catching him in the balls. He doubles over in agony, and I feel a thrill of satisfaction. I don't wait for him to recover, though, backing away until I bump into my bed.

He lifts a palm and shoots a spear of flame at me, wrapping around me and setting my clothes, my hair, and my skin alight. Behind me, the bed ignites. I summon the wind and drape it over me like a cloak, dousing the flames but not the pain of seared flesh. I can't stop the shriek of rage and agony, but I accompany it with a hurled tornado like a spear, pushing him back, and then turn it into a vortex, sucking in the lamp and my keys and books and my laptop, all bashing at him, smacking him, smashing into him. He curses and flails, howls his frustration, then shakes himself and clenches his fists. Flames ignite on his body, eating his form until he is a man carved out of fire, and he stalks through the winds and debris toward me, his pistol dropped to the ground, forgotten. I back up, wanting space between me and those hungry flames.

I push the winds at him, a steady gale that impedes his progress but only builds the fire of his form higher. He darts aside, out of the current of wind and rushes me, bashes into me and sends me flying. I crash headfirst into the wall, seeing stars, dizzy and limp. I struggle to my feet, but he's there in front of me, a man again, smirking, pistol in his fist, muzzle a cold 'O' on my forehead.

I wonder, almost idly, if he's going to kill me. I'd like to think he won't, because I know he wants me, wants my body, wants control of my clan, which he can't have if I'm dead. I stare into his eyes, and I can see him thinking all this too, and eventually his desire overcomes his raging jealousy, and he lowers the gun, not all the way but enough for me to know he's calmed down slightly.

That's all I need.

I summon all my rage, all my magic, and all my wind into a single coiled serpent and strike him with it, snake-fast. He is hurled through the window in an explosion of plaster and wood and glass. He lands on his back, rolls several times and comes to a stop. I can tell he's hurt and shocked, but not injured. He gets to his feet, brushes himself off, and approaches the gaping hole where the window used to be. He doesn't say anything, but his anger is still simmering.

He turns and leaves, pulling a cell phone from a pocket, cursing at what must be a cracked screen. He taps the screen a few times and puts the phone to his ear. He balls a fist, crouches, and then lunges forward, stabbing his free hand like spear. His hand vanishes up to the forearm, and a blue glow appears where his hand seems to be thrust into midair. He twists his wrist, grasps some invisible edge and jerks sideways, wrenching apart the fabric of reality to reveal the posh trappings of a downtown Chicago loft apartment overlooking Lake Michigan. The vision lasts for a moment, then Hassan steps through the gap, talking on the phone, and then everything closes up behind him.

There are a pair of men standing in the parking lot about fifty feet away, gap-jawed. That's why the djinn are on edge and about to start a war, because Hassan pulls stunts like that in front of witnesses. Reckless, impetuous, selfish fool.

I turn away from the gaping jagged hole where my window used to be, assessing the damage to my apartment. It's extensive. The walls are burnt and studded with wind-tossed debris and charred by flames, the carpet is burnt to a crisp, the door to my bathroom is torn from its hinges and lies half in the tub. Somehow, though, the bed is what sends me into hysterics. It's totally torched. Just . . . gone. My bed is my refuge, it always has been. It's one of things that I did as a girl, a teenager, and now as an adult: when I'm upset I throw myself onto my bed, and I'll scream into the pillow, or cry into it, or just lie there and let my emotions run through me until I'm exhausted.

I'm beyond upset, now. I've had so many conflicting emotions blazing through me in the last twenty-four hours, from hopelessness and anger to . . . god . . . such pleasure and love, to this moment with the pain and terror and anger. Now I can't even lie in bed and think about it and work through it because my bed is a pile of ashes.

For the second time in two days I collapse into a ball and sob.

And then, of course, my phone rings. I can't find it for the longest time and it stops ringing only to start up again, and I finally find it buried in the soot and ashes of my bed. I fish it out of the char and blow it off. I'm covered in soot now, blackened from head to toe, bleeding, emotionally limp, but when I glance at the screen and see that it's my Aunt Talia, I know I can't ignore the call. I haven't spoken to my aunt in a long time, not since moving here. She's holding the party line on this subject, so if she's calling me I know it's important.

Her voice is shaking, tremulous and low. "Leila? It's your father . . . he's . . . you have to come home, quick. *Please.*" She hangs up before I can answer, and I toss the phone aside, my mind running through all the possible horrors that could have befallen my father.

I'm an imaginative girl, and my brain comes up with some grisly things, most of them involving Hassan in some way.

I jerk my keys free from the wall where they're embedded, snag my purse off the floor near the front door, and run to my car. I don't pack a bag, don't leave a note, I just aim my car for I-94 and head for Chicago as fast I can. I'm two hours out of Detroit when I realize my phone isn't in my purse, it's still in my bedroom somewhere.

Carson will be back at my apartment at some point, and he'll find the ruin left in the wake of my fight with Hassan . . . the blood on the carpet, mine and his, and the burnt bed, the broken window. He'll assume the worst, and he'll call and text, and I don't even know what I could say to him, what he could do to help me.

But my father . . . I can't just turn around now, not halfway to Chicago. I don't know what I should do, so I just keep driving.

CHAPTER 15: THE OLD WAYS

Carson

I DECIDE TO SURPRISE LEILA BEFORE HEADING DOWN TO Chicago, but I have no idea what kind of flowers she likes, which only serves to reinforce the fact that we've only known each other a short time. I honestly can't remember how long exactly it's been, because now, when I try to remember my life without her, I just. . . . can't. But I *am* painfully aware that there are a million little things I don't know about her. For some reason roses don't seem right, which is odd since all women like roses, don't they? That's what I'd always thought, but for some nebulous, unidentifiable reason, I just don't think the standard dozen red roses are the right choice for this girl, for this situation.

I stand in front of the glass walk-in refrigerator at the florist, staring at the overwhelming assortment of flowers and arrangements. There are so many, all so different. There are roses, daisies, lilies—isn't that what those big white ones are?—and then there're the arrangements of flowers whose names I'll never know all placed in vases of all sizes and shapes, ranging in cost from fifteen bucks to several hundred.

I sigh and glance around the empty shop, wincing at the awful smooth jazz emanating from the ceiling. There's not one "may I help you" person in sight, and I've been standing here for at least ten minutes trying to make a decision, but nothing seems to stand out.

Finally, an older woman with short gray hair comes out of a back room, wrapping a bunch of flowers in crinkly cellophane, unaware of me until I clear my throat.

She jumps, putting a hand to her ample chest. "Oh, goodness, sweetheart, you scared the liver out of me. I'm sorry; I must not have heard you come in. May I help you?"

"Yeah, I'm looking for flowers for my . . . girlfriend . . ." I'm not entirely sure if that's the right word for Leila.

"Well, roses are always a good choice," the woman says, pointing at a glass vase with a dozen crimson roses.

I shake my head. "Nah, that's not quite what I'm looking for. I don't know what I *am* looking for, I just know roses aren't it."

She comes around the counter and stands next to me, smelling of old coffee and roses. "Well, what kind of flowers does she like?"

I grin sheepishly. "I don't know, to be honest. I haven't been dating her that long, and we've never talked about her favorite kind of flowers."

The woman nods sagely. "Well, that's not the kind of thing that just 'comes up,' you know. You have to actually *ask* her at some point. But, anyway. How about a nice arrangement? These would look pretty in any woman's home." She gestures at the most expensive arrangement in the display case.

"No, those aren't right either." I shake my head and shrug. "I'm just going in circles. I don't know why this is so hard."

"Well, what's the occasion?"

The woman starts every sentence with "well," I'm noticing, and it's driving me crazy. "No special occasion. Just because."

"Oh, well . . . some nice Gerbera daisies are always good for 'just because' occasions."

I'm not sure I'll be able to keep back a snarky comment if she says "well" one more time. "That's those big red, yellow, and orange ones in the front, right? Those are fine. Six, please."

By the time she wraps them, charges me, and sends me out the door, the woman has said 'well' at least four more times.

The flowers are nice though.

I find myself wondering what Leila's doing. I texted her to say that I'm on the way, but I haven't gotten a response. We haven't done a lot of text message communication yet, so I'm not sure if she's the kind of person to respond right away or an hour later.

I set the flowers on the passenger seat, hoping the motion of the car won't send them to the floor and crush them. God, this whole buying-flowers thing is stressful. No wonder I've never bothered before.

I'm a mile or two away from Leila's apartment when I start feeling uneasy. It's a slight thing, at first, just a fluttering in my gut, and a tingling of my instincts. But as I draw closer, the fluttering turns to a churning, and by the time I'm pulling into her parking lot and see the flashing lights and milling crowd of firemen and patrolmen, I know I'll find them coming in and out of Leila's apartment.

I step under the caution tape, flashing my badge. I'm not on duty, but these guys don't know that. Sure enough, the crowd is centered around Leila's apartment. There's a hole in her wall, as if something or someone crashed through it, and the interior is completely demolished, the various responders looking thoroughly perplexed. It looked like there was a tornado *inside* the apartment, but that obviously made no sense. There was also fire damage, the bed had been reduced to ashes, there were scorch marks on the walls and the carpeting . . . something odd and violent happened here, but no one could make sense of exactly *what*.

I have a pretty good idea of what happened, but I'm keeping my thoughts to myself—they wouldn't believe me anyway.

I stand in Leila's bedroom, trying to contain my fear and rage. Her car is gone, so I've got a feeling she left on her own. I'm about to leave too when I happen to glance at the floor: Leila's cell phone is barely visible, hidden under a layer of ash and bricks, looking as if it has been kicked there by careless boots rather than buried when the wall had fallen. I kneel down and grab it while pretending to retie my shoe. It's an old and tired ruse, but it works. Under normal circumstances I'd never remove evidence from a crime scene, or potential crime scene, but these guys will get nowhere fast digging through the rubble, and I need to know where she went, when, and why.

I leave the apartment and get back into my car, sliding the unlock tab on Leila's white iPhone, browsing through it and hoping for a clue as to where she might have gone. I see my own message to her—un-read—and several old threatening messages from Hassan, which make my blood boil. I scroll back through the messages from Hassan: *two weeks, Leila; Don't forget, ten days, Leila. Ten days and you're mine; I hope you're ready, the wedding is less than a week away* . . .

As I get to the more recent messages I see there's at least one text from Hassan every day, some containing veiled threats and reminders as to what will happen to Leila's family if she refuses to cooperate.

I hit the green phone icon, and see a phone call under the 'recents' tab: *Talia; incoming calls; 10:40am; 45 seconds.* Who is Talia? There's no indication on the phone itself, and the phone call wasn't long enough to have been a real conversation. But bad news could easily be delivered in forty-five seconds. . . .

A knock on my window startles me into almost dropping the phone. I look up to see a tall, beautiful woman with thick black hair and dark eyes standing at the passenger window.

I turn the key enough to engage the battery so I can roll down the window. "Can I help you?"

"Are you Carson?" The woman's voice is musical and accented. She seems familiar, somehow, her face jarring my memory.

"Yeah . . . do I know you?" I tilt my head and stare at her, trying to remember.

I've definitely seen her before; a memory flashes through my head: this same woman, but with her hair pulled back in a ponytail, wearing a skimpy cocktail waitress uniform . . .

"Yeah, you interviewed me about Miriam. I work at the MGM," she says.

"Oh, yeah, that's right." I wrack my mind for her name. "You're . . . Nadia, right?"

She smiles. "Nadira, actually, but close." She gestures at the passenger seat. "Mind if we talk?"

I hesitate for a second, then hit the unlock button. Nadira gets in, picking up the flowers and nodding appreciatively at them.

"Why don't we take a little drive, Detective," Nadira suggests.

"All right," I say with a shrug, then turn the ignition, and pull out of the parking lot. I take us in a wide circle of the city, unconsciously taking an old route I used to drive regularly back in my days as a beat cop.

"So, what do you want to talk about, Nadira?" I ask, glancing at her.

She doesn't answer right away, idly crinkling the cellophane around the flowers as she considers her words. "Are these for Leila?" she asks.

"Yeah," I answer, knowing I sound curt.

Chicago is four hours away at least, and my fear

for Leila increases with every passing minute.

"What's the occasion?"

"Do I need one?" That comes out a lot harsher than I'd meant it to.

Nadira smiles at the answer rather than getting annoyed or angry. "No, you don't. That's a good sign. So . . . are you guys together?"

"What? How the hell is that any of your business? Are you a friend of hers?" I'm getting irritated now. "Listen, Nadira, I don't know if you noticed, but that was Leila's apartment all those cops and firefighters were at. Something happened to her, so excuse me if I have neither the time nor the inclination for small talk at the moment. What do you want?"

Nadira doesn't seem perturbed by my rude tone or words. "Bear with me. I won't keep you long. I want to know about you and Leila. I have good reasons for asking. Trust me."

I try to rein in my irritation. My detective instincts are telling me this isn't a purely social call. She wants something specific, but for whatever reason she's not willing to come right out and say what just yet. I glance at her again, assessing her. Now that I remember her, I realize there's something else about her that feels familiar, but I can't put my finger on it. It's a feeling, a notion, something unidentifiable in my gut, something about Nadira that strikes a chord in me. Something that reminds me of Leila, although I doubt they're related in any way.

Nadira eyes me quizzically. "You're staring at me. Why?"

I return my attention to the road and shrug, trying to pass off my growing suspicion. "Nothing. Sorry. It's just . . . there's something about you . . ."

"If you're trying to hit on me, I'm going to punch you." She doesn't sound as if she's joking.

"No! That's not—no. Sorry. There's just something . . . familiar about you. I can't . . ." I shake my head, afraid to say what I'm thinking. "You'll think I'm crazy."

Nadira narrows her eyes and crosses her arms under her breasts, leaning back against the door. "Try me. You'd be surprised."

"Fuck it," I murmur under my breath and then address Nadira. "Like I said, this is probably gonna make you think I'm a nutcase, but . . . are you an ifrit?"

Nadira's eyes widen and her fingers clench into fists. She's tensed and ready to attack in the space of a single breath. I take my right hand off the steering wheel, rest it on the console on my right and sit up straight in the seat to allow myself more room to draw my gun if things get messy. But then if she's an ifrit or whatever, I'm not sure what good a gun will do, or if I'd even have time to draw it.

"*What* did you say to me?" Her voice is a hiss, vibrating with threat.

"I asked if you were an ifrit . . ." I say again. Her nostrils flare at the word, and I suspect that word is the cause of her sudden aggression, though damned if I know why. "Or a djinni, maybe?"

Nadira doesn't answer immediately. She uncrosses her arms and leans forward, eyes fixed on mine, and I'm mesmerized, unable to look away from her. The car is stopped at a red light, which turns green, causing cars to honk angrily before pulling around me. I can't look away, can't form a coherent thought, and I can't unwrap my fingers from the steering wheel. I'm frozen in her mental grip, and I feel a strange, terrifying pressure on my brain, in my mind. But "pressure" is not the right word. It's a *presence,* a cool liquid slipping between the spaces in my brain, stirring past the synapses and into the deepest part of my being. I'm being examined, weighed, probed; I know it's Nadira inside me, and the power of her presence is overwhelming, alien and awful and terrifying in its intensity.

After what feels like a lifetime, she pulls away, and I see that her eyes are no longer whites-and-iris like mine—like a human's—but are instead roiling liquid blue, oceans contained within the ovals of her eye sockets. I tear my gaze away, knowing I'm only able to do so because she allowed it. I rev the engine, stomping the accelerator and peel away through the red light, turning the intersection into a snarl of near-misses, blaring horns, and infuriated curses. I then pull into an empty parking lot, flashing my badge at the attendant, who waves me through, backing away.

I skid to a stop and turn to face Nadira. "What the *fuck* was that?"

"I apologize, Carson. I don't usually use such invasive methods, but there isn't time."

"But you could waste ten minutes asking stupid questions about my fucking flowers?"

Nadira shrugs. "I couldn't just come out and ask what I needed to know, especially if Leila hadn't told you the truth. I needed to know how much you know. Now I do. Like I said, I'm sorry. I know it was unpleasant."

I press my fingers to my temple and rub in circles, forcing my anger and embarrassment and confusion away. "So what do you need to know?"

"What are we going to do about Leila?" Nadira asks. "She's left for Chicago, and she's going to be forced to marry Hassan if we don't stop it. I know Hassan, and I can't let that happen, for many reasons, most of them personal. And you love her, so you can't let it happen either."

"'We'?" I ask. "What do you mean, 'we'?"

Nadira laughs at that. "You don't think you can take Hassan by yourself, do you? I'm sorry to laugh, but that's just . . . funny. He's so far out of your league it's comical. I don't mean to insult you, Detective, I swear. You just . . . you have no clue what you're getting yourself into. None at all." Nadira pulls a cell phone out of her back pocket and taps at it while she speaks. "It's nothing against you, I swear. It's just . . . Hassan is an heir to a very wealthy and very powerful clan, and he's also one of the most powerful ifrits to come out of the al-Jabiri clan in several centuries. I know him personally, unfortunately, and I know what he's capable of from experience. You'll need my help if you're gonna get Leila back."

"Why do you care who Leila marries? She's never even mentioned you."

"She wouldn't have. She's only met me once." Nadira puts the phone away and leans forward. "We don't have the time for me to explain everything to you right this very second, Carson. Either you trust me, or you don't. Your choice. But I guarantee you, if you try to rescue Leila on your own, you'll be dead before you know what hit you. You really don't understand what you've gotten yourself into with her."

I lean my head against the cool glass of the window, thinking. My gut tells me to trust her despite the mental invasion. I also have a feeling she's right about Hassan, about not really knowing what I've gotten myself into. These people, these djinn and ifrits, they all have powers I can't even fathom, much less defend myself against. The destruction of The Old Shillelagh and Leila's apartment both hint at monstrous power and a capacity for destruction that chills me to the bone.

"You never answered my first question," I say, by way of putting off the decision.

"Your first question?"

"Yeah. Ifrit or djinni? Although gauging by your reaction, I'd say djinni."

"You'd be correct," Nadira answers. "Listen. Let's not waste time talking, because right now, we have to get to Chicago. Like, *now.*"

I nod. "Do you need to do anything before we leave?"

Nadira shakes her head. "Just drive."

The drive is long and uncomfortable. Nadira won't explain anything that pertains to her, or how she knows what's going on, or what her involvement is, nothing. All she'll say is that it's critically important the alliance between the Najafi and al-Jabiri clans not happen.

"Why?" I ask for the tenth time. "I don't get it."

"I don't expect you to get it. It's a lot of socio-political clan business and, unless you were raised in the culture, it wouldn't make any sense to you even if I were to try to explain it."

I hiss in frustration: she's so circuitous, answering questions with more vague non-answers that only serve to spawn more questions. "But if I'm going to be involved with her, shouldn't I try to understand all this?"

Nadira looks at me with something like respect. "You can try, but then she should be the one to explain her own familial position to you, not me." She waves a hand. "Plus, I'm a djinni, she's an ifrit."

"That's something else I don't get. Are djinn and ifrits enemies? What's the difference between you? Leila explained it to me a little, but I'm still having trouble sorting it all out."

Nadira thinks for a moment before answering. "Think *Romeo and Juliet*. It's like the Capulets and Montagues: they were social enemies, but they were of the same race, hailing from the same country, living in the same city. Yet for whatever reason, they hated each other, but they didn't really fight violently, until things got totally out of hand. The tension was there, and if they weren't careful, it could turn bad.

"It's sorta like that with us. It's a loose analogy,

but I think you get it. We're not enemies in the sense that we kill each other all the time, although there have been periods of history where that has happened. Right now, it's just tension, ratcheting up with every incident, especially those incidents caused by the ifrits being careless and needlessly violent against humans. Things are escalating, and quickly. If Leila marries Hassan and their two clans are allied like that, it would give the ifrits a huge advantage in the brewing war. Not really the ifrits as a whole so much as Hassan specifically, though. And believe me when I say *no one* wants Hassan to wield that kind of power. Not me, not my friends within the djinn clans, and not even the rest of the ifrits, for the most part.

"But the ifrits won't take action unless Hassan goes totally crazy and starts killing humans on a mass scale or something, which he's totally capable of—yet another reason why we can't let Leila marry him. My people—the djinn, and specifically my particular . . . subset within the djinn—are willing to wage war—a private, *quiet* war—against the ifrits, especially if it keeps humans off our scent. The world isn't ready to know about us. They may never be. A messy, public war, however, is the *worst* possible way for your kind to find out about mine, and that's what we're trying to prevent." She pauses briefly, then continues. "So, in one sense, I'm here as a representative of my people, who have a vested interest in preventing this marriage. But I'm also here on a personal level. I've met Leila, and I know Hassan, so I can say with authority that *no one* deserves to be married to that vile creature. It's in everyone's best interests if we can stop this, and if we can do it quietly, so much the better."

I try to process all that, but it's hard. "Where do I fit in?"

"I'm honestly not sure. I doubt Ibrahim Naja-fi would approve of his daughter dating a human, much less allowing a marriage between you. You have to remember that marriage among our kind is an archaic thing. It's a business arrangement, a social and political alliance. Love almost never enters into the equation." Nadira's face darkens, and I wonder if she's experienced this personally. "See, our clans are a lot like individual kingdoms back in the Middle Ages: The heir is basically a king, and the clans have shifting alliances and treaties, sometime a skirmish here and there over some issue or plot of land or control over supply lines, with marriages to seal clans together and all sorts of intrigue going on behind the scenes."

This sinks in. "So then Leila is a princess?"

Nadira nods and glances at me. "Basically, yeah, although women aren't allowed to lead a clan, so she can't inherit the patriarchy even if something happened to Ibrahim. Leila is an only child, which means no male heir to the partiarchy. That's why this marriage is so important to Ibrahim: without a male heir, if something happened to Ibrahim, control of the clan would be up for grabs, creating a power vacuum, which could spark a rather nasty and violent internal conflict within the ifrit clans. So the pressure for Leila to marry Hassan isn't just coming from her parents, but from *all* of the clans. Ibrahim is *old*, Carson. You haven't met him yet, but you'll understand when and if you do. He doesn't look it, and doesn't act it, but he's ancient, even for an ifrit. Ibrahim is almost a thousand years old. I'm not shitting you. He was born during the Almoravid dynasty in the late eleventh century. So needless to say, the other clans are just waiting for him to die, as the Najafi clan wields a huge amount of power and influence over the workings of the clans, not to mention the fact that Ibrahim is filthy fucking rich. He's had a millennium to amass wealth, and he's damn good at it."

I'm stunned speechless. "I had no idea . . . I knew she came from an old and rich family, but . . . Jesus. A thousand years old? How is that possible?"

Nadira just shakes her head. "It's complicated. We don't age the same." She sighs and pinches the bridge of her nose, trying to figure out how to explain it. "The mythology surrounding ifrits and djinn is all kinds of mixed up, and most of what humans know is a complete fabrication. The stories you hear, Sheherezad and all that . . . that stuff contains a nugget of truth, but the rest is invention, bastardizations, and just plain confusion. Our kind has lived so long among humans *as* humans that we've evolved to become more like them. With every new generation born, we are less and less the same brand of ifrit and djinni that existed when Ibrahim was born."

"So, when I get old . . ."

"Leila will outlive you by several hundred years, at least." Nadira looks away. "Taking human lovers is considered a temporary sort of . . . indulgence. *Marrying* a human? It's just . . . not done. It's cruel to the human, for one thing. They age, they get old and decrepit and weak and senile, and we . . . don't. We stay hale and strong and they watch us keep living and staying young, but they continue to age. And it's tough on us, too, if we love a human. We have to watch them grow old and die, and we can't do anything about it. There are stories among our people about this, fables, basically, meant to warn us about the dangers of consorting with humans long-term."

"And Leila knows this?"

Nadira nods. "Of course. Better than most, I'd say, if she knows anything about her father."

"Meaning what?"

Nadira shakes her head. "Now we're getting into

stuff that Leila should tell you herself."

There is a long silence then, as I think about everything Nadira told me. She seems to be brooding, staring out the window and lost in thought, watching the yellow lines flash past as if seeing long-ago memories. I suspect she has personal experience with a lot of what she's told me, but I'm not willing to pry into those memories.

"Just . . . remember that she loves you," Nadira says out of the blue. "If you can handle the truth, if you can handle what it means to be with her, then the best gift you could give her is to love her for as long as you can."

A tear escapes from Nadira's face, a bright blue droplet that carves a line into her face, revealing a roiling cerulean ocean beneath the surface of her skin. She wipes away the tear, roughly, angrily, and her skin returns to normal.

"Sorry," Nadira says, clearing her throat. "Old hurt still hurts, you know?"

Don't I know it?

Evening blankets Chicago in a golden haze as we arrive on the freeway. We make our way through the city, following Nadira's directions to a high-rise building facing Lake Michigan. She guides me to a parking garage and up to a tenth-floor apartment.

Before she knocks, Nadira turns to me, placing a hand on my arm. "Listen, I'm not really supposed to be bringing you here, and they'll know you're a human on sight, so just . . . be cool and let me do the talking. All right?"

I can only nod, wondering what I've let her drag me into.

She raps on the door a few times, and it opens to reveal a slender older woman, beautiful and serene, a thick black braid shot through with silver hanging down her back. Her eyes are dark and exude what I can only think of as ancient wisdom. It sounds silly, even in my own head, but I know by the way she pierces me with a searching stare that the woman in front of me has seen century after century come and go, crash and recede, like waves on a shore.

"Aunt Noura," Nadira says, embracing the woman. "Thank you for having us."

"You failed to mention your . . . friend, my dear." Noura's voice is quiet and disapproving.

"I'm sorry, Aunt. We won't be long. And he *is* a friend, nothing else."

Noura steps closer to me and looks up at me, touching my forehead with her middle finger. When her fingertip touches my skin I feel an electric contact, the same insistent, alien presence probing through my mind, sifting through my memories and desires and fears. It's a violation.

I wrench myself away, anger flooding through me. "Would it be so fucking hard to just *ask* first instead of mind-raping me?" I can't help the outburst, the words pouring out of me unfiltered. "I just want Leila back. I didn't sign up to have my brain ransacked by every damned djinni I meet."

Noura doesn't seem upset by my outburst in the slightest. "I'm sorry, Mr. Hale. That was inconsiderate of me. But you must understand my position. When my niece, whom I haven't seen in . . . a very long time . . . shows up at my doorstep with *another* human in tow . . . it is only prudent that I take precautions. I needed to find out your intentions, that is all."

I glance at Nadira and see a flash of something like anger and embarrassment cross her face before she schools her features into a still, calm mask once more.

"It's not like that, Aunt. I promise," Nadira says, then cuts me a look, her eyes telling me, *Don't ask.*

Noura looks from me to Nadira and back, then smiles. "Ah. I seem to have mistaken the situation. My apologies once more. Please, come in."

She opens the door the rest of the way and ushers us into a spacious apartment with many wide windows letting in the sunlight. She shows me to a tan leather couch and I sit down, sinking into the soft leather. Nadira and Noura go into the kitchen, leaving me alone in the living room while they stand together having a whispered conversation. Water heats in a kettle on the gas range. The way Noura glances at me from time to time tells me they're discussing me.

My phone vibrates in my pocket and I withdraw it, grateful for the distraction. There are half a dozen work-related emails that I answer quickly, slipping the phone back into my pocket when Noura returns bearing an elaborate silver tea service. She places the gleaming tray on the coffee table and sets about pouring the tea into the fine china cups with a sense of dignity and ceremony. I feel myself unconsciously sitting straighter, taking the teacup in careful hands, sipping slowly and trying to match the graceful dignity of the women. I feel hopelessly out of place suddenly, holding a tiny teacup in my big rough paws, unable to join in the aimless small talk of the women, who discuss family matters in quiet tones.

Eventually I can't contain myself any longer. I set down the teacup as gently as I can. "Look, this is all very pleasant, and thank you for the tea, but—"

Noura interrupts me. "My niece has apprised me of the situation, Mr. Hale, but please be reminded that you are a guest in my home, and that I have not seen my niece in at least an entire human lifetime.

Your problem will not change in the few minutes it will take for me to catch up with Nadira. Please, be patient."

I open my mouth to argue, then close it again. I take a deep breath and pick up my teacup, sipping the black, bitter tea. I don't understand what we're doing here, or what Noura has to do with Leila, or how any of this is helping me get her back.

After what seems like an interminable amount of time spent chatting idly, Noura finally removes the tray, returning to sit next to her niece.

"I know this must all seem very strange to you," Noura begins, "but what you must understand is that this is not the type of situation you can solve by just barging in with guns blazing. You would only worsen things, and most certainly get yourself killed. The reason Nadira brought you to me is because I am related to the al-Jabiri clan. I am a djinni, as is my niece, but my husband and his brothers are ifrits—distant relations to Hassan, as a matter of fact. This is a delicate situation, as is my and my husband's place within our respective clans, as well as between the two tribes. The wrong action could precipitate a war between not only the clans, but between the tribes. Certain sectors within the djinn actively wish for war—" Noura cuts a hard, meaningful glance at Nadira, "but they haven't lived through a djinni-ifrit war . . . they don't know the devastation such a thing would cause."

A look passes between the two of them that I can't interpret. Nadira looks away first, and I could swear she's acting as if her aunt has rebuked her in some way.

"I admit I don't understand why Nadira is involving herself in this in the first place," Noura continues. "But she has, and now you're here, for better or worse. I can tell, from merely looking at you as well as having viewed your intentions, that you will not let this go. I cannot expect you to understand that Leila Najafi's marriage to Hassan al-Jabiri really is the best thing for everyone involved."

"It's not best for *her!*" I say through gritted teeth, with more force than I intend.

"Perhaps, but as the daughter of a man like Ibrahim Najafi, she has more than just herself to consider. The Najafi clan is the subject of much speculation within the ifrit community, since Ibrahim never sired a male heir. That leaves a power vacuum, which would incite a power grab when he dies. And a power grab would then spill over into the human world, cause human deaths, cast scrutiny upon the existence of our people. She has her entire clan, her parents, her tribe, and our entire species to think about. No offense to you, Mr. Hale, but you are an intrusion and a distraction she didn't need, and can't afford. If she had exercised patience and restraint, she might have realized that marriage to Hassan wouldn't have been so bad, after a while." Noura holds up a hand to stall my protest. "No, please listen. You do not know the situation. Hassan is a businessman, and he is a very unique heir, for all his . . . moral shortcomings. He is a staunch believer in the old ways, which is rare among both tribes, as well as being a very modern and successful practitioner of human business practices.

"The old ways, Mr. Hale, mean that marriage is an arrangement and, as such, both individuals typically perform only a perfunctory lip-service to the reality of the marriage. Leila would likely be given free rein to live as she wishes. She wouldn't have any expectations placed on her beyond attending a few functions here and there. She would be free to do many things. Many women in her situation have taken a lover, and have enjoyed long, satisfying relationships."

"You want me to be her *affair?*" I stand up and stalk to the window, trying to calm my boiling blood. I speak without turning around. "This has *got* to be a joke. If you think Hassan would be content with that kind of arrangement then you're fucking delusional. *I* know that much and I don't even know the asshole, yet *you* claim to be related to him? You can't honestly sit there and suggest that I just let her marry that evil sack of shit, and then just . . . what? Show up every now and again and fuck her in the back of a limo? Be her side-piece?"

Noura shakes her head. "It is common in our culture. It wouldn't be secret, just . . . discreet."

"There's so much in what you're suggesting that's *so* fucked up."

"Please, Mr. Hale, calm down. I am only trying to help. Your cursing offends me."

"My cursing offends you? Really?" I turn around finally, letting my anger show. "Your suggestion that I just sit around with my dick in my hands while the woman I love marries someone else, someone like Hassan? . . . that offends *me*. This isn't the eighteenth century, lady."

"Please, Mr. Hale, your vulgarity is unnecessary. You can't be expected to understand. You are only human, after all."

"*Only human?*" I shout. "Are you for real? You're straight out of a fucking movie! This is stupid. I'll figure it out myself. I really don't care if I start a war. I'm not about to let Leila go through with this marriage just because you people are too fucking backward to let go of archaic traditions that should have died hundreds of years ago."

I stomp to the door and slam it behind me. I've got no idea where to go next, but I'll figure it out. I'm in Chicago, I'm close; I can almost *feel* her.

I find my car and start the engine, but before I can peel out, Nadira slides into the seat next to me.

"Look," she says, "I know my aunt is a little old-fashioned, but there was some truth to what she was saying."

I hiss between my teeth; Nadira is the closest thing to an ally I have in this whole mess, and I can't afford to alienate her. "You can't honestly think I'd—"

"No, I know you couldn't do that, and I agree with you about the whole tradition of arranged marriage. I do, more than you could ever know." Nadira grabs my hand and squeezes it, meets my eyes, pleading silently. "But you do *not* want to start a war. If the two tribes started fighting . . . you don't understand what that would mean for your kind. You really don't. The last time there was open warfare between our tribes, the fighting spilled over into the politics of the human countries, and it turned into a war that killed hundreds of thousands of people. And that was five hundred years ago. With weapons being what they are today . . . with how deeply our people are tangled into this society . . ."

"What's that mean?"

"It means we have people in positions of power in this society. Politicians, mayors, governors, policemen, FBI and CIA agents, generals and admirals . . . crime bosses, arms dealers and drug runners . . . it could drag the entire country into civil war. I'm not exaggerating."

"And all this hinges on Leila's marriage? Is that what you're trying to tell me?"

"Yes, Carson, that's *exactly* my point. That's my aunt's point, too."

Nadira seems perfectly serious, and that scares me. But it just doesn't seem possible. I met Leila when she was slinging drinks at a tiny little pub in Detroit, and now these people are trying to tell me the fate of the entire country hangs on her marriage to a bastard like Hassan?

"What am I supposed to do?" The words are whispered, more to myself than to Nadira.

"I don't know," Nadira answers. "I wish I did."

"Weren't you the one telling me I couldn't let the marriage happen?"

"Yes," Nadira agrees. "I did, and it's still true. It's a complicated problem. If Hassan gained access to the wealth and power and influence of the joined clans if Ibrahim were to die, he'd be unstoppable, for all intents and purposes. What's more, Hassan is one of the ifrits who wants a war with the djinn, who wants to reveal our existence to the humans, openly exist, and he's willing to spill blood to make it happen. He's not content with one little clan, either, and that's another problem. He'll want more."

"How do you know so much about him?" I ask.

"I just do. Leave it at that." Nadira's features are hard and cold, her eyes lost in memory again.

She keeps dropping hints and snippets that suggest she used to be involved with Hassan somehow, but then always clams up again. It's driving me nuts.

"So I can't let them marry, and I can't let them *not* marry? Real fucking helpful, Nadira. Thanks." I groan and slump back into the driver's seat. "What am I supposed to do?"

"I don't know. I was hoping my aunt would be more helpful."

"Well, she wasn't." I sigh. "Look, if you don't have any better ideas, then I'm just gonna crash the wedding, consequences be damned. I can't let her do this. I *can't* let it happen. I love her, and she doesn't deserve to be railroaded into this. The idea that one girl not marrying this one guy could start a war, which would in turn drag all of America into war? That's idiotic. I just can't . . . can't believe it. I've reached my limit of believing impossible things."

"I know it sounds that way," Nadira says. "But you have to trust me. It's real. It's true."

"Too bad." I pull my pistol from the small of my back, eject the clip and check the load, slam it home, then replace the gun in my waistband. "Where the hell is this wedding happening?"

Nadira lets out a long breath, wiping her face with both hands. "I guess I'm going with you, then. God knows you'll just get yourself killed without me."

Chapter 16: Thunderheads Approaching

Leila

The gate is locked, and I have to announce myself on the intercom to be let in. I push the button and wait.

"Who is it?" The voice on the other end is unfamiliar, gruff and male.

"It's Leila. I'm here to see my father." I don't bother to hide the exasperation in my voice.

The voice on the other end doesn't respond; the gate swings silently and slowly inward. I drive forward, marveling as always at the sculptured beauty of my parents' estate. The driveway is long and wide, lined with imposing poplars and cool green grass, a line of bright flowers edging the blacktop. Beyond, the lawn stretches away in all directions, an ocean of wind-rippled green. The trees sough and sway, the flowers nod, the topiary shrubs tremble, the water spouting from the fountain at the center of the circle shivers and casts diamond droplets; there is always wind here.

I park my car at the top of the circle, leaving the door open and the keys in the ignition. Father's valet will park it somewhere hidden, so its ugliness won't mar the perfection of the surroundings.

I need a few moments to gather myself before I go in and face them, so I sit on the ledge of the fountain. I've always loved this fountain. Ever since I was a little girl I've found peace here, listening to the water gush and splash endlessly, admiring the Grecian curves and lines of the perfect Carrera marble. It's a scene from Greek mythology; Father told me the stories, but I don't remember the names. There's a young man depicted on the side of the fountain, handsome and muscular, chasing an equally beautiful young woman. The artist caught them in the act of the woman being clutched at by the man, his fingers tangled in the folds of her robe. Now, it seems to express how I feel at this moment: chased, caught, captured.

I don't know what to expect when I go in. Father could be dead. That's my worst fear. I might be angry at him right now, but he's still my father, and I love him. He gave me a wonderful life up until the moment he betrothed me to Hassan. He gave me everything I could ever want and so much more, despite the strictures and rules and expectations. If he were dead . . . I would be devastated, of course. But that's not where the fear comes from. If he's dead, he can't protect me from Hassan, from the horror of marriage to Hassan. If Father is alive I still have hope that I can persuade him to find another way to fix everything without me having to marry Hassan. There's still hope for this to work out another way.

There's still hope, however slim, that I can be with Carson.

I wrench myself away from those thoughts. Carson isn't here, and he can't help me.

I go to the door and lift the monstrous brass knocker, molded into a serpent's head. One echoing rap, and the door swings open.

"Leila, my dear. It's good to see you've come to your senses." Mother, tall and imperious, cold and distant, hair always perfect and fluttering in an invisible breeze.

I stifle a sigh. "Hello, Mother." I give her a stiff embrace. "Aunt Talia called me. She was upset, saying something had happened to Father."

I step inside to the cool grandeur of my parents' home. I see Mother's face contort in confusion briefly, recovering quickly. Now I'm curious. That look of confusion tells me Talia was lying. I feel myself tensing. Something is wrong. The house, ever silent and still, breathes with a new air, a new kind of coiled tension.

I turn to Mother. "What's going on?"

She doesn't answer, only stares at me, almost vacantly, for a long, awkward moment. She draws a deep breath, holds it, then blows it out over me slowly in a magic-laced wind. I feel the spell clutching at me, seeking entrance into me, and I recognize the feeling. My anxiety loosens, my shoulders relax, and the fear starts to bleed away. Mother used to do this to me when I was a little girl, if I hurt myself, or woke up with a bad dream. She would blow on me, weaving a soothing spell into the breath to calm me and put me at ease.

I brush the magic aside and clench my anger around me. "No! Don't you *dare* do that," I hiss. Raising my voice to yell at her is inconceivable, even now. "Don't you dare. Tell me what's going on. Where is Father?"

She remains inscrutable as ever. "Do not speak to me like that, child. Yes, your father is fine. I apologize for Talia's untruth, but it did serve a greater purpose, in the end. Come with me into the living room and all will be made clear." She turns and glides away, expecting me to follow.

Which I do, damn it.

She always makes me feel like a little girl again. I hate it.

My anger almost boils over and gets the best of me when I see what's waiting for me in the living room: my aunts, my grandmothers and great-aunts and my cousins, and my mother's friends' daughters; every female in the entire clan above the age of five is here, plus Hassan's mother and his many aunts, and all the cousins from that clan as well. There are easily two hundred people between the crowd in the kitchen, living room, and backyard, and they've been waiting all this time.

There are streamers and ribbons, vases of flowers, all of them white, and there are round tables set up in the backyard, draped with white linens and sparkling silverware and tall centerpieces with snow-white irises. There's a table piled high with gifts, all wrapped in silver and white. There are tables groaning under the weight of trays of cheese and meats, vegetables and fruits, lamb kebabs and a thousand other hors d'oeuvres and finger foods. Servers float through the crowd, dressed in white robes that would be ridiculous anywhere else, but manage to seem regal and ethereal here.

It's a wedding shower. On the face of it, at least. But as I look around, I see other decorations that make me suspicious. An arch woven through with hundreds of white roses with a podium in front of it, facing ranks of white wooden folding chairs.

A wedding shower, or the wedding itself?

I turn to leave but, suddenly, there is a pair of guards flanking me. Normally decked out in all black, even they are wearing white slacks and button-down shirts. They aren't holding weapons openly, but I have no doubt they have them hidden somewhere, not to mention their ifrit birthright powers. I try to push past them, but they close together, forming a massive shoulder wall between me and freedom.

"Don't be foolish, child," a dry, amused voice says in my ear.

I turn to face Aida, Hassan's mother. She is a short, voluptuous woman with chin-length black hair touched with silver at the temples.

"Excuse me?" I demand.

"You wouldn't want to ruin the party, would you? Not when we've all gone to so much trouble." Aida leans forward and puts her mouth to my ear, whispering like a snake slithering in knee-high grass. "You cannot get out of this. Do not try. You wouldn't want anything to happen to your family after the wedding, would you? Too much is at stake for you to play the part of a spoiled child."

I resist the impulse to send her flying across the

room. I turn to Mother. "Where is Father?"

"He is with the other men, of course," Aida answers.

Mother remains silent, and I wonder at that. I know my mother and Aida al-Jabiri have no love lost between them, so Aida answering for Mother shows all too clearly where the balance of power resides. Mother glances at me, and for once I see actual emotions brimming in her normally flat and emotionless eyes: she is afraid. She clutches at the fabric of her skirt at her hips, knotting the cloth in her trembling fingers.

I look around at the gathered women, ranging in age from children and young girls to aged grandmothers. They are all watching me, waiting for my reaction. Silence reigns, tense and heavy. I glance at the wall of male muscle standing impervious and immovable behind me, and I notice that they clutch their hands behind their backs, and I know their callused hands hold the grips of pistols.

The gravity of the situation permeates my anger. If I cause a scene, the punishment will not be meted out to me, but to others. The clans are tense enough as it is, and if any one of these women gets hurt, the clans will all fall to fighting. There are tenuous alliances between clans, solidified through marriages exactly like the one being 'celebrated' here. My cousins are married to men with business partners in other clans, who are related by marriage to other clans, which in turn bear long-standing enmity to yet other clans. One shot fired, one bit of magic carelessly cast, and the fragile peace would collapse like a house of cards.

Seconds of silence drags out into minutes as I struggle to contain my anger. Can I allow a civil war to be sparked over me? I love Carson, but at what cost? I feel magic thrumming in the air, and I notice the guards' eyes are glowing, one pair liquid blue, and the other orange pits of flame.

I grind my teeth, unclench my fists, and storm out to the backyard. I watch the other women loosen up and begin to mill about, resuming their chatter, suddenly cheery and happy. My stomach revolts at their blasé attitude to what almost happened. Perhaps they don't know, or just don't care. I sip the wine and try to hold back the tears that threaten to spill out. It doesn't work, and I turn away from the house.

I feel a presence near me, the cold and familiar stolidity of Mother.

"I can't do it, Mother," I whisper. "I can't marry him. You don't know what he's like. He destroyed the bar I worked at, just to get my attention, and he almost killed a human police officer in the process. He's threatened me, you, Father, Aunt Talia, everyone. He attacked me in my apartment, and then shifted in front of humans. He's the reason the djinn are threatening a war of suppression. Not to mention, Hassan is a pig."

Mother doesn't answer right away, considering her words. "Listen, Leila," she says. Shock runs through me: she never, *ever* speaks to me in so intimate and informal a tone. "I know what you're going through. I also know you see me as being ice-cold and uncaring.

I actually gasp, hand flying to my mouth. I have never heard my mother refer to herself this way in my entire life.

She smiles, a small smirk of amusement. "I *am* cold. 'Ice queen' is a term I've heard all my life, and I suppose I earn it. But that doesn't mean I don't know what you're experiencing, to a degree. My marriage to your father wasn't my choice, surely you realize that. I was betrothed to him when I was fifteen and married him at sixteen. I was very young, and I had barely begun to understand who and what I was. My parents were wealthy and powerful and important. They were always too busy for me, so I was raised by my nurse, Hoda. Then, one day, my parents sat me down and said to me, 'Leena, you have been betrothed to Ibrahim Najafi. He is a powerful man, and very wealthy. Marriage to him will cement the alliance between our clans. He is a good man, and he will take care of you.'"

Mother stares out past my shoulder, not seeing me. Her fingers toy with the rings on her finger, one a platinum band, the other a massive diamond worth a rather large fortune. She's silent so long I wonder if maybe she's forgotten she was speaking, then she draws a deep, shuddering breath and continues.

"I was terrified. Everyone knew Ibrahim Najafi. He was one of the most ancient and powerful ifrits in all the clans, even then, but he had always refused to marry despite the many suits he received on an almost daily basis. You see, despite his age, he was still a handsome and virile man. I know you don't want to think about your father that way, but it's true.

"All it meant to me, however, was that I was even more terrified of him. Why had he finally agreed to marry, after so many centuries of bachelorhood? And why to me? I was a slip of a girl then, a sheltered, frightened little thing. I begged and pleaded with Father to call it off, but he'd Sealed the agreement with Ibrahim. He couldn't back out, and of course I had no more say in such matters than did Mother. Less, really. So a year came and went, during which time I never left my room unless forced.

"The wedding arrived, and I hadn't even set eyes on my betrothed, a man several hundred years older than me. Oh, the stories they told. All the bridesmaids and the cousins, they all talked about how lucky I was. He was born into the Almoravid dynasty, and was a prince of one of the most powerful empires in history. But he was a bastard, spawned by an ifrit warrior on a wayward daughter of the emperor. He was raised with a scimitar in one hand and magic in the other, wind always swirling around him like a cloak. He was trained by all the best of the warriors and mages and ifrit advisors in the land. It was whispered that he fought against the European invaders during the Crusades. He was a pirate, and a Berber king, and . . . oh, for weeks leading up to the wedding I was regaled with tale after tale about the man I was to marry. His adventures were the stuff of legends, and I do mean that literally as well as figuratively. All of Córdoba was abuzz with news of the wedding, for both our clans were known across the lands, his more so, though the Almoravids had long since fallen from power."

I wonder why Mother is telling me all this, what it has to do with Hassan, and I open my mouth to ask, but she holds up a hand, silencing me. She's never spoken so many words to me in all my life, and I'm enthralled despite my confusion as to her purpose.

"My legs shook beneath my gown as I approached your father on our wedding day, and I think it was only my own father's hand on my arm that held me up and kept me from running away. Ibrahim was tall and his skin was darkened by the sun, and his muscles showed even through the ceremonial warrior's garb he wore. He *was* handsome, devilishly so, though this did little to help my nerves. It made them even worse, I think, for he was watching me approach him down the aisle with open desire and anticipation. As if he knew me, and this was a marriage of love rather than a political alliance. When he took my hands in his, I nearly fainted. Yet . . . he was gentle, and his eyes were kind.

"I knew then that I wouldn't mind the marriage so much, although I was still terrified of him, of the stories told about him. They were all true, it turned out, but I didn't discover that until later.

"The point to all this, Leila, is that you never know what the man you are betrothed to is like until you marry him. Some of the stories told about your father were every bit as horrid and distasteful as the ones told about Hassan. And I must say, every time I have met him, Hassan has been polite and charming, and he is your own age, furthermore, a consideration I didn't receive." Mother pauses, but I keep silent, sensing that she isn't done. Besides which, every moment here is another moment I don't have to spend in *there.* "I know this is hard, my daughter, and I know it's not what you would choose for yourself. But, really, you'll grow to care for him, if you let yourself. It was many years before I stopped being terrified of your father, and I came to realize that he was in fact a kind and loving man. You are a child, Leila, and you see with limited vision and experience. Please, give this a chance. There is too much at stake . . . for everyone."

Finally she's done, and I'm bursting with questions and protestations, but none of them come out. I don't know where to start.

"Mother . . . you don't *know* Hassan." I've told her this a hundred times. "He's charming and polite around you and Father, yes. But underneath . . . he's a monster. He's violent and cruel, and he wants me as a trophy, as a possession, not as a wife. He wants me only for what I represent, Mother. Don't you see? Father isn't young anymore, and the clans all know this. . . . *you* know this and so does he, and so does Hassan. Everyone knows that without an heir, patriarchy of our clan is up for grabs. That's all this is about: power." I sigh, knowing I'm getting nowhere. Mother knows the situation, better than I do, probably. I'm not sure why I'm bothering.

Mother only looks at me sadly. "I know, Leila," she whispers. "I'm sorry. I wish there was something I could do."

She stands up and floats away without a backward glance, without a hug or a touch. Her story was interesting, but it seems so . . . pointless, so non sequitur. Was she trying to make me feel better? I know my father is a good man, and I know he cares about me in his own way.

But Hassan is not anything like my father.

Aida beckons to me, and I realize I've got no hope left. The guards stand behind her, glaring at me with blank, dead eyes. They would kill everyone here if Aida commanded it, I think. I consider for a moment letting that happen, just opening up with all my powers and blasting them as hard as I can. Perhaps Aida sees my thoughts, somehow, because she lifts a hand and a dozen more white-clad guards materialize all around the party, magic falling from them as they cast aside the spells that had rendered them invisible. The threat is obvious: cooperate, or blood will run.

I see the true hopelessness of the situation, and I have to fight away tears yet again. But I can't cry, not in front of Aida, not in front of my mother.

I force myself to my feet and make my way back inside. A mask falls into place, slamming down between the world and me. Carson is out there, but I know now there's nothing he can do. Even if he showed up here by some miracle, all that would happen is that he would be killed. I can't let the clans fall into war, and I can't let my family suffer at the hands of these hard-eyed killers.

Aida appears beside me, eyeing me. "Your father is Sealed to this arrangement. Don't forget that little fact, my dear."

A sob bubbles up and escapes my lips. I clamp down on it, swallow it.

I must do this. I have no choice.

Carson. I can feel him, out there. The night we shared together, it bound us together, somehow. My magic is twined around his heart, I think, and now I can feel it returning to me, drawing closer. He's coming.

I try not to let this translate into hope, but I'm not entirely successful. I can't help the feeling that arises within me at the thought of his presence. He's coming for me, and I know he won't stop until he's either dead or has me in his arms. That's the most cliché thing ever, I'm pretty sure, but it's true. I know it is. I'm sitting in my bedroom, the sprawling room in the house where I grew up, big enough to hold my apartment twice over. I'm on the balcony, guards are posted outside the bedroom door. My heart throbs, both with the anticipation of Carson's presence and with fear for what it might mean.

If he shows up, all hell will break loose. I haven't told Mother or Father about him, and if they know

I made love to a human . . . if Aida knew . . . blood would run. I want to tell him to stay away, to save himself. I want to believe in the impossible, that he could somehow get me out of this. But even if he did accomplish the impossible, the consequences would be . . . outside both of our capacities to understand.

My father is Sealed to the agreement, held to the oath not only by his honor but by magic. I'd forgotten about that part, that Father had let himself be Sealed to the arrangement. Agreements are law to our people, and breaking them holds dire consequences. I don't know exactly what would happen if Father were to try to break his promise, but it wouldn't be good. Knowing how the magic of my people works, he'd probably be killed instantly.

God, my head is pounding with all the variables. The agreement, my father's Sealing, the escalating tensions between the clans, and between the tribes . . . Carson's love, his hands on me, his lips pressed to mine, warm and tender and intense with passion . . . the rage in Hassan's eyes, the threats from his mouth, my mother's oddly-timed and confusing revelation of her own past . . .

I can't make sense of it all, I can't put all the variables into an equation that makes any sense to me. It's too much for one girl to bear, but bear it I must.

Carson my love, if you're coming, come quick. I pulse the thought out into the ether. *I'd rather die with you than live without you.*

CHAPTER 17: IBRAHIM'S PLAN

Carson

MY PULSE POUNDS IN MY EARS, AND MY BREATH IS COMING in short, shallow gasps. I've got my Glock in my hand and extra clips in my pocket. Nadira told me such things won't do too much good against Hassan, but I've got to try. I feel better with a pistol, whether it'll do any good or not. I need the pretence, at the very least.

I park the car on a quiet, tree-lined side street. I can see the lake in the distance, and the highrises of downtown Chicago. I slide out of the car and lock the door with the fob. Nadira is beside me, eyes boiling supernatural blue, the roaring sound of crashing ocean waves accompanying her every step.

We're down the street from Leila's parents' home, the mansion looming in the distance surrounded by expansive green lawns and surrounded by a huge stone and iron fence, extending half a mile in both directions. As we draw near the gate, a steady wind kicks up, gusting around us in violent eddies.

This is definitely the place: the crawling of my skin, the churning in my gut, these are clues, along with the ever-blowing wind that smells oh so faintly of Leila.

I flex my fingers on the grip of the pistol as we stand on one side of the closed gate, the driveway stretching away toward the house packed with cars, all of them expensive luxury vehicles. Valets stand at attention near the top of the circle, and four security guards flank the wide double front doors. I can't quite believe the opulence of the estate. It's like something out of a movie, unfathomably grand and imposing.

"How do we get past the gate?" I ask as we follow the fence out of sight of the guards.

Nadira smirks, an 'I know something you don't know' kind of smile. She lifts her hands, flexes her fingers, and the glow of her ethereal cerulean eyes brightens. I feel a pressure at my feet and look down to see a fountain of water lifting me up inch by inch, foot by foot, slow and steady and impossible. The water guides me up and up and over the spiked wrought-iron fence and to the ground on the other side, evaporating the moment my feet touch the grass. I expect Nadira to rise over the same way she'd lifted me, so I'm shocked when she merely presses herself against the fence and her entire body turns liquid, allowing her to squeeze through the bars.

"Let's stick to the fence and move towards the back of the house," Nadira suggests. "I want to avoid the guards as much as possible. The more people that get involved, the more likely we are to spark fighting, so try not to shoot anyone if you can help it."

"I'll do my best." I'm not sure what to expect. I could be walking into a trap, with dozens of armed guards waiting for me. Or they may not know I even exist, which would work in my favor, up to a point.

We skulk along the fence a few hundred yards away from the mansion and the attendant guards until we come to a point where the fence angles away into the distance and we're forced to cross the open yard. Nadira breathes a word, and I see a cloud of glowing golden particles spring from her mouth to shower down around me, coating my skin.

"That should keep you from being spotted until you get to the house," Nadira says. "That's about all the assistance I can give you, though, and it won't last long. I've got to conserve my energy. I've got a feeling we're going to need it."

I step carefully through the grass, moving as quickly as I can while still staying silent. I can see myself, my body, and I don't feel any different, but a guard rounds the side of the house and looks straight at me but doesn't raise an alarm. I must have been rendered invisible by whatever magic Nadira used on me. I don't dare think about it too closely, though; I've got other things on my mind.

Nadira strides next to me. She's turned herself into a statue of woman-shaped water, her body outlined by a faint shimmer in the sun.

I focus my attention on the house, watching for guards and trying not to be distracted by Nadira. She's beautiful in her human form, but like this . . . there's something alluring about her liquid body, especially since she may as well be naked with the way every curve and detail of her body is carved in ever-moving liquid. Despite the strange and ethereal beauty of Nadira in her elemental form, it's disconcerting and distracting and difficult to look at her for too long. I'll be glad when she reassumes her human form.

After what feels like an hour of silent advance, we finally reach the side of the house, pressing ourselves against the brick. The backyard is only a few hundred feet away at this point, and that's where the crowd is gathered, milling in and out of the house, sitting at tables and chatting. There are several hundred people here, mostly women and children, but also many men including many male attendants.

I risk a glance at Nadira, who has returned to human form, and looks decidedly uncomfortable.

"What's up?" I breathe. "You look like you're about to puke."

She takes a deep breath and lets it out, swallowing several times. "I am," she mutters. "I'm a djinni, remember? It's like a lone cat walking into a dog pound. Plus, I know some of these people. But, never mind, I'll be fine. Let's go."

"What's the plan? Just . . . walk in and say 'I'm here to stop this wedding?'"

"Basically," Nadira says. "I don't see any other option."

"I don't either. I just hope they don't all attack me at once." I'm sweating, my palms are clammy and my stomach is roiling.

"Oh, most of them will stay out of it, whatever happens. They'll let the guards and Hassan handle it. If things get violent, you take care of the guards, however you have to. Leave Hassan to me."

"Shouldn't he be my responsibility?" I ask. "I mean, I'm the one trying to stop his wedding."

"Yeah, but you're no match for him. Not by a long shot. No offense, you're just not. The guards will be trouble enough, trust me." Nadira takes a step toward the backyard, but pulls up short, glancing around as if she hears something.

"What is it?"

Nadira only shakes her head, holding up a hand for silence. "I thought . . ." she starts, then trails off. "Do you . . . do you feel anything unusual?"

I go still, listening, straining all my senses. "No, I don't feel anything."

As soon as the words are out of my mouth I feel a breeze curling around me, a susurrus in my ears, ruffling my hair, smelling again faintly of Leila and strongly of something else, wood and leather and pipe smoke and brandy.

"You shouldn't be here," a deep voice says behind us.

I jump and spin around, my heart thudding crazily. "Who—who are you?"

The man is tall, maybe an inch taller than my six-foot-three frame, elegant and impressive in a slim-fitting tailored tuxedo, salt-and-pepper hair carefully oiled and combed backward over his scalp. His features are sharp and attractive, resembling Leila enough that I'm sure this is her father, Ibrahim. He is a stern, commanding man, his eyes piercing and penetrating, coal-black and hard.

"I am Ibrahim Najafi, owner of this estate," the man says. "And you are?"

"I'm Detective Carson Hale, and this is—"

"Nadira Nasri. I know who you are." Ibrahim's voice is hard, cold, and sharp with threat. "You are trespassing on my property. Why are you here? What do you think to accomplish? A human and a *djinni?*" The last word is spat like a curse.

"Please, Mr. Najafi," I say. "You're making a mistake, making Leila marry Hassan. You can't let it happen."

"What could you possibly know of such things? You are a human, and you think to tell *me* I'm making a mistake? Why should I not kill you where you stand?"

"Because I love Leila, sir." The words come out unbidden, unrehearsed. They emerge and as soon as they do I feel the danger in the air thicken into a tangible frost.

"*What* did you say?" Ibrahim hisses.

I know I can't take it back, so I repeat myself. "I said I'm in love with your daughter. And she loves me back."

Ibrahim stares at me for a long moment, and then turns on his heel, saying, "You should go. I have no wish to do violence at my daughter's wedding."

Wedding? Already?

I react without thinking, grabbing Ibrahim's arm and spinning him around, stepping close to the older man. "No, please, listen—"

Ibrahim snarls, jerks his arm free and I'm assaulted by a punching fist of air crushing the breath from my lungs, sending me flying. But before I hit the ground I feel myself reeled in by an invisible hand, and then an all-too-real hand clutches my throat and lifts me an inch off the ground. I'm dangling and choking in front of Ibrahim.

"You *dare* lay a hand on me?" Ibrahim is livid, veins pulsing visibly in his neck.

"I'm sorry," I rasp, gasping for breath. "I'm sorry. I just—I love her too—too much. "

Beside me, Nadira is silent, watching, not interfering. I understand her reticence, but I sure could use her help right about now. I'm released abruptly, and I collapse to my hands and knees. A wave of nausea rolls over me, accompanied by the all-too familiar sensation of being violated in my mind. I'm aware of a presence ransacking my mind and memory. I fight against it, knowing it's Ibrahim in my mind and knowing it's futile. The presence sorts through my mind, shuffling images like playing cards: my childhood in Ferndale, Mom taking me to the library, Dad coming home, setting his briefcase on the floor at the front door; the first time I shot my sidearm in the line of duty, a too-young face contorting in confusion as the bullet pierced a chest; my first girlfriend lifting her shirt over her head as fluorescent parking lot lights bathe her white skin even paler in the dank heat of the backseat of my car; Leila kissing me, whispering to me, sobbing against me, naked above me—

I rip that last memory away from the invisible presence in my mind and slam a wall down between Ibrahim and those most private memories. I'm surprised to feel his presence is suddenly gone, and I find myself lying on the ground, puking violently, cursing past drool and bile.

"What is it with you people?" I demand as I wipe my face. "Every one of you does that to me. I'm fucking sick of it!"

"Most impressive," Ibrahim says. "You shut me out of your mind. Not many can do that. But I saw enough. Too much, perhaps. You do indeed love her, and she does love you in return. Unfortunately, such things are irrelevant in the face of the current situation. I can't stop this, whether I want to or not."

"You have to . . ." I struggle to my feet, spitting bile onto the grass. "You can't make her do this, please—"

"You do not understand, Detective Hale," Ibrahim says, each word precise. "I have been Sealed."

I open my mouth to ask what that means, but Ibrahim holds his hand up for silence, glances around, and then punches a hand forward, ripping a hole in the air and sinking his fist up to his elbow in some invisible pocket of reality. I blink, not believing what I'm seeing. Ibrahim then shoves his other fist into the hole and pulls his hands apart, and the hole widens to show a library or study. Ibrahim gestures for me to go through, but I can't make myself move, too stunned and confused to make my limbs cooperate.

"Go, you idiot," Nadira whispers in my ear, shoving me toward the gap in the air.

I stumble through and find myself standing in front of a huge desk, the walls of the large room lined with glass cases containing old swords, axes, ornate round shields, silver-and-gold encrusted bridles, curving, jewel-studded knives, yellowing parchment maps curling at the edges, crumbling strips of paper lined with scrolling Arabic script. I'm drawn to a sword hanging on the wall, a matching sheath beneath it. It's a long, curved blade, the metal swirling with intricate designs clearly not carved or etched or painted onto the blade, but which rather seem to be a part of the metal itself. The hilt is simple, black leather wrapped with silver wire, a huge ruby in the pommel, the sheath etched with intricate gold-leafed Arabic script. The sword is mesmerizing, and I find myself wanting to hold the blade even though I know nothing about swords.

Ibrahim speaks behind me. "That is a Damascus

blade. It is one of a kind, crafted for me by a master swordsmith in the year 1292. No one alive knows the secret of crafting sword blades such as that. Few such exist anymore at all, and certainly none so fine as that. I slew a thousand infidel Christians with that blade."

"It's beautiful," I whisper, awed by the blade.

"Yes, it is." Ibrahim's voice is pitched low, almost tender. "If I could swing that sword and with it win my daughter's freedom from Hassan, I would. Please believe that, Detective Hale. I would. I love my daughter, and I know all too well what kind of man Hassan is. But I am bound by the Sealing."

"What does that mean?" I ask. "Sealed? I've heard the term used several times now, but I don't understand it."

"Please, sit, Mr. Hale. The wedding is still more than an hour away." Ibrahim pours a generous finger of brandy into a cup, hands it to me and pours another for himself.

"The wedding is *today?*" I ask, confused.

Ibrahim hasn't so much as looked at Nadira, who sits next to me, silent. It's almost as if she's trying to become invisible again.

"It has been moved forward, to today. Hassan and his father are eager to finalize the alliance. To get their hands on my clan." He sounds more than a little bitter. He takes a swallow of brandy and then continues. "Sealing is a complicated business, but, basically, it's an oath, a promise. It's not merely a matter of my word, however. It's a contract sealed between the two parties by blood and by magic. I am incapable of going against my word. Not unwilling, I must emphasize this, but rather rendered magically *incapable,* and if I were to try there would be disastrous consequences. I would be struck down dead on the spot by the magic of the Seal and my assets would be seized, my clan taken over by another patriarch. My wife would be given as a gift to another man and my daughter married to Hassan anyway."

"That's pretty harsh," I remark.

"Yes, I suppose it is. But that's how we do business."

I'm struck by a thought. "Is Hassan Sealed the same way?"

"Well, yes, of course," Ibrahim nods. "What are you thinking?"

"Just . . . what if we could somehow force Hassan to violate his end of the Seal?"

"How would we accomplish that?" Ibrahim asks. "He would not do anything to risk this. He has too much to gain."

I shake my head and shrug. "I don't know. It was just an idea. If we could get him to void his end of the deal, then Leila would be free, wouldn't she?"

"Yes, I suppose so," Ibrahim agrees, "but I don't see how that's possible at this juncture. The wedding happens in one hour, out there in my own backyard." He waves toward the window.

Silence hovers between us as we try to think of a solution. Eventually it's Nadira who speaks first. "What if Hassan was somehow *unable* to marry her? What if something stopped the wedding?"

Ibrahim tilts his head, considering. "Well . . . that would work temporarily, but he would still have the right of claim and the Seal would be intact. We would have to make sure he couldn't ever possibly fulfill his end of the bargain." Ibrahim hisses in pain. "I can feel the magic of the Seal working on me even now. Even discussing this is activating the terms of the Sealing."

"What if I were to banish him to the elemental dimension?" Nadira asks. "He might be able to find his way back, but by then we could figure out a way to break the contract without risking your safety."

"I would still be bound by my side of the oath, to see my daughter married. The oath does not say *who* she must marry, though," Ibrahim says, his voice low and thoughtful. "I have an idea, but I have to be careful in my phrasing of it. Even thinking it causes pain. The clans are gathered for the wedding. They would be displeased if they were to be made to leave without witnessing one. Perhaps if Miss Nasri were to do as she suggested—banish him to the elemental dimension, which is a one-way trip, correct, Miss Nasri?"

"As far as I know it is, yes. I cannot say with one hundred percent certainty, however."

"Good enough for our purposes, I suppose, and the best chance we have." Ibrahim waves a hand toward the backyard. "So Nadira banishes Hassan, at which point a different wedding could take place . . . just not the one everyone was expecting. Do you see? I would have fulfilled my end of the bargain, and in returning to the elemental dimension, Hassan will have voided his end of the oath, so he would be dead, and thus unable to challenge your marriage to my daughter."

There's a hissing noise, and smoke rises from Ibrahim's palms. He opens his hands flat, and I see the curving script of Arabic lettering seared onto his palms, a reminder of his oath, I presume.

I see his plan, and it's insane. I love her, but . . . marriage? So soon?

Ibrahim seems to sense my hesitation. "It will only work if you are totally committed, Carson. I must warn you. Ifrit marriages are not like yours. The vows made are a contract as well, and they are a kind of Seal, though not so draconian as the one binding me. They are permanent nonetheless, and they are magical in nature. The magic would work on you, though you are not an ifrit. You . . . joined with my daughter, Carson, and that union has imbued you with a certain amount of magic, binding you to Leila, albeit loosely." Ibrahim pauses, his face schooled to stillness, though I can see pain etching lines in his forehead, tendrils of smoke rising from his flesh, the scent of charred flesh filling the room. "Were you to do this, it would complete that binding, and you would be united with her in a very unique way. It is the only way, if you truly wish to free my daughter from the fate set out for her.

"It is not without risk, however, Detective Hale. Besides Hassan himself, his clan has provided the security you saw around my estate. They are loyal solely to Hassan, Aida, and Farouk al-Jabiri. They will fight to the death to prevent anything from interfering with their plans. And I am rendered powerless to work against the Sealing I agreed to. You and Miss Nasri would be on your own." He glances at Nadira. "You are positive you are able to perform the banishment? It is a difficult piece of magic known to few, and comes at a price."

Nadira nods. "I can. I've done it once before. It's not fun, but I can do it." She in turn looks to me. "This is for real, Carson. There's no divorce in our world. It's not possible. It doesn't exist. You marry her, it's forever. You try to leave, you *think* of leaving . . . well, you can't. You won't be able to, no matter how unhappy you may be. You could cheat on her, but even that would come at a price. So you'd better be really damn sure you love her enough to go through with this." She lets out a long breath. "Plus, there's no guarantee this will even work. There's two of us, and a lot of them."

My mind is racing. I love her, and this is a way out. Am I willing? This isn't something I can just get out of later if it doesn't work out; I can't undo this. It's permanent. I will be bound to Leila for all time.

My hands shaking, I can only nod.

"Are you sure about this, Carson?" Nadira asks again. She seems incredulous. "This is a little crazy."

"No more so than storming an ifrit wedding," Ibrahim points out. "You are a djinni, Miss Nasri. Your presence itself is the height of insanity, whether you are related to the al-Jabiris or not."

Nadira's only response is a laconic shoulder shrug.

"How do we do this, then?" I ask.

"My kind are somewhat addicted to the Old-World notions of honor, Mr. Hale," Ibrahim says, each word carefully chosen. "Hassan in particular fancies himself an ifrit of the ancient world, though he is but a child himself. He holds himself to a code of honor, though not as you and I would know it. If Hassan is challenged in front of a crowd of witnesses, he would not have the freedom to simply strike the challenger down with all his fury and magic, as he might in private. This is especially true if the challenger is not of the same race as he, not possessing the same abilities. If Hassan were to be provoked in front of such a crowd, he would be honor-bound to challenge that person to a duel."

"I see," I say, my blood running cold as I begin to grasp the true shape of his plan.

"Are you familiar with the most ancient rules concerning duels, Detective Hale?"

"No, not really," I admit. I'm curious as to what exactly Ibrahim is suggesting, since by all accounts if I challenge Hassan I'm guaranteed to lose.

"Well, you don't need to know the rules of seconds and all that, because it wouldn't be that kind of duel. What you need to know is that the one who is challenged always picks the weapons and the terms for the duel. So if one was to provoke Hassan into challenging him to a duel, he would be able to choose terms that would be most beneficial to him. For example, one could specify the use of fists only, preventing Hassan from using his natural advantages. Do you see?"

I nod. If I can get Hassan to challenge me to a

duel, then I might be able to make sure I can fight Hassan on more equal terms. Take away Hassan's elemental powers, force him to fight me man to man, and I might just have a decent chance at winning.

"I get it," I say. "But if I win, then what? That doesn't void the contract, or get me Leila. I'm not sure I can just kill him like that."

"No, you certainly could not. You might win the fight, but I doubt you could kill him, and I wouldn't suggest trying. If Hassan was to be incapacitated, however, Miss Nasri could perform a certain bit of magic that banishes the victim to the elemental realm. That is when the marriage Sealing would occur." Ibrahim fixes me with a penetrating look. "You understand, by agreeing to this Sealing, this marriage, assuming you win and all works out as planned, you would be then bound to me and my clan by the same terms as Hassan was. The Sealing itself is simple, needing only the verbal repetition of the oaths by the bride and groom."

I shrug. "I don't bring much to the table besides myself, Mr. Najafi. I don't have any family. I'm just a cop."

"Which in itself presents certain problems, but we can figure that out at another time. A human and an officer of the law at that . . . no one would stand for you inheriting the patriarchy. Such a thing is unthinkable. But you present me with an opportunity to avoid handing my daughter—my only child—to a monster like Hassan. I still owe Farouk a rather large sum of money, but that can be worked out some other way, and is not your concern. Not yet, at least. It might become your concern, should you succeed at his, and you must know there would be far-reaching repercussions should if you succeed at banishing Hassan and circumventing the alliance. I would have an heir—technically, but the clans would be mightily unhappy at exactly whom—and *what*—my heir would be. And war between the djinn and ifrits is still possible, even after all of this is done with, regardless of the outcome."

I nod, pointing at Nadira. "Yeah, her aunt made that pretty clear," I say.

"Ah, you spoke to Noura?" Ibrahim seems amused. "I don't expect that went too well for you, did it?"

"Not exactly. She suggested I let Leila marry Hassan, and then I just hook up with her on the side, like a . . . what's the word . . . a consort? Is that right? I might have gotten a little pissed off. How do you know her, anyway? I thought djinn and ifrits were enemies?"

"Enemies . . . yes," Ibrahim says, "although we haven't been at risk of outright violence in many centuries. In recent decades, however, we've slid inexorably toward war, and we are closer now than ever before. There are many, many factors at play here, but if you are determined to do this, then we cannot worry about what we cannot control."

"You didn't say how you knew Noura."

"No, I didn't. It's complicated, and ancient history. The short of it is Noura is married to an ifrit from Hassan's clan. Her husband and I have had some dealings in the past, so I have met Noura on several occasions. She is . . . a unique individual."

Nadira laughs, a harsh bark. "Yeah, you can say that again. I wasn't sure who else I could talk to. I was kind of desperate."

Ibrahim and Nadira exchange a weighted glance, one that I can't decipher. Nadira has secrets, that much is clear, but I can't spend time thinking about that right now.

"Desperate is right," I say, rising to my feet. "This whole thing is desperate, but I don't see another way. I can't just sit around and let it happen. So . . . let's do this."

Ibrahim shakes his head. "I'm afraid you'll have to wait. You need to time this exactly right. Hassan is sequestered with his groomsmen and friends. They would simply rip you to shreds and burn the remains. You have to make your appearance when all the crowd is watching."

I slump down into my chair, cursing. I hate waiting.

I focus on breathing, bringing Leila's face to mind, picturing myself marrying her, saying "I do," feeling the magic bind us together. It's scaring me shitless, but it also seems right somehow.

I can sense her somewhere close, and I know that she's afraid, which is enough to remove any remaining doubts.

I'm here, Leila. I'm here.

Chapter 18: The Wedding March

Leila

Carson's here, somewhere. He's so close I can feel his presence on my skin, almost hear his breathing in my ear. My door is heavily guarded, and I cannot leave or even look out into the passageway.

There's a deep, boiling rage in my gut, anger building inside me that these people would do this, would force me to marry at gunpoint. If the only one to suffer was me, I would loose all my rage and take the consequences. But it's not just me. They've made sure of that, they've arranged everything so I have no choice, and that helplessness is what makes the anger flicker to life, morphing from mere emotional response into a howling typhoon of barely-contained hatred. I cannot let the winds free, not yet. But soon. Oh yes, very soon they will all know the mistake they've made.

But god, Carson. I know he's here, but I don't know why, or how, or what he's planning. I can't get out of this room, I can't communicate with him. I can't tell him to flee, to run, to forget me.

So all I can do is sit on this stool, sweltering and sweating, this heavy dress belled around me, an explosion of ruching and lace with a long veil and hijab, long-sleeved to cover me to the wrist, beautiful and traditional and lacking any sensuality. I will walk down the aisle at my father's side, and I will speak the words of Sealing to bind myself to Hassan, and I will die inside with every footstep, every word.

I may say the words, but I will never belong to him. I will not allow him the pleasure of consummation. He will kill me first; I will make sure of that.

Father has not come to see me. He hasn't shown his face even once. I am tempted to think he is ashamed, feeling guilty that he allowed this to come to pass. He should be. I will never, ever forgive him for this.

The first time I will have seen him in more than a year will be when he takes my arm to walk me down the aisle in the backyard of the home where I grew up. There is a window—sealed shut to prevent escape—

and through it I can see a clear blue sky dotted with shreds of cotton clouds, a sparrow wheeling in the bright air, free and chirruping joyfully. It's maddening torture to see a bird so free and happy to merely be, to fly and wing and soar, when here I sit, alone and trapped and forced to complete the Marriage Sealing to a monster, all so my father will have a male heir, because I am nothing but an irrelevant woman, a possession, a thing to be bought and sold, traded, given away.

Tendrils of air stretch out from me, seeking gaps in the walls, cracks under doors, anywhere that I might fade and filter and fly away. They've done their job well though, blocking every avenue of escape. This room is airtight, air-conditioned and cool, but escape-proof, even for an air elemental like me.

I am tempted yet again to send the winds to bash and batter at the door and window, to fall into a screaming tantrum. But it won't do any good, I know. It's best to wait, to bide my time and conserve my strength, hoard my anger and let its potency mount.

Soon, now. I can feel it. The moment is nearing. They will open the door, level black muzzled assault rifles at me, their eyes flat and dead, power held ready and thrumming and far more dangerous than their guns.

Yes, here they are. The door is unlocked and

pulled open. Four hard-faced guards enter the room, followed by Aida.

"It's time, dear." Her voice is sickly-sweet, grating on my nerves.

She takes my arm, and I snatch it away. She reaches for it again, and I cannot help my reaction. I blast her with a ball of wind, sending her flying through the open doorway and into the opposite wall.

The guards rush to me, rifles pointed at my head, all four surrounding me like an inward-pointing star of death. Aida emerges from the rubble of the crumbled wall, dusty and bleeding, her face a rictus of hatred. She stomps back into the room, fists balled at her sides.

"Touch me again, and I'll kill you," I hiss at her. "I have nothing to lose. Your little dogs here can shoot me if they want. They'd be doing me a favor." I want her to touch me. I want a reason to rip her foul little body apart with gusts of wind sharp as knives.

She trembles, eyes hating and sparking fire, but she keeps her distance. One of the guards shoulders his rifle and reaches for my arm as well, and I step away from him.

"Keep your filthy hands off me," I snarl.

He lowers his hand slowly. Perhaps he recognizes the glare in my eyes, the look that says I won't hesitate to shred him like paper. A vortex of wind blows around me, tousling my hair and plucking at the hem of my dress. I know my eyes have turned white, the edges of my body fading and reappearing. I silently dare him to touch me again.

His lip curls into a snarl, but he keeps his hand to himself, gesturing at the open door. I force the winds back within, lifting the hem of my dress off the ground and walk with all the dignity I can summon.

They lead me, Aida in front, two guards behind her, then me, then the other two guards. We pass doorway after doorway, turning down one hallway after another, and I realize once again how mammoth my father's house is. It's excessive and exorbitant to have this much house. We descend the wide, curving staircase to emerge in the foyer, my heels echoing off the high ceilings and marble floors. To the right of the front doors is my father's study, the doors pulled closed. I can see straight through the house to the backyard, and now my nerves begin to jangle. There are easily five hundred people seated on white fold-ing chairs. A white carpet stretches like a wide ribbon through the green grass, coming to an end at a high, lily-wreathed archway. Hassan stands to the right of the dais with six groomsmen, his cousins and best friends lined up behind him. To the left of the podi-um are the bridesmaids, three of my distant cousins, none of whom I've spoken to in at least five years, and the other three are Hassan's sister, her friend, and another girl I've never seen before. The officiant of the wedding, the Sealer, is an ancient man, liver-spots on his bare scalp, back bent and knuckles trembling. He holds a thick book in both hands, and I can see his eyes flashing fire as he struggles to retain his form and stay upright.

The doors to my father's study open and he emerges, tailored tuxedo perfect and creased just so. He looks at my entourage and waves for Aida to leave, and she does, after a moment of hesitation. The guards remain until Father barks a command in Arabic. Their expressions pale and they scurry to follow Aida.

He stands inches away from me, eyes for once gentle and showing his emotion. "I'm sorry, Leila." It's all he says.

You should be, I think, but the words don't come out.

He flourishes his hands and a magnificent bouquet of flowers appears, which he hands to me. They are all white roses, wrapped in pale blue silk. I take them in my trembling hands and grip them tightly, as if they could provide strength somehow.

He glances at the guards standing by the door, then back to the study. He hasn't shut the study door all the way, as he normally does. I see a flash of a body through the crack in the door, a brief glimpse of brown hair and blue eyes. Carson. He's in there, mere feet away. Father steps into my line of sight, meeting my eyes and shaking his head, a slight movement that I almost miss. I feel a twinge of hope. Perhaps they have a plan. All I can do is carry on as if I've seen nothing, despite wanting to burst into the study and wrap my arms around him, bury my face in his shoulder and let him kiss me, let him take me away from here.

I take a deep breath, hold it, let it out slowly, and ready myself. I nod to Father, and he takes my arm. We begin the slow, measured pace, unpracticed but automatic. I want to drag this out, hoping the walk to the altar will take a lifetime, hoping some miracle will happen between here and there.

I ignore the eyes on me, stare at my feet and refuse to look at Hassan. My father's arm is all that steadies me as I finally approach the dais. I know I'm near to fainting, so hard is my heart beating, so violently is my stomach heaving. I don't quite stumble, but almost. One step, two steps up, and then I'm facing the officiant, the aged ancestor from a neutral clan. He takes my hand in his parchment paper palm, turns me to face Hassan, and places my hand in Hassan's. I jerk my hand free, and the fear drains away, replaced by rage.

Everyone present knows this is a farce, knows

this is a forced wedding, and they all understand the reasons behind it. I see no reason to play along with these stupid games of pretend.

Hassan reaches for my hand, and I pull free. The flowers held in one hand are nearly blown away by the sudden gust of wind, and Hassan's eyes flash.

"Don't make this harder than it has to be," Hassan whispers.

"I hate you." I don't quite whisper it, and the microphone picks it up. The crowd murmurs, and there are a few gasps.

Hassan pales with anger, grabs my hand before I can move, grips it with crushing fingers. There is a moment of struggle, but then Hassan glances from me to Father and Mother, his glance meaningful.

Father seems nervous somehow. He glances back at the house, almost as if expecting someone.

The officiant begins his ritual speech, reading from the heavy tome in his hands in a language that was already ancient when humans were still learning to forge iron. I tune him out and look around, taking in the familiar faces and the unfamiliar, the white-clad guards standing motionless and alert in strategic locations. I can see into the house from where I stand, and my heart stops beating for a moment when I see Carson leave the study, Nadira beside him.

I see two interior guards step forward and then

Nadira lashes out with twin jets of water from her palms that split the guards' heads like melons, striking with enough force to paint the wall red. No one else notices.

Carson catches a glimpse of me, and our eyes meet. Nadira moves away from Carson's side, gliding on cat-quiet feet to stand behind a guard who is positioned just outside the door to the backyard. She claps a hand over his mouth, and I see him struggle, thrashing around as if drowning. Her hand glows slightly, and I realize she *is* drowning him, water gushing down his throat from her hand. The guard struggles once more, then goes limp and she drags him inside. The other exterior guard must have heard something, because he steps inside, and Nadira smirks. She shoots a hand out, sending a serpent of liquid to coil constrictor-like around his neck, a wrist-thick rope of water that seems to take on a life of its own, forcing itself into his mouth and down his throat, into his eye sockets and in his ears. A moment of thrashing, grasping at his throat, eyes terrified, and then the guard drops to the steps, twitching. Carson drags him further inside the house, settles the corpse quietly to the floor beside the others, and then exits the house, approaching the [carpet?].

Hassan follows my gaze, sees Carson standing on the white carpet just behind the rows of chairs. The officiant sees him at the same moment, falters to a stop, and then the crowd turns to look as well.

I can't pull my gaze from Carson, and I don't try to. Hassan lets go of my hand and descends the dais.

"Who are you, and what do you want?" Hassan demands. "This is a private event. How did you get in here?"

"My name is Detective Carson Hale, and I'm here for her." He gestures at me. "This sick joke of a wedding is over."

By this time Nadira has snuck up behind two more guards and made them both vanish, though I don't see how she's done it. There are four more and now Nadira emerges to face the remaining four. They form up and close in on her, withdrawing pistols and firing at her, but the bullets are stopped midair by a column of water and then fall harmlessly onto the grass. With a haughty laugh, Nadira flashes into her full elemental form and rushes at them, swelling in size as she moves until she's twenty feet high and rolling down upon them like a tidal wave. She slams down on the guards before they can react, before they can summon their own magic or elemental powers. They are crushed to the ground, everyone in the crowd forced to listen to their bones crack and crunch, and then Nadira is a woman once more, clad in skintight black pants and a tight black V-neck shirt, knee-high leather boots, simple warrior garb.

Ten men, dead in under a minute; Nadira is a little scary.

"What is the meaning of this?" Hassan demands, a little slow on the uptake, it seems.

"I told you, *dickhead,* I'm here to stop this wedding. She doesn't want to marry you." Carson hasn't moved, hasn't even looked to see what Nadira is doing. He hasn't taken his eyes off me, and even now he answers Hassan while holding my gaze.

God, I love him.

Hassan snarls, his eyes flash fire, and he summons a crackling globe of fire in one hand, prepares to throw it, then hesitates, looking around at the seated crowd. He has realized Carson is a human, offering no overt threat. If he were to strike now, Hassan would be in the wrong. To attack a human who poses no threat would be breaking a cardinal rule of our kind, and Hassan knows it. He's done it before, to Carson himself no less, when he and his thugs attacked him in the Old Shillelagh, but to do so in public would be to invite dishonor. It would be cowardly.

Hassan lets the fireball dissipate with a muttered curse. He also cannot allow Carson's insult to pass without an answer.

"You don't know what you are meddling in, human. Leave now, while you still can." Hassan speaks loudly, so all can hear his response.

"Pussy," Carson spits the insult, his voice dripping contempt. "That's all you are, Hassan. Nothing but a pussy. You can pick on women, and you can attack me when my back is turned, but you're too much of a fucking *pussy* to face me like a man."

He's trying to provoke Hassan, and it's working. The crowd is whispering, nudging each other and muttering. I want to warn Carson, tell him to stop, tell him to save himself before it's too late. But I can't. All I can do is watch, and hope Carson knows what he's doing.

"This is your last warning, human. Leave . . . *now*." Hassan is furious, livid, outraged. His control is slipping, wisps of smoke and fire are rising from his tuxedo.

"Or what? What are you going to do? Set me on fire? You already tried that, when you attacked Leila and me at The Old Shillelagh. And then you attacked Leila again at her apartment. You must get your kicks attacking women. Why? Cause you're a *pussy*, that's why." Carson is spitting the words, and he's moved up the aisle as he speaks until he's standing less than three feet away from Hassan. He's several inches taller than Hassan, far more muscular, a tight gray T-shirt clinging to his torso, thick arms stretching the sleeves. Hassan, by comparison, looks small and weak. Carson towers over Hassan with his arms crossed over his burly chest, head back and eyes flashing contempt, lip curling in disgust.

Hassan can't handle the intimidation. He puffs his chest out and stands as tall as he can, steps close to Carson and glares up at him, posturing, cocky and vibrating with rage. Heat is radiating off Hassan. I can see it from here on the dais where I'm frozen in fear for Carson, the heat billowing in visible waves. A bead of sweat drips down Carson's forehead, and he lifts a finger to wipe it away, flicks it into Hassan's face with a contemptuous snap of his hand.

Hassan snarls and wipes his face, shoves Carson backward. Carson doesn't retaliate, only laughs, catching his footing easily.

An ugly expression crosses Hassan's face, a look of sudden inspiration and returned arrogance. "How about a challenge, then?" he says, his voice pitched to carry. "How about a duel, man to man? I challenge you, Carson Hale."

Carson grins, a brutish baring of teeth. "I thought you'd never ask. As the one challenged, I choose fists and feet. No magic, no fire, no guns, no special powers or tricks of any kind. Just you and me, man to man. Or man to . . . whatever the fuck you are. You're certainly no man, that's for damn sure."

Carson smirks as Hassan goes still, realizing he's

been out-maneuvered. He thought Carson wouldn't know about the rules of challenge, and he was wrong. I didn't think Carson would know that either, but then I look to Father, and he's got a ghost of a smile on his face. This was the plan, then.

I can't interfere, I know this much. The rules forbid it, and this is my only chance out of this, so I don't dare speak out. My fate rests in Carson's hands, now. I follow the two men as they circle behind the dais with its arch to face off in the open grass. The crowd has gathered around them, and I stand behind Carson, still absently clutching the bouquet of roses in my hands. Hassan peels off his tuxedo coat and vest, takes off the bow tie and the button-down shirt, stripping until he wears nothing but a thin white tank top above his tailored black tuxedo slacks. His arms are toned and he obviously works out, but it's also obvious that he's outmuscled by at least fifty pounds.

It's Carson's turn to strip off his shirt, which is unnecessary but impressive. He's a beast of a man, his stomach rippling with cords of muscle, pecs and biceps and triceps bulging and flexing as he swings his arms. He jumps up and down a few times, curls his hands into fists. He turns to face Hassan, and then lifts a hand in a 'hold on' gesture. He pulls a pistol from the small of his back and hands it to Father, then bends down and pulls another from his ankle, then pulls his cell phone from his pocket and hands that to Father as well.

"Remember, *asshole,*" Carson says to Hassan. "No magic, no fire, no powers of any kind. Hands and feet only."

Hassan spits on the ground at Carson's feet. "Prepare to die, *human.*"

CHAPTER 19: FACING THE DEMON

Carson

MY BODY TURNED SIDEWAYS, MY FISTS HELD LOOSE NEAR MY
face, I bounce on the balls of my feet, circling Hassan,
waiting for the right opening. Memories of hour after
hour spent sparring with Juice in the tiny ring at the
gym flood though my head, and I cycle through possible moves and blows. Hassan assumes a rough paro-
dy of a fighter's stance, making it obvious he doesn't
have a lot of experience in hand-to-hand combat.

Adrenaline rushes through me, blocking out the
world around me, fading the crowd into silence. It's
harder to block out Leila standing behind me, so beautiful in the dress, so tempting, so alluring, so strong.
All that exists is Hassan, elbows sticking out, his body

facing me full-on, presenting me a wide-open target.

Hassan's gaze flickers away for a split second, and that's the opening I need. My right fist thunders into Hassan's exposed torso, and his breath blows out in a wheezing huff. My left knee follows into Hassan's kidney, and then my right fist again.

Hassan gasps and his eyes blaze, the pain replaced with rage. He bellows like a bull and charges me with both hands flying at my face. I block easily, forearms barred vertically, dance back a few steps, then lash out with my left foot, heel crashing into Hassan's chest and knocking him backward. I immediately dart in swinging before Hassan can catch his balance or his breath, and my fists smash into his ribs—left, left, right, left, right—and Hassan has no chance of blocking any of them. Curling down over his torso, Hassan takes the last two blows to the ear and the back of the head, and then I bring my knee bashing upward, breaking Hassan's nose and spraying blood onto the grass.

I hear the crowd muttering, and I realize with unease how one-sided the fight is: Hassan hasn't landed one hit yet, and I'm not even winded. Hassan stumbles backward, nose sluicing blood, eyes sparking fire. Magically, the blood evaporates and the break straightens, and I realize my mistake: I could batter Hassan all day and never win since, as an ifrit, he can keep healing himself that way. I'm not sure if healing is automatic or an infraction of the rules, and I don't know if he can keep healing himself indefinitely. Too many things I don't know.

Hassan smirks, knowing he has just surprised me, and then he charges again, this time with a flurry of clumsy but powerful blows, a few breaking through my defenses, one landing on my cheekbone, splitting the skin open. The sight of my blood seems to send Hassan into a frenzy, and he rains blow after blow on my torso, most of which I'm able to block with my forearms, but a few hit the mark, inflicting pain I know I'll feel later.

I curl up and absorb the worst of the blows on my arms and shoulders, waiting. I peek through my shell of defense, waiting for Hassan to leave an opening; I don't have to wait very long. A momentary pause between punches, a brief glimpse of a torso and a face, and I explode forward, leading with a left jab, following with a right hook and a driving knee. Each one lands, and with each one Hassan wilts further in pain.

This time I don't let up, but hammer in with punch after punch, not bothering with style or technique or finesse, just powering in with a hail of brutal blows, each one spearing down with all the force I possess. Blood flies and the crowd backs up, a few turning away, sickened by the display. A woman sobs and faints, another vomits into the grass.

Hassan curls up again and I see the pulp of his face dripping gore, but his eyes burn still with bright fires of hatred, so I continue to pummel him. I don't dare let up, now. Some instinct tells me Hassan is about to explode, about to reach a threshold, and I know I have to deliver as much punishment as I can before that happens. I drive in with my knee, knock Hassan backward and lash out with a foot, slice an uppercut to bare his battered face and grab a handful of gelled hair, jerking his face downward as I smash up with a knee, crushing his face so brutally that had he been a human he would have been killed instantly.

Honor can only push a man so far, especially a man like Hassan.

Hassan crumples, his face a mask of blood, spitting teeth and fragments of bone. A woman shrieks and rushes forward to his side, followed by Leila. The woman is short and resembles Hassan; I guess this is his mother. Leila pulls at the woman, spins her around and shoves her away. Hassan's mother screams in rage, her hands igniting in red flame, heat billowing to force me away. Leila holds her ground, finally dropping the bouquet she's held in a death-grip all this time, and I hear the freight train roar of a tornado, watch in awe as a spinning storm cloud howls into existence around her. Leila's eyes glow white and her hair streams out behind her, reminding me of that night in Hart Plaza, only this time there's no seduction in her face, only hate and fury.

The two women face off now with Hassan between them. I watch, helpless, as they clash. The tornado vanishes, only to reappear as a horizontal spear of wind, crashing into the older woman and knocking her flying. The sky above darkens, gray-black thunderheads materializing out of nowhere to cover the blue of the sky and the bright orb of the sun. The glow of magic fills the air around Leila, and I realize the storm appeared at Leila's behest. Lightning flashes blue-white, filling the air with the thick tang of electricity, thunder crashing all around, shivering my bones.

A wall of fire sears the air between the women, and my heart leaps into my throat. The flames are diverted by a gust of wind, blasting past Leila to either side, leaving her unharmed. Leila retaliates with a raised fist descending like a hammer, and the other woman is smashed to the ground by a wall of air that breaks bone.

The older woman coughs, gags, and goes still.

I rush to Leila's side and gather her in my arms. She's wind now, barely substantial, shifting and fading in my arms, eyes white, edges bleeding into nothingness, becoming storm, becoming wind.

She looks up at me with inhuman eyes, kisses me, and puts her lips to my ear. "This isn't over," she whispers. "It's not that easy."

"I know," I murmur in response.

"We've started a war."

"I know that, too." I smile and kiss her again. "You're worth it."

"That was a *huge* mistake." Hassan's voice echoes from behind me, tolling with awful power, reverberating endlessly.

Turning, I see Hassan in full elemental form, a pyre of red flame a dozen feet tall with clawed fingers and eyes like dying suns. The rules of the duel have clearly been tossed aside. I bend and retrieve the Walther PPK bound to my ankle, the one hideout pistol I didn't give up, because I'm no fool. I crack off three shots—*BANGBANGBANG!*—each one impacting dead-center between Hassan's demon eyes. The hell-thing doesn't flinch, only bleeds bright yellow flame from fiery red flesh and keeps approaching me, each step shaking the ground and scorching the grass black. I empty the clip, and the apparition soaks the ground in blood-flame, which spreads like lava. The empty clip drops to the ground and I back up, slamming my one spare into the handle, dragging the slide to chamber a round. I fire again and again and again, backing away, the crowd widening the circle around

Hassan, Leila, the mother, and me, all of them watching and waiting in complete silence. There will be no interference.

I know I can't win this way, but I feel the fear freezing my blood. I refuse to succumb to its paralyzing hold. I see Nadira slinking, unnoticed, a hundred feet away. She's a barely-visible figure of sky-colored liquid slipping between blades of grass to rise up behind Hassan, translucent hands waving and circling in a bizarre dance, body jerking and coiling, magic sizzling and sparking and crackling, visible as golden particles of energy that pop and snap and flare, coalescing into a shimmering veil of raw power, which twists and spins in synch with Nadira's motions, circling like a whirlpool. The maelstrom rages silently, growing in size and violence, a dot of blackness appearing at its center. The dot grows, stretches, spreads, and becomes an expanding hole in the golden veil of magic.

Nadira needs more time, I realize. She needs Hassan distracted long enough to allow the portal to fully form. Leila shrieks behind me, her voice feminine thunder, all rushing winds and hurricane rage.

I drop the useless pistol, and stalk forward toward Hassan with no other weapon but my fists. I have no chance against a force like him. I know this, now. I never did. But I can't give up. I won't.

I hear my name called as if from a great distance,

and I turn to see Ibrahim tossing me the sword from the study, the ancient, priceless Damascus blade. I catch it, draw the sheath free and toss it aside, marveling at its featherlight weight and perfect balance.

A dozen feet separate Hassan and me, but they flash beneath my feet in a single impossible bound, the blade slicing down to split Hassan's arm from his shoulder, the disembodied limb dropping to the ground still flaming and flexing fiery fingers, still grasping at me. A sidestep and a swipe of the sword, barely missing Hassan's head, and then I feel a blow smash against my chest and I'm hurtled across the charred lawn, my skin sizzling and smoking. I roll to a stop, gasping, heaving, agony shooting through me, the sword still clutched in my white-knuckled fingers.

The crowd has become wild now but no one heeds their noise, not Ibrahim, nor his wife holding their still-screaming and thrashing daughter back, not one-armed Hassan bellowing and clawing for me, and certainly not me, the lone foolish human wielding an ancient sword, facing an enraged ifrit twice my size.

Fear pumps through my veins, but I refuse to give in to it. I take the fear and transform it into fury. I charge at Hassan with the sword stabbing forward, aiming for the wide, heaving red-flame chest.

Hassan pivots aside at the last moment and plunges his claws into my back, grinning evil glee as a scream of pain bursts from my lips. Hassan with-draws his talons and steps back, evidently assuming victory as I stumble backward, consumed by agony, using the sword to prop myself up, feeling fire and blood leaking down my back, carving a path of ago-ny through my flesh. I feel my strength begin to ebb away. I marshal the last dregs of my strength and turn to face Hassan once last time.

I push the sight of hysterical, weeping Leila from my mind, knowing I can't spare a thought for any-thing but a final, fatal strike.

I take a single, tremulous step, and then a second and third, pretending to be weaker than I actually am, although it's not much of a farce, now. I'm dying, and I know it.

But I'm not dead yet.

Hassan stands his ground. "You are a fool, hu-man," he sneers. His voice echoes, causes the earth to tremble under my feet.

"Perhaps," I answer, lifting the sword to rest the back edge on my shoulder, taking another step for-ward. "But I know something you never will."

"What?" Hassan demands.

"The taste of Leila on my lips."

Hassan roars in fury, and I lunge forward, crash-ing into Hassan and knocking him backward, toward the portal Nadira has finished summoning behind him. I accept the torment of flames licking at my skin and hair and face, stagger backward a single step and then throw myself forward and plunge the sword up to the hilt into Hassan's chest. He stumbles backward, surprised, and I slam my heel into his stomach, feeling the rubber and leather and cloth of my boot flash-burnt into ashes, feeling my skin sear and bubble. Hassan staggers a step closer to the portal, and I use the last shred of strength I possess to kick him one last time, my foot slamming into the pommel of the sword protruding from Hassan's chest, forcing him off-balance. He topples backward through the portal.

The world beyond the gap in the shimmering golden circle is one of fire and brimstone, an ancient vision of hell, a lake of blue-white-yellow-orange-red fire, the sky blood-red, jagged black claws of mountains skewering the sky, bat-winged demons soaring through curtains of flame, hundred-foot-tall giants lumbering past the opening, small darting creatures flicking and fluttering like sparks, horned beasts with gaping, toothy maws roaring.

Falling backward, arms pinwheeling, Hassan screams, flails, grabs for the edge of the portal and catches it with desperate claws. I lurch forward, dizzy and seeing double, afire with agony, weak, collapsing. I knock away his hand and he falls, spouting a spume of flame at me in a final act of hate, enveloping me in heat and hell and horror and pain.

Nadira brings her fists together, and the portal closes on Hassan's roar of futile rage. I tumble to the blackened earth, my skin and clothes and hair burning. Nadira douses the flames consuming my flesh, but then she too collapses, still in elemental form.

Leila finally breaks free from her parents and rushes to my side, weeping, sobbing, kissing my charred lips. My eyes are barely open and I see Leila above me, a white-gowned angel with tender lips. I gasp, struggling for breath, each gasp of oxygen causing a searing pain to rip through me. It feels like a building is sitting on my chest, making it impossible to breathe. My vision fades, my body no longer blackened meat but still throbbing with agony. I clutch for Leila's hand, feeling my breath fail me.

Her eyes are locked on me. I hear her whisper my name, hear her whisper the three words that make it all worthwhile: "I love you."

Darkness subsumes me.

CHAPTER 20: WORDS OF SEALING

Leila

I WATCH HIM FALL, AND SOMETHING INSIDE ME BREAKS, DIES. My parents let me go, finally, and I'm at his side, kissing him, desperate and pleading with him to live, to breathe, to be okay. I don't think he hears me, but he's looking at me, and I know he did all this for me. He fought Hassan and won, for me.

He did the impossible, for me.

And now he's dying, for me.

I deny it. Refuse it.

No.

Nadira, weakened to the brink of collapse from summoning the portal, is somehow still upright and running water-blue hands on him, magic-laced liquid soaking into charred flesh. His skin heals at her touch, his hairless scalp pinking and sprouting brown follicles, muscles returning to their heavy, rounded perfection. His eyes, however, retain their dying, fading listlessness, the encroaching darkness clouding his gaze. I can't even speak, can't make the words form. All I can do is kiss him, weeping, as Nadira heals him to the best of her abilities.

Finally, she topples to her back beside him, and I know she can do no more. It will be days before she can resume her human form.

"Lungs," Nadira murmurs. "He . . . can't—can't breathe. I'm too weak. Can't do . . . anything else." Her eyes meet mine. "Leila . . . you have to help him. You have to be—you have to be his breath."

Shock runs through me as I realize what she's suggesting. It's possible, but I'm not sure it's ever been done, or if it will work.

I look back at Carson, and my heart cracks further. He's gasping for breath, shuddering with every lungful. His eyes are latched on mine, and I refuse to look away.

He's still breathing, but barely, his breaths coming in slow, long-spaced gasps. His heart still beats, but barely. Carson's fingers clutch mine weakly, as if holding on to me is synonymous with holding to life. I am so tired, so sapped of all strength. But Carson is slipping away from me, and I have to summon the power to save him.

"I love you," I whisper. His eyes flutter closed, open again and search for me, then roll back into his head.

His breathing slows, a ragged gasp every second or two.

No, no, no. Pleasegodno.

I take his face in my hands, press my forehead to his and delve down within to the sea of magic. It surges to my command, but I know it won't be enough. Not for this. Desperation rips through me. It has to be enough. This has to work. I can't lose him. I can't. I hear a whimper escape from my lips, followed by the swish of skirts.

I feel a presence beside me, and I recognize the cool hardness of Mother. She puts a hand to my shoulder, and a surge of power ebbs from her into me, then from me into Carson.

It's not enough.

I draw deeper from myself, pull harder at the siphon from Mother; I hoard the power, wrap myself into it, curl it around myself like a shimmering cloak.

Carson's breath shudders. Time is nearly out. I clutch the power to myself and dredge up the strength to turn incorporeal, feel the edges of my body fade and meld with the gentle breeze. I let the fading spread through me, match my breathing to the rhythm of the wind. Between one moment and the next I have transitioned from woman to zephyr, and as a breath of wind I clutch in my slippery fingers a ball of thrumming blue-white magic.

Before I can question the wisdom of the act, I force myself into Carson's nostrils and mouth and down into his lungs, where I let the orb of power burgeon and expand, filling in the spaces and pushing against the walls of his lungs. The wounds have been healed by Nadira's ministrations, but too late. Carson's lungs still and deflate, and now I must force them back into motion.

I swell and push against the walls of his lungs, spreading myself in every direction, darting through bronchi and bronchioles and alveoli, splitting my essence smaller still to enter his bloodstream and into cells, pushing, pushing, forcing his body to resume motion, forcing his blood to pump, forcing his lungs to bellow open and closed. In weary, desperate circles I flow within him, willing his body to work, willing him to live.

If I could sob, I would. If I could beg, I would. But wind, motion, and air have no words, no identity. This is the danger in my action: I risk losing myself in him, I risk becoming mere air, spreading myself too thin until there is no *I*, until there will be no way to become a single, discrete entity once more.

The strain of retaining my identity is beginning to take its toll on me. I have a few moments more before I will lose myself entirely. I pulse the circuit once more, and feel his body respond, the various systems beginning to churn on their own with sluggish but growing life. I withdraw from the smallest particles, slowly and carefully, until I am once again a breath of wind in his now-pumping lungs.

Finally I am able to emerge out into the sunlight, and it takes the last dregs of my strength to regain human form.

Carson is now gasping, sitting up and heaving in desperate lungfuls of air.

I'm limp and exhausted, collapsing to the ground, but I take joy in his life. He regains his senses after a fit of coughing, sees both Nadira and me on the ground, turns to look around himself at the stunned crowd, at Father and Mother, and finally back to me. I fade, now, weakened, dizzy.

He kneels beside me, scoops me up and sits cross-legged with me in his arms. "You're my breath," he whispers.

I didn't know he'd heard that. Maybe he didn't, maybe he came to that understanding on his own. I don't know. All I know is his arms are around me, and I feel the tender, impassioned touch of his lips on mine.

"I love you, Leila," he says, and I know he heard me whisper those same words to him just before he died.

No one speaks, no one moves. I have no strength left. All I can do is lie limp in Carson's arms as he clutches me desperately, kissing my face and my neck and my forehead and my temple.

A crackling, rasping voice breaks the silence. "There must be a Sealing." It's the officiant, insistent and hunched. "The magic demands a Sealing. The groom is absent, so the burden must be passed." He looks to Carson, and my heart clenches as I realize what he's saying.

There *has* to be a marriage. The nature of the Sealed marriage contract is such that the terms must be fulfilled today, or the penalty for breaching it will occur at midnight.

There has to be a marriage.

Everyone is looking to me, to Carson, expectant. Panic fills me. It's too soon. I love him, and we've both saved each other, but . . . marriage? An ifrit marriage, especially a Sealed one like this, it's not merely a legal agreement, it's permanent, magically binding.

My eyes find Carson, and I expect to see equal panic in his eyes as he realizes what the officiant is saying.

Instead, I see . . . acceptance. Love. Knowledge. He knew this would happen. I look at Father, who is nodding, smiling, and at Mother, who seems confused but somehow relieved.

My strength is returning, and I sit up. "You . . . knew?" I search his eyes; feel his hands tangle in my hair and in my fingers. "This was the plan all along? Banish Hassan and marry me?"

Carson nods. "The contract must be fulfilled. There has to be a Sealing." He smiles, kisses me. "But if we're going to do this, we should do it right, shouldn't we?" His eyes twinkle and shine as he stands up with me still in his arms, lifting me effortlessly. He kisses me again and then sets me on my feet. Carson looks at me, then at the crowd gathered around us, mainly my clan now that Aida has vanished with hers.

He lowers himself to a knee, takes my hands in his. My heart throbs in my chest as I realize what he's doing.

"Leila Najafi . . . I don't have a ring, and I'm not an ifrit, but . . ." He hesitates, licks his lips, takes a deep breath and continues. "Will you marry me?"

I thought I'd wept all my tears, but I was wrong. I laugh and sob and hiccup, nodding, lift him up to his feet and throw my arms around him.

"Are you sure?" I ask him, whispering in his ear. I pull back and look at him, search his eyes for doubt or hesitation. I see none. "This isn't . . ."

"I know," he interrupts me. "Your dad explained it. I know what it means. I love you, and I know it's crazy, but . . . this is right. Everything between us, it all happened so quickly, but it's just. . . . perfect and natural and right. I can't remember what my life was like before you, and I can't picture my life without you."

Carson takes my face in his hands, kisses me with all the passion he has, and I feel my soul rise up to meet his, feel the essence of all I am, natural, mortal, magical, elemental, all tangling about him. When I healed him, when I forced his lungs to breathe, I left a portion of myself in him. When we made love back in Detroit—what feels like weeks ago but was only days—I know part of my essence was imbued in him then. I can feel him inside me, in my heart and my mind, and I can feel a new kind of power surging through him.

I look closely at him, and I see his eyes glowing slightly. It is the same white that mine become, the same as Father's and Mother's. He's absorbed some of my nature, and now he is changed. He knows it, too, but he's smiling and laughing as he feels the wind skirling around us and blowing through us, teasing and tangling and twining with us both.

I don't know how we got here, but we're standing in front of the officiant, the arch rising above us, the flowers somehow changed from lilies to irises, a few violets here and there now, and I know that's my mother's touch, lending color, lending hints of herself to it all. I look around us, and see the same touch everywhere now, hints of purple touching everything. Mother herself stands a few feet away, smiling for once, a genuine, loving smile, and Father too, his arm wrapped around her waist in a rare gesture of affection.

I can see the strangeness of it all in their faces, but they're happy enough that we've all escaped the specter of forced alliance to the al-Jabiri clan. I push those thoughts away, as well as the knowledge that we've started a war on several fronts, most likely.

I turn back to Carson, who hasn't taken his eyes off me. My dress is smudged and filthy from kneeling in the ash next to Carson, who is clad in only a pair of Levi's and boots. All of the al-Jabiri clan left hurriedly at some point and now there is just my family, my clan, left. They resume their seats for the ceremony. The bride's side is full of happy friends and relatives; the groom's side is empty. That's apropos, I realize. Carson has no one. Nadira is now awake again and smiling but still in elemental form, a woman-shaped figure carved from living liquid.

She recognizes the situation and takes an empty

seat on the groom's side. "I'll fill in for your family," she says. Carson nods, and I can tell the knowledge that he has no family to attend his wedding, abrupt or not, is still painful.

The officiant looks around at everyone, sees that we all seem to be ready.

"Who offers the bride in marriage?" he asks, voice reedy and weak and heavily accented.

"We do," Father and Mother say together.

"Who stands in witness for the husband?"

Nadira rises and comes up to the dais. "I do," she says.

"Very well," the officiant intones. "Let the bride be offered and the husband witnessed."

Mother and Father speak in unison: "We offer this bride, pure and willing, into the Seal of Wedlock."

Carson's brow furrows in confusion; he'd expected the typical American church ceremony, and this is definitely not that. I squeeze his hands and smile at him.

Nadira recites her part flawlessly: "I stand in witness for this husband, bearing testimony to the purity of his troth."

The officiant nods, waves a purple-veined hand and swirls golden particles—the essence of magic—that eddy around me and Carson and my parents and Nadira, sinking into all of us, igniting the magic of the Sealing. Mother, Father, and Nadira take their seats, and now it's only Carson and me standing face to face. I can feel the magic of the Sealing swirling and coiling around us, pushing through us, preparing to bind us.

"The husband will now repeat my words," the officiant commands. He speaks the words of Sealing, echoed by Carson. "'In the sight of these witnesses I pledge my troth of my own free will. I offer my life from this day until the ending of time, and I offer it freely in the spirit of love and loyalty. I seal myself, heart and mind and body and soul to my bride for all of time. May the thread of my life be cut if my pledge be broken in word or deed or thought.'"

Carson's voice is strong and confident as he repeats the words. I can hear the promise in his voice as he understands what it is he's agreeing to, and I know he's offering himself to me wholeheartedly. When the last word is spoken, the letters rise up from the pages of the officiant's book, glowing cursive script floating with semi-sentient purpose to surround Carson in a skein of words, in a train of binding, burrowing into his skin, into his temples and his chest, inked tangibly upon his skin as the magic enters Carson and tangles with the essence of his being, residing there and waiting for the Seal to be completed.

The officiant reads the words again, and I repeat

them, but my voice is not nearly so strong. It cracks and I find myself fighting back tears yet again, and I swear to myself in the back of my mind that I won't cry again for at least a year. This time, however, I don't mind. The words of Sealing are woven of magic in their very essence: when you speak them, their meaning is driven into you word by word, phrase by phrase. You speak them and you understand the permanence of marriage. In our culture, among ifrits and djinn, marriage is forever; the words of Sealing make sure of that. What isn't guaranteed to last forever is the happiness and love of the marriage.

When I speak the final word, the same sweet strain of magic wreathes around me, spreading through me and into me, and then there is a soft susurrus echoing within me and within Carson; I know he hears it, I know he feels it, for his eyes widen and his hands tighten on mine. The sound is the breath of magic becoming real, becoming a physical tangible psychic connection between us. The wind blows, and we are caught up, we fade and twist and twine and tangle into a torrent of joined currents of earth-breath, two souls reaching together into the farthest spaces of the sky; there is naught but we two, there is only our merged sense of *I*, only one self coruscating and scintillating in the bright hot sun far above the commonality of human and ifrit and djinni. This is beyond wedlock, beyond union, beyond marriage, this a new and rare kind of Sealing, a perfect and inimitable morphing of souls caused by magic and by a prior meshing of essences in the vulnerability of a love-made sexual union and in the presence of my unique magic now residing in the structure of his very cells.

He is breath, and I am wind; he is motion and I am air.

I know not for how long we glint and glide in the wide sky, but at long last, after a mere moment or an echoing eternity, a day or an hour, we return to the earth and split and regain corporeality. The wedding has moved inside, where the clan smiles and drinks and celebrates. They are all happy, relieved, if a bit puzzled as to what just happened and what it means for the future of the clan. A human, a police officer, no less, the heir to the patriarchy? Unheard of. Impossible. Yet, there it is, an unavoidable fact.

Before we go in to join them, we stand with arms wrapped around each other, lips touching, our breathing synched.

I've heard of what is possible in the purest of Sealed Unions: *I love you, Carson Hale.* The words are thought, not spoken.

He starts and gasps, curses in surprise. I see the dawning of understanding filter through him, and he smiles slowly.

I love you back, Leila Hale, he replies in the same manner.

I hadn't even thought of taking his name, but hearing it from him, it sounds perfect, it sounds right. He said it himself, and I know he's right: I cannot imagine a moment in my life that hasn't contained him. All the years before the moment he sat down on the stool in my bar seem as distant and half-remembered as a dream, and as easily forgotten.

Now, he is my reality.

THE END

Continue Reading for a sneak peek of

DJINN & JUICE

By
Jasinda Wilder

DJINN & JUICE

Nadira
Alexandria, Egypt; June 1882

SEAGULLS CAW AND WHEEL IN EVER-WIDENING CIRCLES ABOVE the sapphirine surface of the Mediterranean. Cargo ships creak and bump at anchor, the salt spray drifting in tangy mists in the constant breeze, the smell of fish and unwashed bodies sits heavy in the air. People of all nations bustle in a constant crush as far as the eye can see, hawking wares, conducting business, eating in the myriad cafes, puffing on hookahs in jabbering groups, cursing and jostling and shouting in a dozen languages. There are kaffiyehs and hijabs, long white

robes and black ones, western-style fedoras and bowl-
ers, English soldiers in brilliant red and white uni-
forms, business suits, and khaki clothes favored by the
influx of explorers in the city. There are men with red
hair and blond and black, men with long thick beards
and those who are clean-shaven, men with swarthy
skin and fair. Arabic and Urdu and English and Dutch
and French and Bedouin and German and Spanish
rise to mix in a cacophonous babble.

I take it all in as I walk by my father's side. I tug
at the veil across my nose and mouth, wishing I could
simply take it off. I don't often leave Father's house, so
I seldom wear the full head covering and veil. Today,
however, Father has finally acceded to my constant
badgering and has allowed me to go with him to his
business meeting. Sometimes I just want to get out of
the house, away from the stifling silence and endless
hours with my tutors.

We push through the crowd to a small café
tucked away from the crush of people, the entrance
hidden in a narrow alley. The interior is dimly lit, with
low ceilings, and the hookah smoke hangs in thick,
fragrant clouds. My father and I are met by the proprietor, a short, older man with a long beard hanging
over a round belly.

"Come, come," the owner says in florid, formal
Arabic. "I have your table ready, your Excellency. All

is waiting for you. Your guests are here, and I have taken the liberty of serving them. I hope all is to your satisfaction, Excellency. Is there anything you wish, any further instructions? I can have anything you wish brought to you, immediately, at no extra charge of course—"

"Enough," Father murmurs. "Leave us."

The proprietor bows as he backs away. "Yes, Excellency, as you wish. If you desire anything, you have only to raise your hand. I am at your service, ready and waiting to attend to your pleasures."

Father waits until the effusive proprietor vanishes before addressing his guests. Both are Englishmen, one older with graying brown hair and a neatly trimmed full beard; the other is younger, perhaps twenty-two or twenty-three, clean-shaven with platinum blond hair.

I sit beside Father, trying to keep my eyes demurely cast down as is expected of me, but I don't quite succeed. I have met a few of Father's European business associates before, but none of them have ever been so young and handsome as this one with the hair so blond as to be almost white. I stare at the rough wood grain of the tabletop, but my gaze keeps wandering back up to the young man's finely-chiseled features, intelligent blue eyes, and broad shoulders.

"Good afternoon, Abdul," the older Englishman

begins in clipped English. "It is good to see you. I see you brought company with you, this time. Who is this lovely young lady?"

"This is my daughter, Nadira." Father waves his hand, dismissing me. "You had a successful journey, I presume, Captain?"

"Very. Best yet, in fact. Although I fear things are growing tense here in Alexandria. I might be forced to avoid this particular port until things settle down somewhat, politically speaking."

"Nonsense," Father says, puffing on his hookah mouthpiece. "It will all blow over in time. It's just the nationalists at it again. They make this noise every so often, but it never comes to anything. The Suez is too important to your government and to the French to allow a fool like Urabi to threaten it. Urabi won't last."

The captain waves his head from side to side, fingering his mouthpiece but not sucking on it. "I don't know if you're correct, actually. I think Urabi is a worrisome threat already. I think we'd all best be on alert. Don't take offense, Mr. Nasri, but you're so often shut up in your home that I doubt you see the unrest in the city. The people listen to Urabi. My countrymen won't abide him, you're right about that much, and neither will the French. If he seizes control, we'll all be in trouble."

I hear the question leave my lips before I can stop

it. "Why are the people upset?"

The young blond man answers the question, much to the annoyance of Father and the captain. "It's not everyone, it's the nationalists, led by Urabi Pasha. He wants Egypt to be controlled by Egyptians and he wants us Europeans out. The problem is, we're too heavily invested in the Suez to let that happen."

"What's the Suez?" I've heard of it, of course, as it is a name on everyone's lips, but I'm not sure exactly what it is. Something to do with the European boats, I think.

"It's a canal," the blond man answers. "A big ditch cut between the Mediterranean and the Red Sea. It allows boats to travel from Asia to Europe without having to go all the way around Africa."

"Well, why is that so important? Is it enough to start a war? That's what you mean, isn't it, when you speak of unrest?" I can't help the questions from tumbling out.

"Well, it *is* that important, because it cuts the trip in half, which cuts costs to merchants and—"

"What does it matter to you, daughter?" Father cuts in. "I did not bring you with me to interrupt my conversations."

"Oh, it's no problem, Mr. Nasri—"

"Brock, I think you should—" the captain begins, but Father speaks over him.

"It *is* a problem, Mr. Branscombe, and it is *my* problem."

The young blond man, Brock, nods, chastened, but I see irritation in his downcast gaze.

"But Father," I say, tugging on my veil, "I'm simply curious—"

"If you're curious," Father says in Arabic, "you will speak to me in private, not when your betters are having a conversation in public. Do not embarrass me."

"My *betters?*" I shoot to my feet, shaking with anger, speaking in Arabic now as well. "My *betters?* Just because you're *men* does not make you better than me—"

"Enough!" Father says, not yelling but hissing, which is infinitely more threatening.

He raises a hand and snaps his fingers once, a sharp *crack* in the quiet café. An Arabic man in traditional white robes and a red-and-white checked kaffiyeh emerges from the shadows.

"Escort my rude and disobedient daughter back home," Father says in Arabic, speaking in an undertone. "And see that she remains there until I return."

The man nods once and takes my wrist in a firm but gentle grip, tugging me to my feet and escorting me out of the café. I struggle, but don't scream; if I embarrass Father in public any more than I already have my punishment will only worsen. I curse floridly in Arabic as I'm hauled out of the café, drawing stares from the proprietor and the patrons, eliciting an offended huff from my escort.

"Watch your mouth, girl," he whispers harshly in my ear. "You've already angered your father enough. Do not make things worse for yourself."

I jerk my hand free. "Let go of me, you ugly ape. I'll see myself home."

"I'm sorry, mistress Nadira, but that is not possible." He takes my wrist again, this time holding tighter, but still not enough to hurt.

I curse at him again and jerk my hand yet again. "I said, *let go.* Do not presume to touch me again, you stupid baboon. I do not answer to you."

The man isn't fazed by my insults. He merely captures my wrist yet again and this time squeezes hard enough to grind my bones together, eliciting a whimper of pain from me. "I answer to your *father,* as do you. Do not fight me, or it will go poorly for you, mistress."

I shove him with my free hand, tugging at my pinioned wrist. "What will you do? If you harm me, my father will peel your skin from your bones. Now for the last time, *let go!*" I slap him as hard as I can with one hand and rip my other wrist free, startling him enough to let me dart away.

He catches me easily and when his hand is latched onto my wrist this time, I hear a low rumble like a distant avalanche. My wrist burns, stings, and aches, and then I feel my entire arm being encased in cold and unforgiving stone. I look up at my escort and see his eyes roiling brown and bright, the color of a mudslide, blurring with inexorable power. I force my gaze away from his eyes and down to my arm, and stifle a scream: my entire arm from fingertips to shoulder is sheathed in gray granite, heavy and hard and icy. I struggle and push and pull but can't break its hold. It's a subtle thing, what Father's man has done. My arm is swathed in black fabric and is invisible from the outside. The only evidence of my imprisonment is a flash of stony gray at my fingertips.

"I'm sorry, mistress. I have been tasked with seeing you home, whether you wish my company or not. Please do not make a scene, or it will only go the harder for you." He pulls me into a walk, muttering to himself, "Allah save me from troublesome children."

I watch ships ply the vast harbor from the balcony of my room, their fat-bellied sails snapping in the wind, high prows proud above the azure waves. I lean against the elaborate marble scrollwork of the railing, wondering what it would be like to be on a ship like that, wind in my hair, freedom boiling in my veins. I can almost feel the roll of the deck beneath my feet, almost taste the brine spray on my lips, almost hear the creaking of the ship like the complaints of a beast of burden.

I wonder if the handsome blond Englishman is on one of those ships, hauling on a line, his broad shoulders straining, forehead furrowing in exertion.

"Brock Branscombe." I speak his name out loud, tasting the foreign twist of the syllables. "Brock. Brock."

His name sounds strong and hard like I imagine his hands and muscles would be. I see his eyes when I say his name, steel blue-gray like the barrels of the rifles his redcoat countrymen carry. He'd stood up for me, both to his own captain and my father, which means he is either very brave or very foolish. Probably both.

I turn away from the view of the harbor and the dozens of cargo ships, as well as from thoughts of Brock Branscombe. He is likely long gone, and even if he isn't I'll never see him again. Father will see to that.

My stomach rumbles noisily, reminding me that I'd refused both lunch and dinner in protest. In hindsight, however, refusing to eat had been petulant and childish. I'd just been so angry at Father and at his stupid autocratic nonsense that I'd lashed out the only way I could think of. I'd only managed to hurt myself in the process, of course. My door is locked from the outside, and the day is ending, which means no one will come to my room to bring me food until tomorrow.

The thought of going hungry all through the night makes my blood boil in anger. How dare they treat me like a child? Just because Father and the captain are men doesn't mean they're my betters. Just because I'm a woman doesn't mean I'm not curious as to what is happening in my own city. I deserve to know, don't I?

And Brock had been chastened unfairly as well. All he'd done was answer my questions, after all, so why should he be publicly embarrassed simply for speaking to me? It was all so unfair.

My stomach growls and gurgles again, and I flop down onto my bed, trying to calm my anger. Getting upset and working myself into a tizzy won't help; I need to *do* something about it. Something useful, something productive. This is the nineteenth century, after all, not the ninth, and I won't just sit here locked in my room like a naughty little child. I'm a grown woman, eighteen, already considered old by many. I am the last among my friends to remain unwed. Aziza is pregnant already and she is a year younger than me. Many of my other friends have been married for a year and some of them even for two or three. I, at eighteen, am one of the last girls I know who is still a maiden. Yet, here I am, a grown woman locked in my bedroom in my father's home.

And not just a grown woman, but a *djinni,* no less. My race has lived among the humans for thousands of years, unnoticed and hidden. We possess magic as well as elemental birthright powers. We don't just control the wind or fire or earth or—as in my case— water. No, we *are* that element. We are long-lived, capable of living hundreds, if not thousands, of years. Djinn, in fact, are the source of the human myths surrounding "genies," a bastardization of our true name.

Here I am, a member of an ancient and powerful race of nearly-immortal beings, and I'm locked in my room like a child?

It is embarrassing and infuriating; I'll just have to take matters into my own hands, then.

I stride confidently to my door and stand in front of it, focusing my attention on the lock. I have received at least rudimentary training in the use of my birthright powers, so I should be able to accomplish *something.* It's just a lock, after all, a hunk of dead metal. How hard can it be to force it open with my powers?

Mentally steeling myself, I turn my focus inward, gazing down deep into the corners of my soul where the power awaits. I grab for the core of energy, but it eludes my grasp. It is slippery, like wet stone. It is like trying to grip a handful of seawater. Calming my frustrated nerves with a few deep breaths, I try again, this time slowly and gently, as if approaching a skittish bird. My eyes are closed, the darkness of the inside of my eyelids shutting out all distractions, the sounds of the cawing of seagulls, the chatter of voices from the streets below, the clatter of wheels on cobblestones.

The darkness slowly begins to recede, although my eyes remain firmly closed. Black turns gray, and gray turns blue—subtle navy at first, then deep sapphire, and then a gradually brightening azure, then the brilliant, scintillating blue of sunlit ocean water.

At first, I wonder if perhaps I'm looking down at a pool within myself, an impossible sea of liquid somewhere in my body or mind. Then as the glow encompasses my mental vision completely, I come to the realization that it isn't merely a pool I'm diving into, or a bath in which I'm submerging, but it is, rather, a sea vast and endless and not merely within me or around me, but an ocean that *is* me.

Always before, with the various djinn instructors I've had, I have only ever managed to create a brief spurt of water from my fingers, enough perhaps to douse my younger brother, enough to play with, but that's it. I've always pretended to be in control in these situations. Indeed, the amount of control I have over the liquid I was able to summon was always impressive to my tutors, but I always felt I was merely scratching the surface, merely dipping my pinkie finger in the true depths of my potential powers.

Now, surrounded by the glow of power, I realize I am right; if I can just grab hold of this rippling sea and learn to wield it like a scimitar, I will be unstoppable.

I *have* to learn to control this, have to learn to summon not just a puny little jet of water, or create icicles on my bedroom ceiling, but actually learn to *control* it, all of it.

I reach a mental hand forward, imagining myself grasping a tendril of the power, picturing it like a rope coiled from the larger whole.

My efforts are rewarded by a thrum in my veins, a buzz of vibrating power in my blood and bones. I open my eyes and breathe a curse of surprise in Arabic. Instead of the normal, bland view of my bedroom door I see a thousand, million bluish-white streams of liquid, a web of watery threads surrounding me and wavering and rushing in constant motion, fluttering in the gust of wind from my open balcony door, drifting in the currents of air, weaving around me and twining into knots and coils and bunches. The edges of my body, my fingers and the tips of my hair and the tops of my ears, my bare toes peeking out from underneath the hem of my skirt, the curve of my waist and the mounds of my breasts, all this seems to fade and drift and undulate with the motion of the streams of liquid all around me as if my body wishes to join the play of currents.

With a breath of awe, I slip a hand outward into one of the currents and watch as my fingers turn from tan flesh to cerulean water, the glow spreading from fingertip to knuckles to palm to wrist until I mentally stop the spread as it reaches my elbow, panic fluttering low in my belly.

What would happen if I let the glow spread all throughout my body? Would I ever return to normal? Could I return my arm to flesh and bone now that it is transformed? I have no answers for these questions, but I push the fear away and return my attention to the problem at hand: getting free of this room.

I touch my finger to the metal square of the lock plate and picture liquid wicking out of my body, liquid being pulled out of the air around me and being poured into the lock, into the substance of the door itself. I picture the liquid spreading and growing and expanding, pushing the cogs of the lock and the particles of the metal and the grain of the wood, filling the spaces between molecules until there is no more space at all and then expanding still more, pushing and pushing and pushing to breaking . . .

There is a deafening crack and an explosion of wood, water, and metal, and then the door is simply gone in a shower of splinters and warm rain. The currents vanish as I release my hold on the tendril of power.

I laugh and clap my hand over my mouth in surprise. "I might have overdone that a little," I say out loud to the empty room and hallway.

There's no sign anyone noticed the sound, as my room is on the opposite side of the house from nearly everything else except Father's study on the level below, and at this time of night he would be in the parlor with Mother, smoking his English pipe and reading his English newspaper.

Tiptoeing quietly, I make my way down the empty hallway to the stairs, emerging in the darkened kitchen. Father has already dismissed the cooks. I see a round loaf of bread on the counter, snatch it up, tear a huge hunk free and shove it into my mouth, swallowing hastily. After another hurried bite I force myself to slow down; no need to eat like a pig, I remind myself.

Then a thought strikes me: why be content with a little bread, when I can have more? I've already destroyed my door and snuck out of my room, so why not go further? Trouble is already mine simply for daring to use my powers unsupervised and for breaking my door. Sneaking downstairs is another sin, and thus encumbered by trouble I may as well have a bit of freedom until I'm caught and punished like the child Father obviously considers me to be. A long knife perches in a block on the counter and I use it to cut a piece of bread free, then pocket the knife in the folds of my voluminous black dress, careful to keep the point away from my body.

I'll need money, though, if I'm going to have any fun.

Father's study is silent and dark, lit only by the red-orange glow of sunset through the window. His desk is an immaculate expanse of polished wood, a neat pile of papers in one corner, a few ornate silver pens in a crystal glass in the other corner. A search of the drawers reveals a case containing a brace of pistols, a curved ceremonial dagger in an elaborate gold-chased sheath, and a metal canister of pipe tobacco. And then, most importantly, I find a clinking pile of *gineih* coins in a little leather bag at the back of the bottommost drawer. I've never had cause to use money myself, as Father has always provided everything I need, so I have no idea how much I'll need or what I would do with it. Panic and guilt gurgle in my belly like bile as I take four of the heavy coins, clutching them in my trembling fist. I cinch the leather bag closed and slide the drawer shut, flinching at the dull thud it makes as it closes.

The window slides open with a gentle squeal, causing me to freeze in place before contorting my body through the opening. Once through and crouching on the ground outside, I slide the window shut once more, my heart hammering in my chest, pounding so loudly I'm sure Father will be able to hear it from within the house.

Waiting until I'm sure I've gone undetected, I creep out into the street, glancing around me nervously. I pull my veil into place across my face and make my way through the darkness, winding my way from the heights where the wealthy reside down into the city's pulsing, uneasy heart. The weight of fear clutching my heart bubbles, boils, and evaporates, replaced by a thrilling glut of excitement.

I am on my own for the first time in my life, alone, free, and ready for adventure in the lights and bustle of Alexandria.

Djinn and Juice, coming soon

JASINDA WILDER

Visit me at my website: **www.jasindawilder.com**
Email me: **jasindawilder@gmail.com**

If you enjoyed this book, you can help others enjoy it as well by recommending it to friends and family, or by mentioning it in reading and discussion groups and online forums. You can also review it on the site from which you purchased it. But, whether you recommend it to anyone else or not, thank you *so much* for taking the time to read my book! Your support means the world to me!

My other titles:

The Preacher's Son:
Unbound
Unleashed
Unbroken

Biker Billionaire:
Wild Ride

Big Girls Do It:
Better (#1), Wetter (#2), Wilder (#3), On Top (#4)
Married (#5) ,
On Christmas (#5.5) ,
Pregnant (#6)
Boxed Set

Delilah's Diary:
A Sexy Journey
La Vita Sexy
A Sexy Surrender

Rock Stars Do It:
Harder
Dirty
Forever
Boxed Set

The Falling Trilogy:
Falling Into You
Falling Into Us
Falling Under
Falling Away

The Ever Trilogy:
Forever & Always
After Forever
Saving Forever

The world of *Alpha*:
Alpha
Beta

The world of *Stripped*:
Stripped
Trashed

The world of *Wounded*
Wounded
Captured

Jack Wilder Titles:
The Missionary

To be informed of new releases, special offers, and other important news, sign up for **Jasinda's email newsletter (http://eepurl.com/qW87T).**

ABOUT THE AUTHOR

New York Times and *USA Today* bestselling author Jasinda Wilder is a Michigan native with a penchant for titillating tales about sexy men and strong women. When she's not writing, she's probably shopping, baking, or reading. She loves to travel, and some of her favorite vacations spots are Las Vegas, New York City, and Toledo, Ohio. You can often find Jasinda drinking sweet red wine with frozen berries.

To find out more about Jasinda and her other titles, visit her website: www.JasindaWilder.com.